A Burden of Proof

Jane Doe

Order this book online at www.trafford.com
or email orders@trafford.com

Most Trafford titles are also available at major online book retailers.

Note for Librarians: A cataloguing record for this book is available from Library
and Archives Canada at www.collectionscanada.ca/amicus/index-e.html

Printed in Victoria, BC, Canada.

ISBN: 978-1-4120-7090-4 (sc)

*Our mission is to efficiently provide the world's finest, most
comprehensive book publishing service, enabling every author to
experience success. To find out how to publish your book, your way, and
have it available worldwide, visit us online at www.trafford.com*

Trafford rev. 11/23/2009

 www.trafford.com

North America & international
toll-free: 1 888 232 4444 (USA & Canada)
phone: 250 383 6864 ♦ fax: 812 355 4082

Thanks to all those who supported me through the dark days and kept me going, persuading me to write my story. Escpecially Jasmine and Caleb and my mom and dad for always being there for me.

Almost Perfect!

I was a beautiful summer day in June of 99 in the Midwest. We were in the park with colorful flowers blooming all around the brick pathway leading to the bronze fountain. We gathered an arm full of flowers along the way. Since it had only been two weeks that I had accepted the proposal, we decided to make it a simple ceremony that hardly required any planning. It all seemed too good to be true. Nothing elaborate or expensive. Some of my family was there and so was his. A wedding, not a marriage. All too soon I would learn the difference between a wedding ceremony and a real marriage. Our lives would never be the same. The lives of my children and I, that is. We had a very nice and comfortable life. Looking back now it was almost perfect.

As a child I grew up in a small town, middle class. My Mother was Amish and met my Father, a carpenter, working near her farm. We moved once when I was in grade school. It was a big deal, even though it was only thirty-five miles, but the biggest difference was moving to the country. Before, all my friends were close by, some within walking distance. My father had taken a better job at a different steel mill. The highlight of moving was choosing an animal to have as a pet but I had to take total responsibility of the horse and knew it would be a lot of work but worth it. We took family vacations every year within the U. S. I loved to travel and always looked forward to the next trip. Every summer I spent time with my Aunts and Uncles and Cousins about eighty miles away. I was a Camp Counselor at a Conservation area during summers. On Sundays I taught Sunday School to pre-school and older children. After school and weekends I was a waitress, cook, cashier and hostess and still had time to ride and care for my horse. Later there were more animals, such as lizards, turtles, ducks, raccoons, pet rats, rabbits, an angora guinea pig, dogs, cats, and fish.

At seventeen years old I graduated high school and it could not have been soon enough for me. I did not really like school and did not know what I wanted to do except travel. When I turned eighteen, I worked at the same steel mill where my father worked and would later retire. After being hired I realized there were only about three other women in the mill. Great pay and benefits and paid vacation time! That gave me plenty of money and time to travel. I enjoyed working at the mill, except for the hard hat and steel toed boots. Friends stopped after work at the local bars and had bonfires at the river. I was there for sixteen years.

I had moved into a duplex in a nearby small town by

the park for about eight months while I drew plans for the house I wanted to build in the country. I searched all around within a twenty-five mile radius and ended up purchasing some gently rolling farm and timber property just across from my parents where I grew up. It was perfect and did not bother me to live fairly close to my parents. They were good people and my closest neighbor. By the time I was nineteen, I was moving into my newly built home and began decorating with antiques collected over the years and stored at my parents. My Grandparents on both sides of the family had antique furniture and collectibles and when they passed no one wanted these heirlooms. Some were being thrown out and I asked to keep them. At that time I was still living at home and my parents agreed to store the items in the attic. Other antiques were from sales my mother and I frequented.

My little ranch was just as I wanted inside and out. Large decks and balcony with a long lane and five hundred pine trees and walnut, oak and maples I also planted. The flowers and bushes were for birds and other animals and they bloomed from early spring to late fall. In the timber I made trails to watch all the rare wild flowers bloom, like bloodroots, orchids, ginseng, and bluebells. There were wild animals of all kinds including turkey, deer, rabbit, raccoons, timber wolves, cougars, bald eagles and hawks. Every bird imaginable like hummingbirds and different species of butterflies also frequented the property. There was an albino robin living in the pine trees surrounding the house for many years. Any type of animal that could survive in this area could be found here. Of course many people would drop off their unwanted domestic animals at the end of my lane knowing I would take care of them. I had a spiral staircase built and plants and trees inside with almost all glass on two floors on the south side. Some called it a museum and others said it should be in magazines. I am proud of that. It was my own little paradise.

Every other year I ordered a new car and a few times a year took vacations. When my friends could not afford to go on trips or take the time off, I traveled alone. There were ski trips for one day to Aspen for a New Years celebration or skiing at a different resort for a week all over the Rockies. Once, three of my friends and I just took off driving west for two weeks. We ended up in Northern Idaho where we helped herd two thousand sheep through the mountains. Then my friend's father had a friend who lent us a condo in Nashville to stay for a week. We ended up at a Senator's election party. The trip we also met a friend of Johnny Cash that worked in his band. We also got lucky and were cast as extras in the movie 'Coal Miner's Daughter'. There was the trip to Acapulco and Mexico City with a couple of girlfriends for ten days. We tried everything we could including parasailing. One of my friends went every year so she knew people to show us around that took us to a political gala for one of the heads of government there. Beaches and islands, mountains and snow. I did as much as I possibly could, everything from shopping in exquisite cities to weekends abroad. No matter how long the trip was, it became a new experience. I wanted to go everywhere and see everything. Life was good.

During this time I had only one steady boyfriend and

believe me it was not anything I care to remember. I knew him for a year but never realized he was one of the county's biggest drug dealers, hard drugs. That is how naive I was. We got along well. When he tried to kill me and trashed my house and new car as I tried to escape and ended up in the emergency room, I realized how serious the situation was. Later I discovered, among many other serious episodes, he had put his ex-wife and mother-in-law in the hospital. None of my friends had ever told me what they knew because they said they did not think it was any of their business and thought he had changed for the better since going with me. Time to move on.

So now it is time to settle down? If I could find the right guy and have ten children it would be perfect, not almost perfect. A couple that lived close by set me up on a blind date named Jeb. This went well but we did not agree on everything. Despite that we still decided to marry. After all I had everything I wanted and did everything I wanted so I could see being with someone special and raising children now and having a family.

My theory is that men think with only one side of the brain, and if that is the case, then they only speak out of one side also. Jeb said he was ready for a family when we discussed the future. It probably sounded easy to have a nice ranch in the country when you are living in a trailer park. We were married about a year later and were doing okay until I became pregnant with my first child. It was my child because after Jas was born he decided he really did not like kids around. They were too much work, and that is something he did not want to be involved with. He wanted to go to work and do the same as he used to, but if you have children some things have to change to be a good parent. His family felt the same way about children being around and in the way. Jeb's mother claimed she did not want to be asked to watch our child because she had spent her time taking care of her own. So she was not asked, except for one time we were at her house and went to a couple of stores. Who would want to leave their child with someone that did not want to watch them? Children are a privilege, an honor and a blessing from God. They are not an intrusion on your life, never too much work, time, or expense. My children were their first granddaughter and grandson. I believe it is truly their loss.

Jeb moved out but I spoke to him on the phone a few times and he agreed to move back and try again. That's when I got pregnant again. Jeb decided he could not take it and left us for a simpler life. He had become more hateful because he felt trapped with one child and another on the way. The next time he moved back in, he was only there for a short time and then gone for the last time. If one child was too much, no way could he handle two. He simply wanted no children. Children can sense some things no matter how old. He left and said he did not have to take the responsibility of children and they were all mine. I still tried to talk with him on the phone about the children but he did not want to talk. The last time I had a conversation with him he told me they were my-------kids and he did not care what I told them or what we did. Believe me he was not kidding. It is amazing how much children can change your life for the better.

We were on our own, the three of us. My little princess, as my son and I call her even to this day, and my little football player. The hardest part about a divorce is what to tell the children. It was easier since they were still babies. They don't even remember their father being around. Psychologists report that a child should have their father in their life no matter what he is, a murderer, a rapist, etc. I never spoke in a negative way about Jeb in front of my children as they grew up. Even when they asked questions, I explained in a positive way so there was no blame or bad feelings. Despite their fathers choice to be absent in their lives they have done well. After about a year he and his new wife thought they should have visitation because they were "ready now". That did not last long and it cost me a ton of money to be sure my children were safe.

Our lives would be okay. Jas and Cal would see him at his convenience when he would show up at the Sheriff's Department where the courts agreed to set up the pick up and drop off for visitation. Twice Jeb had come to the house and got a little crazy with us and that was not going to happen again as long as I had the money to pay the attorney I could try to protect my children. Jeb tried to run me over once as Jas and Cal were pulled into his car. I was crossing the street from the Sherriff's Department to my car and he waited for me to get in the middle of the street. The dispatcher saw the whole incident because her chair sat directly in front of the window only two feet away. I was lucky to be quick enough as Jeb squealed his tires racing towards me. The dispatcher immediately checked to see if I was okay. I was shook up. He had just missed me. I insisted they go and check on Jas and Cal. They visited his house and checked them and spoke with Jeb. We wrote up a police report and from then on, I only left after he departed. There were times the kids and I waited for 2 hours for him to show. My lawyer told me that was required. When there were no calls or anything we would just go home.

Jeb worked six miles from my house yet my children never received a phone call or even a birthday card. For children, a birthday is a major holiday and I made sure they always had a party to celebrate. I never regretted taking time off work or cancelling other plans to spend time with my children whenever needed. Now that they are adults they can look back, even though some things just do not have an explanation, and try to understand. Despite their fathers choice to be absent in their lives, they have done well and I am very proud of them.

Most people told me I was too overprotective and spoiled my children. Maybe so, but I was strict in many ways. They were each responsible for their own chores. TV was always censored at home until they were about sixteen and sometimes days would go by before it was even turned on. We were always busy doing something. At first they would keep their own rooms clean and toys in place. As they grew older they would also take care of pets and other household chores and learn to cook. Our basement was finished and a twenty-four by thirty foot room was for them to keep their toys and play. They would help outside with the vegetable and flower gardens and learned to drive the John Deere tractor. When they were old enough they learned house, car, tractor, go-cart, and motorcycle maintenance. If we could do it ourselves we did. These were not temporary chores, it was permanent. They would help each other or trade. I tried to keep gender in mind but believed it should be a mix so that they would not be biased and self sufficient and not think only women do this and men do that. They would be independent and able to do anything they put their minds to. On the ranch there was always something new and different but we made it fun and did it together. Sunday brunches and Saturday night dinners out and meals at home were together. It was a great time for conversations because they were always encouraged to keep open communications so they felt comfortable discussing anything.

Luckily I was able to trade or arrange time off work through the years as I raised my children, never missing sports events, church and school programs, recitals, holidays, or anything they wanted me to attend. Sometimes that meant driving from one end of the county to the other to see half of one event or game then returning to the other and back again to pick them up. Jas attended ballet, tap, jazz, modern dance, tumbling, baseball, volleyball, beauty pageants, and modeling. Cal loved video games and the computer and to be home to ride his go-cart and motorcycle in the timber on trails he made. I taught them as much baseball, volleyball, basketball, and football (not my favorite) as I could. The three of us practiced a lot through the years. We traveled whenever we had a chance even when they had to take a week or more off school. They always made up school work before or after our trip.

Every September and July was birthday parties with a house full of their friends with the cake, games, prizes, swimming, and overnights. My Mom and Dad had a very large in ground pool that kept them busy and worn out. Grandmother loved to help with their parties.

Our house was always full of kids for the day, nights, and weeks. My niece and nephew Zeke and Ann spent summers, weekends, holidays with us like their second home. Zeke is a year older than Jas and Ann, while Cal is almost two years younger. They grew up like brothers and sisters and even helped with chores. They all got along so well and I loved having them around.

As an investment, I purchased a travel business which I owned for twelve years. It was in a beautiful, historic town twenty-four miles from home on Main street with a large store front window and very large front office. Jas and Cal would bring Zeke and Ann or other friends with them whenever they could since they came to work with me when not in school. Sometimes they would stay with their grandparents. The back part of the office building was like an apartment so they had everything needed to stay all day. They enjoyed helping with filing, accounting, decorating, and anything else they were able to do. We would order out and eat there or go out for lunch or dinner. One room was props from all over the world including a mannequin, clothes, antiques, and some of their stuffed animals and toys. We would decorate the whole office and window for holidays or anything special since the Chamber of Commerce was very active and promoted many events. Being a member kept us involved in events like parades which Jas and Cal dressed up or acted in our room sized window or at the door. Cal was the actor and even as a child could come up with ideas no one else could. Jas wanted to oversee the business part. During those twelve years they were always involved with the travel business.

Jas and Cal were professional travelers from the time

they could drink from a bottle. No matter where we went they adapted well. I was very careful with anyone around them when in another country or here in the U. S., although it was a safer time then. Once a month we would take a trip even it was for the weekend. Shopping on Michigan Avenue, Rodeo Drive, Cruise ship stores and Ports, and antique shops in New England were fun because after that we would enjoy the hotels with pools, spas, saunas, game rooms, activities, and great meals. Cruising, flying, RVing, yachting, train travel and car trips were common for us. In Australia we drove a motor home from Sydney and chartered a yacht to snorkel the Great Barrier Reef. Out in the ocean, underwater was amazing until Jas decided some of the sea creatures we were swimming with were much larger than her. Cal was looking for a shark, which she wanted nothing to do with. A motor home is the only way to see every main highway in Alaska, hiking deep in the mountains to pan for gold in a stream, watching the Aurora Borealis, and whale watching by yacht to see the Glaciers. Cal learned to surf in Oahu and Jas was chosen to learn the hula and make leis on stage at a pig roast and luau celebration. They learned local crafts and took lessons of every kind on land and in the water on many Islands. One of our best trail rides was in the Superstition Mountains outside Phoenix led by a local teenager that was off work for the day. Of course Cal asked for the wildest horse and got it. Jas went for the more docile ride so we lagged behind a bit. The young man took us to his favorite place high in the mountains until we came to overlook all of Phoenix and the surrounding valley. A couple other unforgettable trail rides were through the Rocky

Mountains. In Excaret, Mexico we snorkeled down the underground river and explored ancient ruins. On one cruise we stopped at Dominica and walked up and down a trail through the rain forest and were caught in a downpour then minutes later watched the clear skies and rainbow appear. We played on white, brown, and black sand beaches with turquoise shades of crystal water. Once we went snow skiing, tubing, and snow-catting through the western states in the Rockies traveling by Amtrak. That trip made us realize there was another way to travel and to our surprise, elegant dining, delicious food, and outstanding service. We decided we could travel forever and never experience it all. We were blessed to be able to have that life.

At thirty-four I went back to college part time for two years so I had something to fall back on in case I decided to change careers. Criminal Justice and Psychology were my two choices and then I received my Private Investigation Certificate. I had completed many airline courses over the years and when Jas and Cal were old enough they helped with my homework and attended some classes with me. They were always welcome because they were so well behaved and mature. I felt lucky they were able to be with me so much while growing up. They learned and had fun at the same time.

There were a few men in my life but I always ended up focusing on my children instead. Even after a couple relationships of five years each I could not make that change. It was too complicated. I wanted to concentrate on my children and felt it was too much of a burden and responsibility to expect someone else to take on three of us. Maybe that came from my relationship with their father, even after many years.

For many years I held political positions in the county and stayed very active. My titles included County Vice Chairman, Secretary, Treasurer, Sergeant at Arms, and Precinct Committee person. I served as Welfare Services Committee person with the Health and Human Resources Department for the State. I was a member and past President of the Business and Professional Women for three counties. I worked with animal rescue organizations. I completed many college courses for travel, airlines, business, criminal justice, psychology and private investigation.

Choices

The older we get, the harder it is to find someone that is compatible and can blend in with the family structure that already exists. We want the emotional and financial compatibility and stability and the honest best friend and monogamous love of our life. We want it all. Then we want the healthy children and perfect family. That sounds like a soul mate and storybook life but there is no such thing. It is a vision and a need that most of us have but not reality. Some are taught that is what you wait or look for, like in a fairy tale. It is all in a matter of how close to those values we can find a compatible mate. What are we willing to settle for? Or should we wait it out and go through life without trying. At what point in a relationship do we decide that we can or cannot tolerate the beliefs, values and idiosyncrasies of a mate. How well do we really know someone until we have gone through different stages in our lives and through certain life changing events over years, of which no one can predict the outcome. Fate is not ours to change. We can only do so much and depending on those events and how they effect each person differently.

Most of the men I dated were decent but the few good ones I did not stay with. Was there an L on my forehead? The attraction of the psychos was a phrase that came to mind whenever I thought about dating. I was too stable and had my life together and I was very good with my money. When I wanted something extra it meant working overtime. I was dependent on myself. I was slow in comprehending the fact that men had an interest in what I had and since I did not realize exactly what that was, it would later cost me dearly. One does not know what they have until they no longer have it, or should I say until someone takes it all away. Not by choice.

Jas

Jas remembers her days growing up in the same home in the country. Summer days and nights were mostly outside playing in the timber and swimming at their Grandparents house which was just through the pasture and trees through the property. Much of that time was spent with their cousins, Zeke and Ann. They all loved the outdoors and when they tired of swimming they would build tree forts and clear pathways and swing on the vines in the trees. They played in the creek and cooked over campfires and planted wildflower gardens with rare flowers such as bloodroots, spring beauties, jack-in-the-pulpits, orchids, bluebells, lillies, ferns and more. She loved plants, birds, and all animals. They would walk through the pines and check for bird nests and make a list and wait and watch the eggs. At night they played hide and seek and light tag in the trees and if there were enough to play they would have teams. They had a tree fort and swing set along the timber where a turkey had made a nest and laid eggs so they were able to watch them hatch and grow. The turkeys would come to the other side of the house by the back deck to eat grain with the horses. Once, she found a gosling at the back of the house and took it in. She would sit at the pond with it and watch it play in the water. It would follow her around. Many animals were dropped off at the end of our lane over the years. Cats and horses were Jas' favorites to care for. One cat would always sit on her horses back in the stall. Her first horse was an Egyptian Arabian that was too high spirited. Later we found a beautiful Tobiano paint that was perfect. A friend of mine was talking about her horse which had the same name as my daughter and wanted to sell her if she could find a good home. She could ride that horse anywhere on her own and I never had to worry because they took care of each other.

The only animal she is cautious of is the squirrel. The squirrel gets its own story. One day Jas and Cal were playing outside with their dog. The dog thought the squirrel was too close so he chased and caught it, but only injured it. Cal decided Jas should save the squirrel while he held the dog. Jas saved the squirrel but it was so scared it bit into her hand and would not let go even as they tried to pull it loose by yanking on it's tail. When it finally released its teeth it scrambled up the nearest tree. Their grandfather grabbed a baseball bat and got the squirrel while her Grandmother tried to stop the bleeding. It was a very traumatic episode and we were all very concerned until the rabies test results came back negative. The wounds could not be stitched because of the rabies testing and she still has her permanent scars. Now when we are all together and see a squirrel we jokingly call her "squirrel bait".

Jas is the socialite and still likes to go and do things with her friends. She had lots of friends and kept busy. When she was old enough to date she chose some very nice boys. I was happy with her choices and they treated her well and always kept curfews. Maybe they worried about me.

At sixteen years old, Jas met her goal. As I had always promised, she received a new car and a cell phone. The cell phone came with restrictions. They had to be available whenever I called and keep under the minutes. We agreed on both. Jas ordered a Chevy ZR2 four by four truck and loved it. She drove it to her school which was sixteen miles away and helped me to take Cal to and from school until he was sixteen. They always knew I was a phone call away at any time. She worked on weekends during school and with me as a second job.

Jas' favorite trips were Australia and Alaska. Both have wonderful, educational zoos with hands on programs which were perfect for her. Australia had the most adorable animals like the koalas and kangaroos which she learned about firsthand as she played with them at the zoos. In the wild, we watched even more animals. Alaska had the scenic highways, abundant wildlife, and coastal towns like Seward. We walked a lot and watched jellyfish in the water from the docks. A woman we met gave us some fresh scallops and fish that her husband just brought in because she had too much already. We took a yacht through the Kenai Peninsula to see the glaciers and remote winding mountain roads. Since we wanted to look for gold, we went to the local hardware store and purchased a gold pan for each of us and the owner explained to us just how to do it. We did bring back some small pieces. Their zoo had taken in an orphaned moose, and a famous elephant that we watched paint. Jas had breakfast with Mary Carey, author and pioneer who signed her book about Alaska, at her Mt. McKinley Lodge which she built on her homestead. They had a quiet day and we just sat and listened and looked out at the breathtaking views. Jas always enjoyed books and wrote stories. Disney, MGM, and Epcot were always fun. In South Dakota she had to find a buffalo herd down a remote dirt trail just to watch them. Jas enjoyed the history of the New England States visiting a real Pioneer Village, Salem, Plymouth Rock, The House of Seven Gables, and many historical museums and sights. At one Island resort Jas was chosen to model some of the stores clothing and made friends from all over the world. She learned local arts and crafts as we traveled. Once she wanted to take out a paddle boat even though a posted sign warned of crocodiles. Later that day we walked the beach and came across it right in front of us and it was bigger than we were. She liked the more relaxing, sightseeing options like the glass bottom boats, snorkeling closer to the boat or beach, and played on many beaches at the Islands and collected sea shells. Jewelry, clothes, and Porcelain dolls from all over the world were also part of her collections. She liked to try all the native foods but never missed a dinner on a cruise ship. Before our trips she would study about that area so she knew what was important to see and do. She did not want to miss anything.

Jas loves her Grandparents and many times I had to make them get out of the swimming pool day and night just to take a break. I am surprised none of them grew gills because we went through tons of sun block and towels. Jas loved to play school and the lowest level of her grandparent's house was set up so they could have desks, papers, books, computers, Barbie's, dolls, play house, and other girls stuff. Once she learned to write she created her own stories. Sleeping in front of the fireplace and roasting marshmallows was common. There would be late night food fests with cool whip, chips, and cookies. If I would come down to check on them they would hide it under the bed with spoons and all. She remembers her Grandmother waking her on occasion to go for breakfast at six in the morning. Good thing she was an early riser. Many times Ann was there to go with them and since the boys were not early risers they slept. Their Grandfather would take them for a sleigh ride behind his tractor in the winter and into town for ice cream in the summer.

As a waitress on weekends, babysitting, and working for me at a Resort an hour away Jas kept busy when not in school.

Jas enjoyed the serenity and watching all the seasons at the ranch with her pets while she grew up. She liked school and planned to go to the local college for a business degree. It was the slower pace which she enjoyed. She was the youngest in her class and graduated at seventeen.

Cal

Cal was born full of energy and was way ahead of his age. He loved to help me and be outside whether it was summer or winter. Summers were swimming day and night at his Grandparents, playing sports, and anything he could think of to try that he had not done yet. He wanted to do everything from hiking through the timber to building projects. As a toddler he was hard to keep up with. Being the youngest of the four, when Zeke and Ann stayed, he did not get away with much even when he tried. The four of them loved to run the go-cart through our pastures and timber. Luckily none of them were injured, only the trees they ran into. The girls were never interested in the motorcycles so the boys did not have to share.

He always had a dog for a pet. The longest to be with us, Spike, did everything with him. Spike would run through our timber, creek, and pasture to keep up with him. I even let him bring him in the house sometimes because they were like friends. I would have to make him come in at night when it got late because he enjoyed the outdoors so much.

As an infant Cal chewed on toy cars, trucks, and plastic footballs. Then he would play Rambo with his Rambo three wheeler, gear, and outfit. He would dress up in camo clothes that I found for him and play outside. I purchased collectible matchbox cars over the years with a large case to keep them in good condition when he was not playing with them. He would study, draw, and show me how they could be better designed in grade school. Some weekends he spent attending car shows with his Grandfather and learning about new and antique vehicles. Well, we all went but my Mom, Jas, and I did our flea marketing and shopping. He would watch his Grandfather restore a 63 Chevy Impala convertible to mint condition and help with what he could. Since he was always working on something, Cal tried to learn because sometimes it was his something. He started out with pedal cars and trucks, then remote toys, electronics, go-carts, motorcycles, and cars. These 'toys' always needed something. His Grandfather taught him about maintenance too.

Cal learned to water ski, cross country ski, and downhill ski at a young age. My Aunt G and Uncle R spent lots of time with us on holidays and in the summer they brought their boat when visiting since we lived by the river. Cal never wore out and would tube and ski all weekend. Later he would ski and surf in the ocean while staying at the Islands. We all had our own snow skis. He would wear out his skateboards, roller blades, and snow board even though he took care of all his sports equipment which was well used.

Traveling was second nature to Cal and no matter where we went he did not miss anything. His favorite trips included snow boarding and skiing in the Rockies where the main runs were not his idea of fun. Our first trip to Yellowstone surprised him because he did not believe that wild buffalo would be close enough to touch until I stopped the car as we were surrounded by a herd with a bull just inches from his window. He loved surfing in Oahu, seeing Pearl Harbor, and touring a Navy submarine (thanks to a friend), though it was too close inside for me. He loved the Hawaiian pig roast and celebration. Hiking, sightseeing, and visiting local zoos in Australia and Alaska were also at the top of his list. He loves animals as much as Jas, especially when they have interactive sessions with their animals. One koala bear held onto him so tight when he tried to put it down, it left its claw marks across his back while I was snapping the picture. What a look he had on his face, almost the same as when the red kangaroo chased him when we stopped for a picnic in the forest. In Sydney we watched Enduro runners bike races and he could not get over the architecture of the Opera House. The Ocean, coral reefs, and all the different ocean life was never ending. Chena Hot Springs in Alaska was his favorite for panning gold and hiking high in the mountains, then sitting in the outdoor hot tub. He loved all the Islands and country's native markets and local foods at restaurants and cafes and cultures. More stuff to collect. We tried to stay off the beaten, commercialized path so the trips would be a more authentic experience. He would meet other children and talk with them about school, what they did when not in school and anything else he could learn. Sometimes language was an obstacle. In Jamaica a driver we met had stopped and climbed a tree and brought him a fresh coconut while we watched. Later he was chosen to play the steel drums in the Reggae band at the resort then went to the Kids Club where they were taking all kinds of lessons and activities. After snorkeling with barracudas in Barbados he ordered a root beer at a local café and gave it to me because it tasted funny. It was a bottle of beer. I know he would not give it back now. I took them to Cancun for Spring Break one year and took tours of beautiful beaches and ancient ruins. He went jet skiing and hit the local hot spots for young adults. His favorite formal dining experiences were on the cruise ships. He was so impressed with the creativity and imagination of the buffets. He was a connoisseur of the best.

Cal wanted to attend a private Catholic High School which was twenty-four miles away. We did it since Jas could help drive and I could alter my work schedule. He loved football, his favorite sport and liked the more challenging and extensive curriculum. I thought it would be a smart move for him after seeing the recent decline in the public school systems. Cal helped by working at the school, the mall, and at Mc Donald's after school, weekends, and summers and detasseled corn and landscaped. Also during the summer and weekends he was able to work with me at the Resort. He made many new friends and still made time for his best friend from his old school. After he got he driver's license he covered many miles to go out with his friends from all over.

Cal did well and reached his goal at sixteen and as I had always promised, he ordered his new Chevy Camaro and cell phone. He loved his car and it really helped Jas and I now that he could drive to and from school and work on his own. He used some of his money to put after market parts on his Camaro. He also had a 65 Chevy Bel Air that he and his friends drove and worked on. It was his restoration project. Computer programs, pencil, and paper were all he needed to design cars, trucks, and motorcycles. Every time he entered design and engineering competitions he received awards, ribbons, and monetary prizes. We designed an area in his room for his work with a six foot counter top, cabinets, stools, and lights. In high school he could freehand anything and has a portfolio that would be comparable to one with an engineer degree.

After high school Cal planned to attend an Auto Design and Engineering College in California. He would also be graduating at seventeen.

When they were able to understand I explained the three C's which were character, courage, and conscience. If you have these they will have the fourth; class. I am very proud that they have these. I have raised my children since they were babies and tried to keep them in a secure, loving environment, same values, same friends, same home.

After Many Years

After seventeen years being single I married a good friend who was also one of my corporate clients. We had many mutual friends to do things with so it just seemed the next step in my life. He was very intelligent and sincere. But I guess when you are good friends that is just what it is. We did not live together since he traveled all the time and had a house in Florida. We all got along until the marriage. We flew to Vegas and had a nice ceremony. It was easy to set up. We used a limo and the little white chapel with a very nice minister. We booked the hotel ahead but waited until we got there to make the wedding arrangements. Afterwards we took Jas and Cal and my parents sightseeing. Within a couple months it all took its toll. We would talk on the phone to try to decide what to do. I wanted to have it annulled, but no one would do it so we used an attorney and signed a paper and it was over. I had to work all the time and it was stressful. He had no children and it was too much of a change for us both because we lived in two different worlds. The split was amicable.

A note to self: If you have a good friend – do not marry him. Keep your good friend.

Trusting Or Not

It was easy to see the travel industry would change because of on line travel availability. Anything could be purchased on line. My business was very profitable and my corporate accounts extended throughout the United States. National Travel Schools sent interns to my business to complete their training. I trusted my employees for years. I was comfortable and thought I had learned all that was needed to have a decent lifestyle. After one of our trips my books were way off as I tried to catch up and had to start pulling up previous months accounts. When a business handles the Airlines' money, tickets, and transactions, the first requirement is to be bonded and retain a Certified Public Accountant to submit reports to a Corporation that was allowed to withdraw weekly from my business bank account. A never ending, enormous amount of paperwork and red tape. It took me over a month to even comprehend there was a serious problem. At first I told myself it was just an error or a mistake. Since my CPA did not catch any errors or missing transactions I thought it had to be in my end of my accounting. Another month went by and I began to go through each transaction with two accountants and then my CPA had confirmed my belief that three of my employees were stealing and covering for each other. I could not put the pieces together because it was a very intricate scam and I found I am not of the criminal mind. Or is that really just being too trusting? Every week and month my reports were not matching the money received. My money was going out and documents were missing. I questioned them over the next few weeks but they always denied anything was wrong so I tracked down each transaction by each employee with the help of the Airlines, Tour companies, Resorts, Car rental companies, hotels, and so on. I guess I was hoping that they would confess or show regret or agree to pay back at least some of what they stole. After all it was all now in black and white and documented. That documentation took months, but it had to be done. My attorney suggested I turn it all over to the Federal Government as we continued to add it all up. Unfortunately the total amount of money stolen was unbelievable. It was so much more than we thought. It made me sick!! We found everything from illegal signatures, embezzlement, credit card fraud, stolen tickets and documents, and so much more. No wonder why some of my employees had separate post office boxes.

When I presented all the reports to my attorney and he was amazed at the criminal mind of these three employees.

The local Law Enforcement had no idea as to how to handle a crime like this. It is called White Collar Crime and I soon learned how it was becoming more common. A local bank was going through the same thing at the same time, but chose not to prosecute in the end because of who she was and the negative publicity it would bring the bank in the end. The bank ate the financial loss and let the criminal employee go. Of course it began with one person, then two, then the third person who did not have the criminal mentality. The third girl became very comfortable in the scams and stealing so that it was easier for us to track backwards and show all the evidence. My phone bill helped when we matched dates and missing monies. She was sending airline tickets all over the United States to friends and family and would collect the money herself. They had set up post office boxes for incoming money and covered each other posing as myself (the owner and manager) on the phone when needed. Local and Federal Law Enforcement became involved when all the documentation was presented. Two of the three employees were married and started to catch on to the fact that they could be federally prosecuted and go to prison, especially since we had all the documentation needed. They opened post office boxes out of town so the spouses and parents would not receive anything by mail. That is part of what makes a criminal good at what they do, perfection. If no one talks no one can get caught because they can use each other. Denial of any and all wrongdoing. Never admit to anything no matter what. No one wants to go to prison. Still it was so hard to believe. I would never understand. Is it the way a person is raised and the family lives that way, a learned behavior?

Or is it a sickness that develops for some reason? In these cases it was not just for the money because the parents and spouses were medium to upper income level. Each of the employees were given a polygraph test and all three of them failed. One of them told me that she was only doing what she was taught to do by the others and did not know any better. My attorney told me the cost to prosecute these three employees would be extreme because it would all be at my time and expense. Even with restitution ordered they would file bankruptcy and be allowed to walk away after all. But I would incur all the expenses. One had already left the state and disappeared and that expense would be up to me to just find her and bring her back to this state for trial. Another moved and was working at a large corporation, of course, in their travel department.

It did not take long to decide I wanted to sell the business. I now understand why the employee who "taught" the others how to embezzle, wanted to purchase the business. And why I was making lots more money than I knew though she was pouring that money into her own pocket, as she taught the others. Each day I wanted to be there less. Another stressful decision but there were other careers even if I wanted to remain involved with the travel industry. Once my business was sold I could take the time to choose a new career. One thing I had always wanted was to purchase some property in Montana. We traveled many times to that state and always talked about ranching there. We set up an appointment with a real estate agent and took a ride. Many properties were available and one stood out from the rest. The school system, the nearest town, and the ranch in the mountains were perfect.

So everyone wanted to purchase my business, but of course no one had the money. I had all kinds of offers and deals. I just wanted out and one of my employees wanted to purchase the business. We agreed on an amount and began the process of all the red tape. Assets and bonds must be verified and submitted for approval. I did not know she was planning on leaving her husband at that time and was setting herself up for a good life. Everyone has an angle. Some are just evil and selfish and do whatever they have to as long as they get what they want. Another woman had met and called me many times and was trying to get the money together but then dropped it. So this employee had the money and we proceeded at the same time the other woman came to my office and handed me a check for the amount I wanted. The employee threw a fit and told her she could not purchase the business because she was. In the end I said fine, just come up with the money. She did not. It ended up her sister-in-law was buying it and would be giving me the money. I trusted people when it came to business, you know give your word and that means something.

It means nothing. I found out the hard way again. The sister-in-law explained her husband would not let her write the final check, but she expected me to continue to work and help her. That family was having problems and had other businesses. So I call the other woman who had a check in hand and she said sorry, I had all this money and had to do something with it and purchased another travel business. I could not believe what was going on.

This was no joke and so much money and work involved. Lesson learned yet?

My choices were go to court and spend lots of money and time to try to recover or what? My lawyer did not even know how to advise. The problem was with all the airline regulations and travel related corporations were already processing the sale for the new owner or owners who formed a corporation. A disaster for me. We came to an agreement that she would come up with the money if I stayed to help her to run the business and be paid for doing so for a short time. What else could I do but try it. Of course it did not work because then she wanted me to do all the work for her since the business was over her head. Thinking I would stay to recoup my money she held out. I asked for my check and she told me her husband still would not let her take the money. I told her I would not help unless she paid me the money she owed me. She refused. In the meantime, everything was now in their corporate name and the process was final as far as they were concerned and there was nothing they could do. I tried but ran into dead ends and lots of expense. How much money should I spend to recover what they owed me? After the first court appearance and lengthy discussions with my attorney and paying him and my accountant the conclusion was let it go and take the loss rather than to add to it. The person with the most money wins in court, not legal or illegal. Even with signed papers. By this time the business had suffered greatly and I had many calls from clients that wanted me to take it back and stay. She just decided to close the doors, which was quite sad. She was out nothing and actually made out quite well by selling off all the furnishings and supplies, taking the cash and walking away. If I had it to do over, knowing that our legal system does nothing for those with the least money, I would not have lost so much because I would have pursued it to the limit.

I often wonder about the fire in which the whole block burned down to the ground and my business lost ninety percent of the contents. No one was ever suspect or convicted though it was claimed to be arson. It was during the night when I got the call. Believe it or not this happened when I first began to question my employees and rerun all my reports. So obviously I became sidetracked for a while and really did not pick back up on it until I reopened in another building. But then I never realized the extent of what was going on in the beginning. So it was not top of the list when I was trying to decide to reopen and start up new. If I had only known what I know now.

Moving On

Many of my friends owned restaurants and bars so I worked for them after taking some time off so Jas and Cal could go with me on some trips. That was my break from the steady pace. Our break for quality time and to catch up. The toll it takes on everyone is something one would have to go through and experience to fully comprehend. My political constituents had knowledge of some openings for employment with the State if I chose to test for the positions available. Another long process for those on the outside. I missed the travel industry. A major airline was hiring and I applied and was hired immediately. All the training was priceless and I loved working for them. The employees that were currently there were not at all willing to let anyone use their travel perks which is always a priority. A short time later three of us quit because the only alternative would have been to move to a larger city or drive over an hour each way. Back to my friends for work while I decided what was next. I liked the fact that the schedules could be worked around my children. I was just used to that for so long.

My friend Keri's son had a beautiful wedding and reception that I attended. I had matched her with an old friend Ken, who had divorced. They married and we often met for dinner and attended events together. So at this reception she introduced me to an old friend of hers. We danced and even dated and seemed to get along well. Daniel lived with his brother up north and sold used cars with him. It so happened I was due for a new car so I promised to let him price one.

When a vehicle is purchased, the car salesman takes down your driver's license and other information from you. In reality, your whole life and financial records can then be obtained. It is that simple. Our laws allow that type of business to access personal past and present records.

The distance seemed to be too much for me and he was always busy 'working' at all hours. I was always working at least one job, usually more. I had never known a used car salesman and was not familiar with their way of life. He had an explanation for everything. My friend thought he was great. Daniel was best friends with her late husband who had passed unexpectedly. We dated for a few months and then decided we were too busy and I could not place my finger on something that was not right, just off, was all I could explain. Like another friend told me that was a gut feeling which is almost always right. Go with it. It is a red flag. So it seemed no loss, move on. Be comfortable. I had an lawyer friend that I went to dinner with on occasion and his son and Cal, the same age, would go with us. Most of my male friends had sons Cal's age so we would hang out and do things they liked. One of my best friends was my first date in high school and we had always kept in touch.

Keri called me and had seen an ad in her paper for a member service representative, but it would be at least an hour drive for me. She thought it would be perfect for me and it promised great pay and benefits. I called and set up an interview. I spoke with a woman that asked if I could return if they flew a Director from Corporate headquarters in to meet with me. Within a few minutes he hired me on the spot and wanted me to develop their member services department. It was a very prestigious and high paying job so I could not pass it up. I could do that since I had sales background and the resort was beautiful. Then within a couple of months they flew someone to the resort to promote me to Director of my department. I loved it though it was very challenging.

I worked a lot of hours but the nice part was my children and I was able to work around each other. Lots of drugs were used around there, but not in my department. It was enjoyable since I hired my son and daughter to work and when schedules allowed we rode together. On weekends when they had plans, they drove separate.

I started dating a nice man that I had gone to school with. His son and Cal were the same age and did things together. He had a younger daughter and we all got along well. It was casual and we had fun. We worked around our hours and life was good. I started to get further ahead and with Jas and Cal getting older I wanted them to have what I promised.

Springtime rolled around and we planned a trip. Jas and Cal chose Cancun for spring break. Any where was fine with me. I arranged some time off and trained someone to handle my reports to relieve the work load for my administrative assistant, even though she was quite capable. It was a high stress, fast paced business. That is why the money was great. You don't get something for nothing. Never. Everything has a price. Our trip to Cancun and Excaret was one of the best. We stayed at an oceanfront all inclusive resort with two balconies and did everything we could. We came home very relaxed.

Additional acreage adjoining my property came up for sale. It had timber, hills, pasture, and a creek. After speaking with the real estate agent I put in a bid and a down payment leaving only the final contract. My bank approved my loan. All ready to go. The many owners lived in different states so I had to be patient. I planned on making a ranch with cabins and trail riding so it gave me time to put the rest of the business together. All was going well as planned.

It was April, 1999. Then the calls came from Daniel again. He had spoken with Keri who told him I was doing very well with a boyfriend and a great job and I was happy. I told him I was seeing someone but when the time came for my other two vehicle purchases I would let him price them. Keri told me how he found her a great deal on her car. I told him I was taking the children on a trip and he could call later. We spoke on the phone and eventually I drove to the car dealership to price some new cars for Jas. He seemed to have given me a good deal on the Chevy Silverado 4x4. After the trip I did not see much of my friend so I accepted a dinner invitation with Daniel. At that time I was not sure I wanted a serious relationship with him, but he begged to see me. He wanted to settle down and I was the one. He wanted to get married. We were both working lots of hours, or so I thought he was. I never doubted what he was doing. Between Jas and Cal, my hours at work, and the ranch, there was not much time left.

Keri and I talked about Daniel and anything I should know about him. All was good. She said he would be good to Jas and Cal if it ended up a serious relationship. Daniel wanted to settle down and get out of the city and what sounded great was that he said how much he loved me and what a perfect life we would have. I wanted to take it slow and wait so I would not make any mistakes. I have unfortunately made enough to last me a lifetime. It sounded almost too good so I was a little distant. Who better to ask, about him, than a mutual friend? No one else ever said a thing to me about him or his family. I was all for settling down and sharing what I had with someone I loved. After all we wanted the same things and we were old enough to know what we wanted and were financially capable. Jas and Cal were sixteen and fourteen, in high school and his older children were grown and lived in Arizona. His son, Daniel Jr, was studying theology to become a minister and had all kinds of scholarships for college. His daughter, Cindy, was in college but did not know what she would major in yet. That sounded stable. No red flags.

I paid close attention to his interaction when ever my kids were around. When I took my kids to the city or wherever for some event or show, dinner or whatever, Daniel would even meet us. Jas and Cal used to love to go to Dave and Busters and Medieval Times or the museums and aquariums or shopping the big malls and specialty plazas. By appearances, all seemed well. That was very important and top of my list.

Jas and I discussed her sixteenth birthday and decided to look for her vehicle for her birthday present. We were narrowing down which vehicle when Daniel suggested I let him look and price what Jas wanted. He said he had a new car coming in from the factory if I could wait another week, so we did. It was perfect. A Z-24 convertible with everything on it and Jas loved it. The price was comparable. After Jas and I had driven up to look at it and decided we would buy it, I arranged for us to pick it up. She was very happy with it but still liked our truck also. We ended up driving each others vehicles a lot. I drove more miles so I saved lots of gas driving the car. Daniel had also arranged the financing on the car the same as he had on the truck and I saw no problems with that. It made sense to let your car salesman take care of it all since I had little spare time. I just signed and drove home with the new vehicles.

We discussed in detail future goals and finances and what we owned and any liabilities. Daniel kept telling me how he loved the fact that I was so stable and had my life together and had everything he had always wanted but he said he just never achieved that goal. But now he wanted to and could financially. Daniel told me over and over how he was always so overly generous with everyone which is why he has never had anything. He said he had taken good care of his children and put them into college and set them up. He just has always lived with his brother out of convenience and helping him since they always worked at the same car dealership. Even when they lived in other states. I paid my bills on time, had money in the bank and a cash box, kept everything insured, paid for my home I built twenty-five years ago (which I had never missed a payment), and supported two children and we lived very comfortably. I was very honest about my finances thinking that is how to build a great relationship if marriage is next. At that time in April and obviously before, Daniel had already checked and verified my personal information and knew exactly what my assets were through the dealership and credit reports he obtained. He knew it all. Now I know why he was in such a big rush to get married. He knew I was not lying about anything. Daniel had his stories and all about how much he made and what he owned and how he paid for Daniel Jr and Cindy's college and cars and now that they were older he did not have all that expense. I believed it all. Why would someone make up stories going into a marriage. Stories and lies that would quickly catch up with him and there would be no way around the truth then. Things that cannot be hidden or ignored and would not disappear.

After much convincing and pressure to marry him, Daniel and I set a date for June. Unfortunately it was only June of 1999. Less than two months away. It was all so fast, like a whirlwind. Everything he promised and talked about was just so perfect, I gave in. He begged me and told me it was perfect because I could give him three chances or as he called it, THREE STRIKES AND YOU'RE OUT. That was his deal so I did not have anything to worry about. I explained there would be no divorce, no matter. We had to be sure. The only way out would be if one of us died. That is the only way it could be because I would never divorce again, I told him. Daniel agreed. I spoke to Jas and Cal about the marriage and Daniel seemed to be good with them so there was no apparent problems. I asked every question I could think of so there would be no surprises after we were married. No conflict, all ironed out. Daniel asked that I handle all the finances since he could see that I was good with money and he was tired of having nothing and too old to live like he had been. He loved my stability. At forty-five years old he knew what he wanted. It was what he always wanted and it was going to be perfect. That is what he told me over and over.

In the middle of all this, came the call from my real estate agent. I needed to come in to sign the final contract and then I would own this property. That is how it works, right? Or how it is supposed to work. Of course, I had told Daniel about it and he rushed right down from the suburbs to go with me. I did not think it odd or strange that he dropped everything to be there for that. We were going to get married now and he would be involved. He quickly decided since he was making so much money he should jump in and help. For some reason at this meeting one of the owners wanted to hold out for more money. The agent asked if I was willing to pay more. No, it was already done. Daniel abruptly said yes and he raised my offer. More money. But the sale price was already set and signed. I asked to speak with Daniel because I was so shocked. We spoke alone and he assured me that it would be okay since he had plenty of money to pay for it and it was still a good deal. I explained it sounded like a good deal to him because the property costs where he lived were more than triple compared to where I lived out in the middle of nowhere. He said there was nothing to worry about and he should help out financially since we would soon be married. He wanted me to have what I wanted. But I was purchasing it before he was in the picture. This purchase and business deal was way before he was in the picture. I was concerned with the way he went about it without my knowledge. I plan or figure out all the details before I do something serious like that. Not just the snap of your fingers or a whim. That is what I explained to him. Daniel convinced me again to do what he wanted. Another check for me to write. He explained if I really loved him and wanted our marriage to work he needed to be involved and could easily help pay for things and his name should also be on it. That was how it should be. I believed his explanation, or should I say, his 'theory'.

The contract was redone adding his name and the higher amount for the property purchase. I ended up writing my checks for the additional amount because Daniel told me he was in such a hurry he did not bring his checkbook. But as soon as he got home he would get some of the money to me. He had the money but not on him at the moment, it was tied up, and I believed him. Of course I was using the collateral in my house. Luckily, I left the loans separate. My house and the property it sat on remained in my name only. Unfortunately, both of our names were on the new property we were acquiring. I thought it was a better idea because that was going to be my business which I originally planned to keep separate anyway. Daniel explained the loan should be one with everything together. He told me if I really loved him and planned on staying with him and marrying him then everything I had should be in both names. That meant his name on everything I owned even though he owned nothing at all but clothes, a bed frame, a chair and debt. Everything I owned could be his and it just seemed off that he was so insistent. Too much too soon. I had two children to raise yet and fair was fair. I have never in my life asked anyone to just give me a ranch and all that goes with it. I have never expected or even thought of someone just signing over their house and property or any part of it to me. Was I being mean and unfair and not believing I would stay married to him? The bank thought it was fine the way I had set it up because I asked them.

Playing House

In a short time I seemed to prepare for a simple garden wedding and dinner afterwards for our families and a couple of friends at a local restaurant. Daniel Jr. and Cindy had arranged to be there since Daniel had bought them airline tickets. The weeks before the wedding were stressful and Daniel was not around to help except on a weekend that he was able to get away from work. After finding someone to take over some of my duties as director for a couple of days, I was ready. I was busy at the resort but was able to manage a couple of days off to get married. We decided not to take a honeymoon until later in the year since we were both so busy. We talked on the phone a lot. He had planned on moving down to my house at the end of the quarter or he would lose his bonuses at the dealership. His father was going to retire and co-owned a used car business about twenty-five miles away. If Daniel did not transfer to a larger dealership that he had lined up, he could always take his fathers place. That all sounded like a plan. It did not bother me that he would be living in the suburbs until he repositioned himself into a closer location and better job. Even if that meant it might be two or three months. After all we would have all the time in the world.

A curious envelope arrived in the mail at my house just before the wedding. It was addressed to Daniel and Jane Mohy. My first name and his first and last name. But we were not married and I had not changed my name. I opened it and found a collection agency from an unpaid residential utility bill in another state. The collection agency had tracked down this couple to my address after many attempts. It seems these people had continued to live there and let their bills run up and then just disappeared according to the letter. Daniel was coming to my house so I left it on the counter and when he got there I questioned him about it. He said he had no idea who it was and he took the letter and said he would contact them and straighten it out. Do not worry about it because that stuff happens all the time. He had something like that sent to him before and he knew what to do. I never thought any more about it. It was not me and I had never lived in that state. It was just a mistake.

Now we were close to the wedding date and trying to get our things together as a married couple. His ideas were changing because as he said he wanted to get moved in with me at the ranch as soon as possible while we continued to work. So it sounded like he was all in disorder trying to get his checking account closed so we could use only a joint account to take care of the ranch.

It would only make sense to use my bank, at which I was well established. He moved quite often and never kept an account at any bank for long. He said he was short for one account and overdrawn because he could not get money from his other accounts in time but if I could just write him a check to cover the overdraw he would be able to close that account out and be done with it. I wrote a check and took it to his bank to deposit so he could close out the account. I explained I had not overdrawn my own accounts and would not tolerate it if we were to use my accounts that had been set up for so many years. Daniel agreed that it was not a good practice and that it was just a bad time and so much going on. In a couple of weeks he would have about five or six thousand extra so we could get that added to my account to show he was sincere and wanted to do what we discussed. Daniel showed me his two credit card statements that he just paid up because on one he had charged five thousand dollars for his daughters bedroom set. He was trying to get his two credit cards paid off before marriage like I did. That way no extra money was going out every month. I did not ever want to live paycheck to paycheck and there was no reason to. It was all part of the agreement. I had what I could afford and did not want that to change. I had the same house, credit cards, bank accounts, and no need to change any of it. I may not have had the best of everything but I paid for it. I always had plenty of equity in my home and property and told Daniel I never wanted that to change either. Everything was out in the open and each detail was clarified so there would be no questions or surprises. I had dotted every I and crossed every T.

When he was always working and could not get time off to come to see me I would drive to see him and go to dinner. Mack, his brother, usually went with us. Daniel's best friend, Mat, went with us and sometimes brought his fiancé. Daniel, Mack, Mat, and Dan were all car salesmen. That was the only people he ever did anything with. I thought it was due to the fact that they worked the same hours and had so much in common. They would go out after work together but not usually as couples. That was okay with me since I was so far away and worked and kept busy with my children. I was trusting. Being introduced to many friends, business associates, waitresses, and bartenders I felt it not necessary to question anyone. Even his female friends that I met seemed friendly and sincere. Daniel had his favorite places to go and I went along many times and enjoyed their company. That is about all we did together. We thought we would travel and do all the other things we wanted at a later time when it slowed down. For now we planned on working and saving money. My business plan would allow more time and money.

About one or two times a week Daniel had to drive down and visit his mother and father who lived about twenty-five miles from me and a few times I went along. They were short visits when I was there. He would always leave to go to his father's business to discuss Daniel taking it over. They were not comfortable going over the finances and business details with me present so I was not allowed to be involved. Daniel told me when they had it all figured out then we could go through it since I would be helping with the business once he took it over. His dad was ready to retire now but wanted to finalize the details with him. Daniel would bring me up to speed when that was all ready to happen. That was fine with me since there was no rush because the used car business is pretty basic as far as what he told me. Daniel was paying him weekly so he could just walk in and take it over.

One Signature

The time had come. It was June of 1999 already though it seemed to go so fast. Since there would only be a few people for the wedding and dinner it did not require too much planning or money. That was fine with me. Jas and Cal were becoming a little cautious about the whole idea but they were sixteen and fourteen so I did not think much of it. I just passed it off as a big change since everything seemed to be in order. No one had said anything negative. It was a big step for all of us. Daniel Jr. and Cindy came from Arizona and were staying with relatives from their mother's side. My mother, father, Jas, and Cal left our house to meet everyone at the garden in the park and waited for the Judge to show. It went smoothly with all our immediate family and a few friends each there. It was very hot and humid so the Judge breezed through the short and simple ceremony. Then the Judge had us each sign the marriage certificate. One simple signature on a piece of paper and that was a legal marriage. It took five seconds. Just think that one signature on a piece of paper could change your whole life so quickly and dramatically. My life and Jas and Cal's lives would be forever changed. We just did not have any idea how extreme that could be. After it was over we did the picture thing. We had champagne in the park pavilion to get out of the sun. Everyone was getting along well. I was happy and the children seemed to be doing well. We proceeded to a local restaurant for dinner. It all turned out quite nice and at the end of the day everyone seemed to be relieved it was over. One signature and I was married.

Daniel, Daniel Jr., and Cindy returned to my house with Jas, Cal, and I. Daniel had taken another day off work to stay there. We visited a short time and then they all left while Jas, Cal and I remained at our house. I did not feel as though it was an upset of our schedules and our home life was the same, no change.

Over the next few weeks Daniel and I spoke on the phone and if he was unable to come down then I would go to see him on our time off. I could not stay away from home to stay at his brother's apartment and leave my children unsupervised so we did not see each other much but it was only temporary. He was working on either taking over his fathers used car business and/or working at a large dealership closer to my house so he could drive it daily.

We each had our own business meetings and then we would meet for dinner and dance and cocktails when we could. It was relaxing and enjoyable. I still had lots of time for my children and all the animals and country life which I could never give up. It is all I knew, by choice.

A New Life

In the meantime, the property that I was trying to purchase was finalized and my bank had drafted the final check for closing. Daniel easily managed the time off for the trip down at the closing for the additional property. Since the property purchase was final Cal and I cleared more paths and cut firewood in the timber and trimmed trees and added more fence. There were some nice trails and we would ride the horses through and time the ride for the business. Jas was always gone and working and was losing interest in the horses but still interested in the business aspect. She had a steady boyfriend who was very nice and treated her well. They spent most of their time together. We had planned on building cabins and cleared the locations near the creek with beautiful views so they were not too close together. The ranch was looking good and it was a perfect layout and size. It was all falling into place. We would be happy with the new business and be able to live right there where we had always lived. Maybe even purchase a vacation cabin in Montana which was still in the back of my mind because I loved it there. Maybe later but for now I had the plans for the cabins ready and all the paperwork was piling up for everything to get the ranch started. I had previously received most of what was needed in paperwork for a business with guest cabins and ranch. Daniel even came down a couple of times to help. He did not know much about country life and I was far from the city. He knew nothing about horses or animals. I tried to show him some of the ropes and explain the business part of what I was doing. The 'kids', I call them since they are getting older and no longer children, and I were always busy preparing the ranch to become a business. For the most part, the first few weeks of marriage continued as if nothing had changed.

After a few weeks of marriage Daniel decided he could close out that checking account he had and we would use my checking account since it was more stable and I had it for a while and of course I had money in it. I really did not want to close out my account so I reluctantly added his name because he said that it would make it easier for him and he could send money from his paycheck automatically because he was not around. He told me that was the only way for a married couple to keep finances straight, otherwise it was deceiving for me to keep my own money and checks separate. He said if I wanted to keep my own account I was trying to hide something from him. I told him I was not trying to hide anything but I wanted to keep what I have always had and I would not deal with negative accounts like the ones he continued to have. Daniel promised there would always be a few thousand dollars extra left in the checking account. I finally gave in when he showed me he closed his checking account up there where he lived. He promised no more bounced checks and nasty letters from the bank and credit card companies. His two credit card companies were sending letters for non payment. I was using up my money fast so I figured if I just helped him out through this rough, slow time for him we could get where we planned. Even if we were married I would not bounce my checks and I could still pay all of my own bills, insurance, cars and house payments. He agreed he was on track and said he was financially off to a good start again. He said there would be ups and downs in the used car business so I would need to understand and get used to it. I did not know what to say. I was not sure that I liked those explanations now that we were married. I had taken on more financial burdens and I wondered just how much. Prior to marriage it was a different story. Now something was changing and not for the better. I did not understand why and began to see him less as the days passed. More money was always an issue for his next crisis. It was beginning to be the norm. Definitely not the kind of stable and calm life I was used to. It was unfamiliar territory and not just a new marriage going through changes.

Daniels' father had called and told him about this great deal he had for us: Two burial plots for only twenty thousand dollars each and they were right next to his mother and father's plots. Daniel thought we should purchase them right away so if I had the money right now he could pay me back later and we would not miss out on the deal. He explained how he knew we were just married but that should just be part of our future planning together, even though it sounded morbid and cold. He reassured me that his father was just trying to help us out with such a good deal. He said if we did not want to do it now we would never be able to get a deal for forty thousand dollars again. He really wanted us to always be together, forever. The whole idea was too much for me. Why would we spend that kind of money weeks after marriage for burial plots I asked? That conversation went on for weeks but I would not agree to pay for it. Daniel told me I was just selfish and if I loved him and wanted to stay married I would share. I heard that all the time. But was I? Was I being that selfish? Why couldn't he share anything? He explained he did not have any thing right now but when he did it would be different and if I really planned on staying married and loved him and wanted this to work I would help out and share because I could afford to. He said I would see that it would be different later, but I had to help financially until he caught up. Some of the money he was supposed to receive from sales on insurance did not come through and he was trying to collect it. He was sure he would end up with the large check but we would have to wait. That is all. It was that simple. Maybe I was too worried and selfish right now. Maybe it would all change the way he said and I should just help out and be patient.

Once again Daniel reassured me that it would all work out and he came down to my house and stayed for the weekend to show me the plan. We produced each bill and expense we had and our income was plenty to cover with extra. He was just about to pay off his two credit cards. He asked to see my social security statement of benefits so he could show me how he even planned for retirement. Yes, it looked great and sounded great. Perfect. Why was I so worried and concerned about his expenses. There would be all kinds of money. He showed me on paper in black and white, everything we planned and talked about.

As long as Daniel was trying to put the whole future plan together he felt it was only fair that his name be put on everything. I mean everything I owned because he owned nothing. I told him that made me nervous because of what I had already seen. He said we were married and I still was being selfish by not sharing. He told me that if he had anything he would have shared it, I did not feel that was fair. He said he could not help it, he was always too generous to people.

All of these changes came so quick and I would need to get used to these ideas, adjust and move forward. After all I had always overcome the obstacles life had surprised me with, both good and bad. One way or another I managed to put it in the past, move on and have a comfortable life with my kids. So this was just going to be another adjustment, though it seemed to be like a tornado coming across the sky. In my mind I just told myself that I would have to bend more because I was not giving enough or putting enough into this relationship to make things run smooth and move forward in a positive direction. That is how I had always overcome obstacles and negative things in the past. Now I would have to do it again.

It seemed there was an abundance of negative energy, especially for two people newly married. The positive energy between us should have been overwhelming. We were older and knew we wanted the same things in our careers and all aspects of our lives. Daniel agreed whenever we discussed the present and future. How could we go wrong?

Daniel always told me that if I agreed to marry him I could hold him to the three strike rule. Three strikes and you are out. But I told him that we needed to promise instead to just have a good marriage. I would not divorce until death; like they used to say, 'until death do us part'. That would be better than his promise of three strikes. Of course, to me it meant three mess ups, like staying out with the guys drinking late or missing something important, maybe even getting caught in a lie. Silly.

I noticed Daniel had a prescription which he took for Epilepsy. He explained his condition was from being beat up years prior. Did he have medical problems that were serious? Epilepsy – I never saw any type of complications or problems. He told me he could not go without his medication. Then I never saw or heard any more about it. I know he liked sympathy.

Changes

Weeks passed and suddenly everything seemed to go downhill. Not just problems but it became one crisis after another, nonstop. Then Daniel's kids were always having financial crises of some sort every week, too. As I understand it, his twenty-three year old son had lost his sports scholarship for the third time. He was going to stay in college but was thinking of changing his major again. He needed money for college and he needed a new vehicle because of an accident he was in. As far as I knew he never had a job. His daughter, twenty-one, changed her mind on her college major. She also needed some more furniture after moving from her mother's place to a bigger apartment. Even though that move was with a boyfriend. It seemed to be large amounts of cash in a very short time. All large amounts not just a few hundred here and there. Then Cindy was also involved in a car accident and she needed a new car. I never figured out who was at fault but I helped with getting the new car. At least she worked part time at a restaurant. Daniel was lucky that he sold cars for a living. This was all just within weeks. He explained it was just a fluke that it all happened at once right after we were married, no coincidence. He just needed to help them each through a tough spot in their life and it was not their fault. He said that he would not be a good father if he did not help financially right away. After I thought about it I decided that it was strange that all this major expense suddenly occurred, but if that happened with my kids I would also help out. That was fair. I did not want his kids to dislike me for standing in the way of their future. So we assisted financially by sending money and vehicles to each of them. He explained to me that that was the kind of relationship they had. One where they never called unless they needed something. I know everyone has a different kind of relationship with their kids depending on the circumstances so I did not question him. Then as soon as they received that money there were more calls, they each had more problems. Now I was becoming concerned because all this time Daniel was having financial problems himself. He had still not been able to help with anything and I was paying for it all and now helping him pay for his adult kids on top of that. I did not have an endless pot of gold and that is what it was beginning to look like his kids needed. Then he told me his ex-wife called in a panic and needed a new car. She said that she had no money and begged him to find something suitable for her because she did not know anything about cars. She had called my house one time looking for Daniel and the only thing she would tell me was everyone loves Daniel, with the emphasis on everyone. That was the problem, she said. She also lived in Arizona and I did not think it made sense that someone five states away would purchase a car and want it delivered to her. I told Daniel that something was wrong here. I had tried to straighten out his finances and help but there was no end in sight. He told me not to worry because he was making plenty of money but he just had to catch up and then he would be able to help me financially as we planned and as he promised. It was always temporary and I had nothing to worry about according to him. But I was becoming aware of something very wrong and it made me very nervous and even scared.

Daniel would call me at all times of the day and night when it was convenient and he had nothing else going on. He did not want me to talk to my friends because he said whatever we were doing was no one else's business. I was to have my phone on me at all times so when he called I was to answer it no matter if I was doing chores or building fence or at work. If I missed a call he would freak out on the phone when I did answer. My job was becoming stressful because he showed up a couple of times and tried to cause a scene. He began to call me weekly on each payday and demand to know the exact amount of my paycheck. He said he had to plan a budget. My checks would vary, even by two thousand dollars each week. The amount had to be to the penny and I better tell him exactly that amount or he would be down to see me and embarrass me. I was trying to run my department and if my secretary or employees would answer the phone and get him he would be ignorant.

Everyone wanted to know what was going on. Red flags!

Daniel wanted me to work only at certain times so I could be at his beck and call. Then sometimes he wanted me to work for him and quit so he could keep an eye on me, he said. He was always doing some type of 'business' on the side. That way I would always be at home and not have to talk to anyone else. He said we would get along better. Every other day it was different. Sometimes it was work there, work at home for me, stay where you are, and so on. He told me I was trying to monopolize his time now.

The days and weeks all began to whirlwind by me while I put the business plans on hold and was working to keep the cash coming in, spending time with my kids, and the usual ranch chores. I got along well with most of his co-workers and his superiors, like the manager of the dealership, so when I called they knew me and the plans that we were making. Then there were the hours spent trying to speak with Daniel on the phone, when I could reach him at work. Sometimes he was not at work at all and they would tell me if he was planning on being in that day or the next or what his schedule was supposed to be. Sometimes I could get him on his cell. It was making me physically sick. I knew he made good money and probably even more than me but I never saw his paycheck. He always lived with his brother and he owned no vehicle, no furniture, no toys, and had only older clothes. He explained that part of his job as the used car salesman was to take clients for dinners and drinks quite often. Of course, everything was expensive in the suburbs and I knew that. That was part of why we were planning to live further south with the business as income. So I finally started to drive one and a half to two hours to meet with him to try to understand what was going on and resolve the situation. After all we were married now.

Daniel told me it was all in my head when I asked about his kids and ex-wife's cars and cash that they suddenly needed. Then how he was still out of money and always had a crisis week after week after week. He told me I was making such a big deal over nothing and if I really loved him I would help out and I would not question him. He said I needed to start acting like this was a marriage and work it out together so we could have the life we planned. When I would call him on the phone he was never able to afford to come down or could not take time off work. Not even a day because if he was not working he was too tired to drive. It is not that I needed someone around 24/7 but the whole marriage was turning into something that was so off the wall I could not even explain it. Then as all of this was taking place he kept using our bank card, the bank card from my account that I added his name to. He would use the ATM machines where he was living for cash and such. It no longer mattered how much money I would add to the account. He did not care. He told me he knew I would take care of it and cover it because I would not let it overdraw with my name on it. I would drive to the bank or call and find out how much I had to deposit and use my money to cover his ATM withdrawals. When I drove up to see him at work a few of his co-workers and him were sitting in the center of the room and made quite a joke out of the fact that Daniel could spend as much as he wanted with the joint account because I always ran to the bank to cover it with my money. They all laughed about it and I told them it really was not funny that he continued to take money from our account and never had to put money in. They told me how that was the big joke with Daniel and how he told them what he was doing. They walked away after they had a good laugh and I was about to cry right there. I was running out of money and did not know what else to do. I thought about what he said that it was just temporary and tried to ease my mind.

Now it is July 1999 and my life was at two hundred miles an hour. I could not slow it down no matter what I did. One day Daniel came down to tell me that he thought I should file bankruptcy because if all my money was gone he could not help me like he promised. His credit cards were all maxed out and he was out of cash too and car sales were down. He was not going to file but I should. I needed to because that is how it is done. He told me all we were doing was starting all over from scratch and this way we could retire in a few years instead of working so hard and so many hours. It was unexplainable. I knew nothing about filing bankruptcy and had no intentions of doing something like that. I was still raising my kids and paying all of my stuff and working and making great money. I had not changed my financial part of my life and mine was not out of control. I asked him what was going on. I explained he needed to make changes and I could not continue to support him, his two kids and his ex-wife. He became very upset and told me I was just being selfish. I would not help him or his kids and I never wanted to share like a married couple should if they really loved each other and planned on staying together and making the marriage work. He said I did not try or give the marriage a chance. I could not even think straight any more. I tried to understand what was going on. He left and then called me to say he really loved me and we should try to work things out and that he would figure out something if I was not going to file bankruptcy. I told him that was just silly.

Daniel continued to call me and tell me that people file bankruptcy every day and he knew how to do it since he sees it all the time. I told him he was nuts and why would I ever do that? I drove to the suburbs with a pen and paper to find Daniel and show him what I had collected and figured up. I took my checks and bills and wanted him to do the same and be honest about everything if that was his intentions because this marriage was out of control. I don't even think you could call this a marriage. I was a bank and that is all it came down to when I looked at the numbers and documents I collected to show him. That was hard to believe as I sat and looked at the numbers. But in black and white there was no doubt about the amount of money I had already gone through. That money was gone into thin air, just disappeared like blinking your eyes and you are somewhere else when you open them. It made me even sicker than before. This was like a nightmare and I would wake up and it would all go back to "normal". The way I thought my life was before marriage was better than average. It was hard to imagine life being so screwed up emotionally and financially and not knowing which end is up and knowing some one else can do that to your life so easily and so quickly.

After eight weeks into this marriage I had lost, yes I said lost, twenty-eight thousand dollars. Where did it go? I saw nothing for that kind of money as I tried to pretend there had to be something to show for it. Not just a marriage certificate. There was hardly anything left to my accounts and safe box. Daniel now automatically owned half of the property that I purchased. When I showed him what I had spent for him since the marriage and what I had left, he would not believe me and told me I was nuts and he laughed and said that was not possible. He told me I did not add and subtract correctly and refused to listen to me. He would not take the situation seriously and tore the paper up and threw it away. I showed him the bank statements and he would have nothing to do with it. I was very serious. Every day became a crisis for Daniel or his adult kids. It was like a roller coaster speeding away, out of control and I had absolutely no control and no way to stop or even to slow down. The more I sorted through and tried to fix the marriage, the worse every thing got. Daniel was furious that I would go to the trouble to do the math and confront him. I actually showed him my paychecks and his bills that were going out. My bills were few, so I was never concerned until the numbers became out of control. It was beyond my comprehension as to why his expenses were so high, not even close to what we went over before we were married. Why would he lie to me about his debt or all the money he owed his brother and father? After all it would all come out after we were married and would be deceitful not to disclose these things. That is how Daniel explained it all to me before marriage and I agreed. Now his father wanted him, or should I say me, to pay more per week in cash so he could be done with his business. The out going expenses that he needed paid from our account were far more than my pay. Of course Daniel assured me it was only temporary and not to worry about anything. I had plenty to cover my home and auto and monthly bills, but this was not working now. I could not also pay his monthly expenses which had become more than double what I paid out for myself and my two kids together. It was no relief that Daniel kept reminding me that the number one problem between married couples was money or finances and it would all soon be the way we discussed before marriage. But we did not discuss at any time that someday down the road it would be as we planned. I had no idea he was planning otherwise. It is true many counselors will report the number one complaint in a marriage is finances, but this had a different tone to it. I could not put my finger on it and many times thought maybe he was right. Daniel always had a perfectly good explanation in an instant without even blinking an eye no matter what I asked him. It was always very smooth and logical as to make you think, oh, I should have seen that or figured that out. He could always explain everything away, which made me think I should have never asked such a silly thing in the first place or even doubted his intentions. Always! So I decided just to pay closer attention to everything that was going on even if he had a perfectly wonderful explanation for it, no matter what it was. I needed to be very sharp and keep it filed somewhere in my brain wherever I could spare a space.

I drove to the suburbs to find him after work one night and found him at work at the car dealership. Most of the employees and manager were on a first name basis with me since we had been together for dinners. On this trip I realized there was a different side of this marriage. A couple of them came to talk to me while I waited for Daniel and they knew why I was there. Daniel showed up while we were all standing there and when I said I needed to talk to him he laughed and said, oh you want to talk about the debit card charges again. All the salesman were laughing and said Daniel thought it was pretty funny that I kept running to my bank with my savings to keep from overdrawing all his credit/debit charges while my mouth was just opened in amazement and when they all saw I was not laughing and was not happy, they left. Daniel said it was just a joke. But it was not a joke to me, because he was breaking me. He told me it was also my account so I would just have to help him out and stop being so selfish.

Daniel told me he made six hundred fifty dollars a week and then received a check for car insurance sales at his apartment. I never knew how much those checks were because he told me they were not much and never the same. But the expenses which he did not disclose were more than those he listed when making up a budget for us before we were married. There was a shocking difference as the money continued to pour out faster than I could deposit it. I tried to do the math and every time I asked questions Daniel became more and more upset. The more I asked, the more the conversation escalated.

Daniel had to pay rent at seven hundred fifty dollars a month and city, electric, cable, phone, internet, medication, lunches and dinners for clients, hair, clothing, and maid service at eight hundred fifty dollars plus! Every month! Two hundred dollars a month went to his father for payments on his used car business, always cash. One hundred seventy for gas and tolls. Seven hundred dollars for dry cleaning, cigarettes, lunches, and groceries. Also once a month his life insurance came due for one hundred fifty dollars. At least he had no car to pay for. He hit the ATM about every other day for extras and emergencies. These are expenses on top of all the monthly payments that were automatically paid from the joint checking account, those that were in the budget that I knew about. It adds up to something was wrong. Then, on top of the additional expenses that had to be paid every month, we paid car insurance for his mother and two kids who were already at high risk ratings. They also had emergencies like he did on a regular basis. One lost another scholarship again and went over on his credit card and the other could not decide what she was going to do. No, they were not paying for anything. Neither of them had time to work. They could not help it, Daniel claimed.

The amount that Daniel had automatically deposited to this checking account was what I thought was his paycheck or I should say what he told me was his paycheck from the dealership. The biggest mistake was the debit cards we received for that account. When the monthly statements came to my house, almost daily Daniel accrued charges from the debit card with this account. Daniel said he did not realize he was charging so much but now that I had showed him how much he was charging he would refrain. But on the next statement and the month after that the charges he made were well over his paycheck deposit into this account and

I would continually drive to the bank with money from my savings to cover his charges. Daniel was still living in the suburbs and told me that it looked like it would be a while before he could leave this job because he had quite a bit of money coming in the next quarter and it would be silly to leave now. But he still planned on all that we talked about. At that time he explained that this was only temporary while he lived up there if I could just wait until he had everything straightened out to move down here with me. We discussed the fact that some things had to change because even though I made good money, it was not enough to keep his bills and charges to the account paid. Some of my savings was for my kid's cars when they turned sixteen like I had always promised. Any of the extra money I had was running out and my savings was almost depleted. But he always told me wait until next payday or he always claimed to have money coming. I know he was working and getting a paycheck. He made less than me but I thought he made enough to pay his own expenses. Nothing ever seemed to slow down. All the plans on the property that my kids and I had seemed to be moving further away. It was like a thick, thick fog that you could not even see your hand if you held out your arm. And it was all out of my control, no matter what I tried. Nothing like that has ever happened to me before and I did not like the feeling.

Then in the mail at my house I found another utility bill from a home out of state. The first time, prior to our marriage, may have been a coincidence. Not this time. I wanted to know the who and where and why and I wanted to know now. I called the company and started to go through all the departments and write down the details. Yes, they told me all the info on file was mine and that is where I lived and it was totally my responsibility to pay in full. There were late fees and interest charges on top of the already high bill that had gone months without being paid. All the personal information they gave me about myself was mine. However, they were never able to find the Daniel Mohy, who also resided with 'me', which left me solely responsible. They never would find him because there was something wrong. Someone was using my identity because I had never even lived in that state. I took it to a lawyer and they said do not worry about it because that is not you. But I was convinced something was still wrong. The letter with as much information as I could gather was sent to this company. This continued on and on and I continued to correspond and call. I was not paying someone else's past due utility bills. No way, even though this person claimed to be me. I was not going to let it continue. They told me it would go on my credit report as a nonpayment of my utilities with another call. I researched more and waited for the return of information. When I asked Daniel about this again he declared absolutely no knowledge or connection and it had nothing to do with him. He swore to me.

Trying to keep things on a positive note I called Daniel and drove up to the car dealership where he worked and we went to dinner and a movie. When we were driving to the theater that I had never been to before, I commented how large it was and which movie I would like to see, and he snapped that just a week or two ago I was there with him and saw that movie. I asked what he was talking about because I had never been there and had not seen that movie yet and would surely know if I had.

He continued to argue and told me that it had probably been a few weeks ago and asked me why I did not admit to it. Believe me that I saw very few movies and I knew I had never been there. He kept insisting and asking why I could not remember it. I told him it was not me and I finally told him just to stop his "hammering", which is what he seemed to be doing a lot of lately. He told me I was just crazy that I could not even remember a few weeks ago. So now I thought while he continued to yell, he must have just been there with someone else and he was busted. So to try to get out of it and cover his story he turns it around 100% and put the blame on me. That way I had to worry about defending myself and that reverses the blame and defense. Such a heated argument over a trivial and innocent comment. It finally died out when I dropped out of the argument. I chose to let it go.

One Sunday Daniel met me to go to a horse auction because he had never been to one. I actually found a good trail horse and decided to purchase her since the bid was about right. I had ridden her and checked her out and spoke with the owner, another used car salesman. She had great bloodlines and disposition. Just what Jas and I were looking for. I found that she was undernourished and neglected, but had a great spirit with lots to offer. Of course when it was time to pay, I had to come up with the money on the spot with my credit card. The deal was he had the cash back at his apartment where he lived but would get that for me the next day so I would not have to use any checks out of the joint account. That way he could ride her and learn too. The horse was for Jas and to use for a foal as she and I planned. But he could learn to ride her on the trails when he came down since he knew nothing about horses and riding. I spent many months nursing her to the healthy horse she should have been. Jas and I rode her on our trails and she turned out to be an excellent choice. Daniel never had the interest to do anything with her or learn about horses. As far as he was concerned that was something you bragged about having. A person did not really take care of it or do any chores and he never paid for any of it. To Daniel that was all he did, talked about it. I never saw any of the money for her but really did not expect to. It did not seem to matter at that time because the horse was Jas' and registered that way. My veterinarian came out and checked them all and gave them a clean bill of health. Now Jas and I could think about breeding. We loved our horses.

On one trip up to meet Daniel for a dinner with his co-workers, I was surprised at the stories about Daniel's new ranch that he was building for me. I just laughed and said there was no new ranch, no new home, no new anything except the additional acres that I was going to add, but now Daniel wanted to be a part of that. I told them I had been there in the same house with my kids for about twenty-four years. Before that I had been raised just a pasture away on the other side of my horses barn. They were all a little surprised at my facts and I was sure they had just misunderstood the story Daniel had told. After a little history about me they seemed to believe what I had told them. How could they have misconstrued so much and be so far off?

Daniel and I were dancing and he asked that I be very careful what I was saying because it meant a great deal to him as far as his position and income. He asked that I not tell anyone that he was living up there, but instead let them believe that he lived with me and drove almost every day and stayed once in a while with his brother. I asked him what the big deal was but he really had no specific explanation. I would not lie about it, I said, but I am sure no one would ask those kind of questions of me. He told me to remember what he said. I did not think any more of it. When we were at the table some of the managers asked me about my house, my ranch and my kids, just general questions and a normal conversation. Daniel kept kicking me under the table while I was trying to carry on a conversation with them and their spouses. What was the deal? No one was asking about what he did specifically. But then the conversation turned to how tired Daniel was all the time from driving so far every day to work and all the work he had to do at the ranch. No, I said that he was not there often and it was the weekend day if he did drive to see me. Usually I came up here for dinner after I got off work if my kids were going to be gone since I was an hour closer if I left directly from work anyway. On occasion I would drive up on a weekend day because I worked six or seven days a week at the resort as director, I still did a lot of things with my kids and took care of my ranch. I asked Daniel why he was so tired all of the time and he said he worked too hard. That was his explanation as he tried to smooth over the stories that he must have been telling everyone at work. He had been missing work and coming in late and the female co-workers were trying to help him keep up at work because he was getting behind. So when they told me how sorry they felt for him and had to let him take naps and cover for him, I was not playing that game. That was not how it was and I was not going to sit there and tell all these people those lies to cover for him. What was he doing anyway? Why was he so tired that he missed work and had to sleep at work? I had absolutely no reason to lie and cover up whatever was going on. Every one seemed to drift away while Daniel squirmed as he tried to cover himself of the lies he had told. Conversations went in other directions and then Daniel decided we would leave. He was very upset with me and said I had probably cost him his promotion that was due to him for a long time. What I had done and said had ruined his chance of making that extra money so he could help to make any payments that I was making. Now he would have to work in the suburbs much longer than we discussed originally to make enough money to move down with me. It was all my fault that happened. He would have no money now for a while because he could not catch up. He told me that I ruined it and he wanted to know why I would do such a thing. I told him I was not going to go on and on and lie and that this big raise he was due never entered into our discussions when we made our plans when we married. It had nothing to do with it.

As The Storm Approaches

Then later that week Daniel called me to ask a favor. General Cars was scheduled to have their yearly convention in Las Vegas and he was not invited to go and should have been. He was supposed to be given the general manager position of this dealership and someone else had taken it. They passed him over and he needed help to have that opportunity back. It was very simple and he would make all the arrangements. He had booked airline tickets and a hotel room for me to just go to follow these three men, maybe more, and take lots of photos of them if it looked like they were doing anything out of the ordinary. Problem was his credit cards were maxed out and I would need to use my credit card to purchase everything. Of course he would reimburse me as soon as I got back. He gave me flight information and confirmation number and hotel information and confirmation so I could be close to where the CEO's were staying. I made him repeat it all back in disbelief. He was telling me how they used hookers and such and if I could just get some photos for him it would be great in helping him get the position of general manager so he could make more money for us. More money for us to do what we had planned and that besides they would get what they deserved. His exact words. I wrote this down along with many other stories and situations that had been arising to try to sort through the problems. I was seeing a pattern now. I said no way would I be involved in something like that. No way when he asked if he could use my credit card for someone else to do it since I would not help him. It was only to take the stress off of him and give him the big raise he was supposed to have. He continued to call me and beg me all week at work and home and still could not understand why I would not do that or even let him use my credit card for someone else to do it. It was wrong for me not to help him blackmail these men to get his own dealership which he should already have had. It was rightfully his and he was going to do whatever it took. It would help us out so much and things would be good. If I really loved him and wanted to stay with him and make our marriage work I would do it, he told me over and over. He told me I was crazy but I refused and did not hear from him for days.

One night Daniel drove to my house and we went to a local restaurant to eat dinner. About half way through our meal, a friend of mine, Bob, recognized me a couple of tables over and said hello. Just then he realized that I was sitting with some one he had known years ago and acknowledged him. He came over to our table and asked how everyone has been and what brings Daniel to the local restaurant down here. Suddenly Bob exclaimed that I was the one Daniels' brother was talking about the last time he called him on the phone. I was the one from this county that he was asking about and could not remember my name and Mack was trying to explain who I was. Bob could not place who he was talking about until now. Bob said he did not know who he was marrying when Mack told him about the rich girl from the county with a ranch and lots of money. Now he knew who it was. Bob was very surprised as he told the story. I had grown up with him and his family lived just down the road from me. He was Cal's baseball coach in grade school. I repeated back to Bob, "a rich girl in this county, lots of money and a ranch, huh?" Bob was not the only one that was shocked at the story. Later I asked why he would say such a thing and I wanted to know how he knew him. Daniel explained that Bob and Mack knew each other pretty well in high school and spoke since on occasion. The part that bothered me was when Daniel told Bob he was living down here now, even though I told them that he was planning on living down here when he straightened out his work arrangements. I told him I did not care for the story and he told me he was probably drunk and just talking when he called him. I knew Daniel was not present at the time or Bob would have known who I was.

So again I tried to stay married, remember my big fear? Daniel and I decide to have dinner when he got off work and I drove up to meet him. We went to a couple of his usual spots for dinner and dancing. Some of his friends were there. I asked him or anyone if they would like to buy some raffle tickets for Cal's private Catholic school. They all wanted to buy some and Daniel spoke up and said if I would just give them to him he would sell them all for me and I would not have to do a thing. I thought that would be great and I would not have to mess with them filling out the tickets right now. That was nice. But a week later when I tried to collect the money he told me he did not have it right now and I would just have to turn in the stubs and pay to cover them. He would reimburse me later and apologized. Well, my cash was slim now but what choice did I have but to pay it.

The evening continued and Daniel's favorite bartender asked me how the new ranch was coming along and she bet I was pretty excited about it all. I just looked at her and did not know what to say. I asked what she was talking about and Daniel came up behind me and joined in after talking with another couple. She continued to ask about the ranch Daniel was building and all the property he bought for me. I told her there was no new ranch, just my house I lived in for twenty-four years and the horses I had. Daniel stood there, not knowing what to say, because obviously he had been telling every one up there a different story. I explained the only thing new was an addition to the property so far. She asked about all the new horses he bought me because she liked to ride and I told her there were no new horses he bought me. By now Daniel was sweating and abruptly changed the conversation before anymore stories came out. I told him he needed to explain but went on with his own conversation bringing in other friends so we could not talk. He knew I would be quiet. I thought he was just trying to bring up his self esteem because of all the stress and pressure at work. We were on good terms when I left to drive back home. Sometimes it was late and I had to make sure both kids were where they were supposed to be or at home.

Daniel's best friend was getting married and I drove to his apartment and then on to the wedding. Mat was a nice guy and his fiancée seemed to be a good person. The only thing about Mat was his deal with a girl he had lived with and borrowed a large amount of money from and then split up with her and refused to pay her back. Maybe that is the car salesman mentality. She finally took him to court and the judge ordered him to pay her back. He should have done that before all the drama. His new wife wanted that out of the way before getting married they said. His new wife to be was from a very wealthy family and the wedding and reception was elaborate and beautiful.

Prior to the reception Daniel simply explained to me what I could and could not say once we arrived. I was not sure how to take the conversation because sometimes he was way out there. One could never be sure what he was up to next. We were seated at a large table with his current and past co-workers. Most of them I had never met because he worked with them through the years, but they all had their stories about the car sales. Some were still with dealerships and some were not. Daniel pulled me to the side before dinner was served to tell me not to speak at the table. What was going on? I ate and said nothing but I was ready to leave. When he got up and left the table to have a cigarette I was answering the questions and responding to the conversations directed toward me. As he returned to the table, he just lost it. It was a nightmare as he ridiculed and insulted me in front of everyone and he was not being quiet about it. His friends were telling him to settle down and stop. Mack, his brother who was with us as always, tried to settle him down and apologized for him. No one could talk to him as he continued being a crazy. That is as close as I could describe his actions. He continued to become louder and no one knew what to do. Some of them moved to another table. I knew no one else there but tried to figure out how to get away. I did not even know where I was. I was usually quiet and business like. This was unfamiliar territory and I was lost. By now everyone had left our table except for his brother, but not before they apologized for him and asked if I needed help. But who was going to help me and how, since I knew no one. I had tears in my eyes but I thought "I can overcome this and it will go away". Obviously, some of them knew him well and were not surprised by what he was doing. At the table his brother told him to stop again and one of the employees there came to the table and asked if everything was okay and I quickly turned to the other side and asked her if a taxi would be available. She told me she would find something. All I knew was that I was far from any main road or city. It was a long drive and in the timber and at least two hours or more from my home. When Daniel caught me talking to her, as his brother walked away, he yelled at me and asked what I was trying to do. Next, he grabbed my arm and literally drug me through the tables and into the lobby area and was looking for something. I did not know what he was going to do at that point and I was crying which made him even meaner. The staff had tried to stop him and ask him what he was doing but that just made him almost run dragging me behind. They asked if they could get me a ride to get away from him and every time someone said they would help me, he became more infuriated. I was stunned and my only thoughts were to escape. But to where and how? I kept thinking it was not really happening because it was too bizarre, like it was a nightmare or movie on TV. A couple of women and a man that worked there told me they were going to call someone for help. He would just yell at them saying no help was needed and that he was taking me home and just wanted to find the parking lot entrance. As he drug me up and down the halls and rooms full of people I could not stop crying. Mack had caught up with us and tried to get control of him. Daniel was like a madman, a psychotic sociopath, if there is such a thing. Mack showed him the quickest way to the door as the staff and guests watched. Down another hall and lobby he drug me as Mack tried to pull his hand off my arm to no avail. Mack tried to help me as we flew down the steps so that I would not fall and be dragged to the car. There was no stopping him no matter who said what. Like he was not human. I did not want to get into the car with him but Mack talked me into it so we could get out of there.

Mack promised me he would get me home, my home. As soon as I got into the car Daniel let my arm loose. I guess he had seen this before and been through it more than once. As we drove back to their apartment to get my car, Mack tried to calm me down. I could not stop crying and said I just wanted to go home. Mack told Daniel he needed to get it together and stop doing these kind of things because there was no reason for it and I had done nothing wrong. I know I had done nothing wrong and at least everyone else did too. That is what never made sense but it was a long enough ride to comprehend and learn more than I wanted to. After the long ride back to the apartment Mack told me I should stay until morning and he promised to make sure Daniel came no where near me. My purse and keys were inside their apartment. Daniel thought he was justified in doing all that because he told me not to talk to anyone and I did not follow his instructions. Never did he apologize to me even though everyone else did. I would not speak to Daniel even after entering the apartment to collect my purse. I was very sick to my stomach and when I went into the bathroom before leaving I began to throw up and could not stop. The more I realized what had happened the sicker it made me and I could not stop. I was so sick and weak and could not even see anymore because my eyes were so swollen. I could not stand up and laid on the bathroom floor with the door locked. Mack had convinced Daniel to go and stay in his room and to stay away from me and he did. Thank God. God made sure I had a guardian angel there with me. Mack spoke to me through the bathroom door and asked that I stay and when I felt okay I could drive home. I agreed if Daniel stayed away. I slept on the floor after there was nothing left in my stomach and my eyes would not open. I needed to sleep even if it was just a little nap since I had more than an hour to get back home.

When I awoke I left and did not know what I would do. I just wanted to go home. It was not that I could just say no to a date the next time he called. Now I was legally married and I know there would be no simple and agreeable divorce. Yes, I wanted out. What else could I do? It made me very sick and sad.

The month of August was coming to a disastrous end. I went to meet him half way one of the many times to have dinner after we were both off work. The dinner went well until I began the discussion about the finances and he just shrugged it off telling me that all married couples have one problem and it is the one problem that splits them up: money. Daniel wanted to know what the big deal was since he knew it would all pass after the marriage progressed and I got used to how things worked. He said there was absolutely nothing to worry about because of the expanding income he would be receiving soon. Everything was going according to his plan but I would just have to wait. I was exhausted and it all made my head spin. So now he decided he had the time to come to my house but he would have to leave tomorrow. I was in for a real shocker as we left one of the vehicles there in town and drove to my house. Daniel was using one of the dealerships cars as always since he had none. I do not think he ever owned a vehicle.

About half way back to my house, Daniel wanted me to stop at a bar where I had worked on occasion for a friend. I was tired and wanted to go home and he became very irate, yelling at me and grabbing the steering wheel and we almost crashed a couple of times. But I managed to keep my car on the road and came to the next stop sign and put my car in park. After catching my breath and senses, I asked him why he did that. The dinner was a big treat because now that we were married we could not afford to do that. He simply laughed and explained that all he wanted to do was go and have a couple of drinks and pick up someone from the bar. Well, I am not the fastest rabbit in the race, but I did not understand that statement so I asked him what in the world he was talking about. He continued to shift my car and grab the wheel to turn down that road and he continued to scream at me. He finally told me we were just going to pick up a woman to have sex with. I refused to move my car and did not know if I should get out and run or scream or try to get him out of my car. I quickly made the decision to tell him to get out of my car and pulled over. He told me if we did not go to pick up someone at the bar he would divorce me. I told him he would have to because I refused to be involved. Since he would not get out of my car and continued to pull my steering wheel and scream, I wrestled control back and drove straight for my house with him screaming he would divorce me if I did not go back. Of course I did not, but I was sickened and angry and confused all at once. I wanted to go home. After a few miles down the road he realized I was not kidding and was very serious. I asked why would he ever think I would be involved in something like that. Then another blow to my senses, or what was left came when he explained that he did that and all his friends did the same because it was normal.....and that there was just something wrong with me. I was speechless because my brain could not even sort or comprehend what he was telling me. He went on to explain that was one of his addictions and that he went to AA for years. That was for all his addictions. I then learned from him that he has these addictions, as does almost everyone. Not that AA meant alcoholics anonymous but he explained that is only one the many types of addictions they went to meetings for. I had no idea. He said that his addiction just moves around from gambling, alcohol, and sex. That was just the way it was and if I did not understand any of it I should go to some of his meetings so I could get used to it and learn to live with it. I told him he needed to go home. I had a feeling there was a reason he always lived with his brother and worked with his brother and stayed in the cities and suburbs but no one told me otherwise when I asked. So the times he could not talk on the phone when he was at his apartment because someone was there, or the time I went there and found a set of keys for a house and car beside his bed from his 'old girlfriend'. My mind was racing and trying to pick through if this was really happening or maybe it was all just a big joke, or anything but true! But Daniel was sure to make me understand that I should become involved and then he would not have to explain something to me that I could not comprehend. So he was using one of my biggest fears.......divorce. But what kind of life was the alternative. He kept telling me that there was something wrong with me, that's all. That was not a life that he was talking about but something evil! I was so sick. It is not a situation you could ignore or ever forget. I did not want this kind of lifestyle and did not want to even try it. Was I that naive?

Cal told me, after only a few weeks into the marriage, Daniel was bad news and something was very wrong. Cal was fourteen years old but had a sense about the character of people.

Severe Storm Warnings

On the horizon and above the trees a storm was brewing. The electrical impulses in the air were negative and could be felt in everything and every thought. The natural balance was off and I mean off as in a bigger picture, all around me, my house, my kids, just everything. That is all I knew. I did not understand it and hoped it was just a phase, a temporary bad time that would disappear as quickly as it came. I had never felt such a negative aura and it was a dark and scary thing, so tried to push it out of my head and be positive because it would have to go away. It made my head spin and hurt when I tried to sort it out and make sense of any of it. The more I sorted, the more I became sick. I thought maybe if I tried to be more positive it would work itself out. I thought maybe the storm would disappear if I tried hard enough. I wanted my life to be back to normal, the way I liked it. The way it was before I willingly signed a piece of paper that said I was married.

It had been quite the summer and it was not even over yet. I had received some information back from the utility company out of state and decided to call back because something was very wrong. The representative finally gave me more details because I had been so insistent. He told me that in April of 1999 Daniel had quite a bit of debt and there were numerous collection agencies after him. Guess what? My name and address were also on that record. How could that be since I had never lived any where else? The representative of the company told me Daniel had extensive credit history problems and since my name and address was listed as Daniel's current address it now would become my responsibility to pay the large amount of debt. They had all my information in their system and it was a fact. But I explained the facts and told him there was a very large mistake somewhere and I would get to the bottom of it. He was very nice about it as most of them were, and apologized, but it was not my debt. And I was not going to pay it. It was understandable that they had to go by information details that were in their computer system for residential billings.

Within a few more weeks I had received more collection agency letters at my house. They were not mine but my name had been added to the debts and bills were outstanding and the explanation from them when I called each one was the same. Daniel had extensive credit problems and I had the financial ability to pay them. Absolutely not! No way were they my bills or in any way my responsibility. Some bills were addressed to both of us and Daniel's name was reversed. I owned all the assets! So, that's who they would go after because I paid my bills.

Daniel denied all of the letters and bills and claimed to know nothing about any of it. I asked him to check his credit report and accounts before we were married. He threw a fit and went into a rage and accused me of what was going on. He told me if I really loved him I would trust him and not believe anyone else. Someone was just out to get him. That was all it could be. These fits he had were becoming the norm. Any time I asked questions, he said I should not be asking if I loved him and really wanted to stay married. I should never ask him anything about finances because his paychecks were his and he would do whatever he wanted with them. He refused to let me see any of his credit information. He already had total access to my credit report from vehicles purchased through the car dealerships. They are allowed any and all info about credit history, past and current. I had never thought anything of it before.

Finally Daniel confessed that he had more credit cards and even those were over the limit and the late fees and finance charges on all his credit cards were enormous. He really thought I would pay them for him because it was only fair since we were married. He thought I should accept the fact that if I would not file bankruptcy for him, I should at least take out a home equity loan because of equity I had in my house. His point of view was that I was not using all that equity so I might as well just let him use it. If I really loved him and wanted to stay married I would help him financially just during this short time. It would all be okay when he caught up with his paycheck, like usual. It was the same old, short story every time. I told him we were going through my money like water and it had to stop because every time was the same promise of as soon as your next check comes. That check never comes.

One day it was a call from Daniel about how I could help our financial situation if I could do a side job for him. He would come down and make some charts on my computer and show me how to do it. We would have more money so there would be nothing to argue about or upset him. He showed me the charts and the numbers and it all made sense and looked like a good income for shorter hours. I worked so many hours already and I told him I was not sure I could do that yet. I was stalling. Some days he wanted me to quit my great paying job and do this business and then the next day he would call and tell me no, wait. I was waiting any way because it was off a bit and I did not want to get involved because of the way he was. Then he called and said he was ready to start this business, which involved his father's business. Then he could move down here with me and do what we planned. Now the story changed; he did not have the cash, but if I could just loan him some money to get it started.....I said no not right now. He thought I should sell some of the things like antiques and collectibles to come up with the money because it was useless junk I did not need. Jas had three large glass cabinets full of antique dolls that he wanted me to sell. He insisted that they were no good to us but they were worth lots of money. Yes, they were worth lots of money and they had been collected over many years. Some were mine as a child and some were from my mother and my aunt. All of them were in mint condition. And they were going to remain in those three cases and they were Jas's dolls. Cal had a motorcycle and antique comic book collection Daniel also wanted sold. I told him I could not do it. He was very angry and told me I was going to have to file bankruptcy because he was so far behind on his payments and would not be able to help me. His kids were in need of money and if I really loved him I would help him. It would be a long time before he moved down with me because I was not helping and was not being fair to him since I had the money and assets to help. Same old story. But he was going to change he repeated.

On top of these problems, I receive another call from Daniel that he needs to use my credit card for an emergency. I asked what was wrong now and he told me his son needed an airline ticket and had to fly around to about four states and then he would come to see him at his apartment for a few days. That was the crisis of the day. Daniel Jr. expected him to pay in full and if he did not then he was not going to see him. If he does not get what ever he requests Daniel explained he does not speak to him for a long time. I told him that was too bad because I would not use my credit card. Many times we had gone to a gas station, store, or to dinner and at the time of checkout he decided he had no money or no wallet, but always an excuse. I did pay and it was the wrong thing to do but when you are married that should not be an issue. He always just needed some money temporarily.

Daniel's car insurance kept coming to my address with my name on it and I told him I did not want my name included since this insurance was for his kids. He owned no vehicle and there was no reason for me to be involved. I had my own insurance and my own vehicles and the rates were good. That was okay if he wanted to pay for his kids insurance even though they were in their twenties, but not me. He told me it was cheaper if he used me and my address and I told him absolutely not because of all the accidents they were in. Daniel said that was no fair and that I really did not love him if I could not do that. I refused and he screamed and told me how terrible I was for not helping. I was too selfish and that I was not a very good wife.

Daniel seemed to get over it when he called about a vehicle he found for Jas. He knew I would follow through with my promise to my kids to buy them new vehicles. That is how it went. He would be furious and say nasty things and then he would be nice and do something positive. You just never knew what and when it would be. Was it all the pressure on his job?

Jas and I had looked at some trucks locally because things were negative with Daniel and I wanted it for her birthday. When I told him we had seen a truck like she wanted he went off and crazy again. He said it was a slap in the face and I had better not look at any more because he would find one for me. Under the circumstances I believed it was fair because when I asked him about it earlier he told me she did not need one and that I could not afford it if I could not help him and his kids. He stopped the screaming on the phone and asked if I would like to come and look at the one he found. I agreed if he would be decent about it and stop the screaming and acting like I should be taking care of his adult kids. I told him I did not have maxed out credit cards and could still take care of my household even though my two kids were still in school. I was paying for it all so I would make the decisions. So we made a date. Jas and I went to look at this truck and she loved it. Brand new Chevrolet, dark blue with black trim, 4x4, bed liner, ZR2 decals, all the extras. We decided I would keep the Z24 convertible and she could get her new truck. It only took a short time to sign the papers and it was done. Jas was very happy.

I had the Chevy Silverado I was going to trade in for it but Daniel said he could get a better trade for it with his father's used car lot. All of a sudden he had to take it to him, so he drove down and spent the night and took it to him early the next morning. Everything was okay and we talked about what was going on. He was going to change, he promised again.

He always seemed to have a shortage with his finances. How could he always be broke if he owned nothing and shared living expenses with his brother? Did he get his insurance policies for his kids cars straightened out and out of my name and address? We never saw each other unless I drove up there and made an appointment? My money would not hold out much longer trying to pay for everything for him and my own family. He had no limits, just use the ATM and call me to tell me to run to the bank ten miles from my house to deposit money into the new joint account because he spent too much and it would be overdrawn. I told him it all had to stop. Nothing made sense anymore. I told him I could not handle his mean side. He apologized and said he was just having a bad time and things were going to change now. He was going to catch up. He had my information removed from his insurance and I would have nothing to worry about. I had spent over twenty-eight thousand dollars for his extra expenses that I had saved. In the last couple of months, I was down to nothing. He tried to tell me I had not covered him that much and I said I would show him and I did. He knew. He was going to make up for it all now he claimed, he just had not realized how much. Everything he showed me on paper, everything I kept covering for him, but it never happened, he never paid me back. It all looked good when he wrote up a budget, but that is all it was, a piece of paper. He begged me to let him start all over again because that was everything he wanted and he loved it there at my house. It was perfect for him and he would show me he was serious. He got on my computer and made up charts and payments he owed and wanted to make a new budget. He asked for my bills, payments, social security statements, paycheck stubs, and all. We had a plan again. I told him it was our last chance to try it. He begged me not to split up or do anything until we tried again. I told him I was worn down and things would have to change and change now. He agreed. Things seemed to be a little smoother, but I now knew it was not my imagination and I was going to be very clear and attentive to everything I saw. The next few times we spoke on the phone it seemed we were on track and I hoped it would be okay now.

No one, even our mutual friend, Keri, had anything to say when I called her or stopped on my way home from work. Keri and Ken had not been around much to do anything as couples except for a few dinners that went well. They thought I was over reacting when I told them some of the things that were going on. I believe Keri thought he was not capable of being so mean and abusive. Ken did not know him well, only through Keri after they were married. Or they just did not want to get involved. She had told me a few stories about him from long ago that were not nice. She said everyone has things in their past they would like to leave there. I filed it in the back of my already full mind.

Daniel called me to let me know his kids were going to be coming to stay with him for a few days. Daniel Jr. had a basketball game scheduled up there. He wanted us to come and see the game to show family support. Jas did not want to go and I talked Cal into going with me. I had to be sure I had enough money for the round trip. We went to his apartment and were shocked to find his son and daughter.........and his son's friends and girlfriends and that they would be staying for a week. All of them. I was invited to bring my kids and have dinner and stay one night because the game was going to be late. But when we arrived at his apartment they decided they did not want to go to dinner since they had all been out the night before with Daniel. So Cal and I grabbed a sandwich and went to the game. We even rode in the same car with Daniel since I did not know how to get there. At the game Daniel sat beside his ex in-laws and never introduced any of us to them. He turned his back to us and never spoke to us until after the game when he told us we could go sit in the car and wait for him. His son stopped to talk to him and Daniel told him to be sure to be at a club at 11 pm. to meet with his last x-girlfriend and her brother. Daniel was not going to be able to go with them now that we had come up. He would be back at the apartment. They all decided to meet at the apartment and go from there. They were all upset because Daniel would not be going with them. Probably because he would have paid for it all night long. Cal and I chose to stay inside to wait. His ex in-laws even asked why he had not introduced us and he turned quickly, introduced us and then walked away with his in-laws, talking to everyone else like we were not even there. Cal and I sat on some steps for about an hour waiting for him to return because my car was at his apartment. Cal asked what was wrong and I explained that was how Daniel was. Why was he doing that? I was embarrassed, perplexed, and sad. I felt bad for Cal and asked if he wanted to go home. He said we could stay because it was late and I told him we would leave first thing in the morning. We slept on the floor, but not before we were told about all the plans they had with Daniel and how he took them out to every hot spot and club around. And how nice it was that he paid for everyone all night, their dinner, drinks, and all. Did I miss something? But he did not have any money, right? I was not to go out to eat a three dollar breakfast as we had always done because we had to be careful with money for right now. No, he only wanted me to spend money to cover himself and his kids. I saw that very clearly. He was very rude even in front of all of his kid's friends. They did not seem to mind because they never really spoke to us either. What had he told them? I certainly did not know what to say. I should have stood up to him then and there. Then they talked about shopping and going to some more places Daniel knew of. But we were not invited because we did not have enough money to go he said.

Cal and I sat on the sofa at the end of the room and Daniel came and sat beside us after a while and we were watching something on TV. I tried not to listen to anymore and just wanted to go to sleep so we could leave early. I asked for a couple of blankets. His explanation was that he had to use his last two paychecks to take care of these kids and be sure they had a good time. I asked him why he was spending so much money when we did not have it and he just said he had to. It was his paycheck and he would spend it however he wanted.

While everyone was still there Daniel decided to tell Cal a story. At this point neither one of us wanted to hear anymore. He went on about something he had done that was on the movie we were watching. He told us he had put a gun to his head and was going to commit suicide but his mom came in and stopped him from pulling the trigger. He laughed as he told the story and thought it was funny. I told him to stop and that we really did not want to hear about it even if it were true. He just kept on telling the story and all these college kids were twelve feet away. It was like being in a psycho movie, when the psychopath uses that to get someone to do what he wanted. It is something that stands in your mind forever. I was hoping he was joking and would tell us that was not true, but when I told him that he said oh, no, that is exactly how it happened. Then he moved to the other side of the room. Cal and I went to sleep and got up early and took off. On the way home we had a long talk and I told him I did not know what I was going to do. I did not hear from Daniel for a couple of days, which was fine.

Daniel called to ask why I was so upset. He did not understand why I would be so mad at having to foot the bill for his kid's friends that I did not even know. He did not apologize for what he did because he thought he was well within the rules to be sure everyone else had a good time at my expense. Even his ex girlfriend and her brother. I felt I was right to feel the way I did. Since I had married him it was one financial disaster after another. It was still as though I were a bank with an unlimited spending account. I had to scrape and watch everything I spent, including gas and groceries. My kids and I were no longer able to do the things we were so used to doing like going for breakfast. Daniel had called once while the kids and I were having breakfast at a restaurant in town and he went crazy on the phone because I spent money. He told me I no longer had the money to go out to a restaurant to eat with my kids and I would have to change the way I was living now that I was married.

I knew there were more serious problems and issues than what was on the surface and it was not just my imagination. He kept trying to persuade me that all this was my fault and it was just a common newlywed problem which everyone goes through. That was the story I wanted to be true and maybe even pretended for a short while that it was that way.

Gut Instincts

We all have a gut instinct but most of us do not know when to trust that feeling. Some people do not even know they have it because they have never allowed themselves the luxury. If something were going on and the situation made you feel funny or a little off edge, it was not right. Other circumstances come into play and those instincts are not acknowledged and you move on and all is forgotten. You never gave those instincts the chance to kick in and just let it pass by. If you were in a situation or circumstance and your stomach just turns into a knot and you allowed yourself that feeling and took the time to realize what happened and why ... surprise... a real gut instinct that you could trust. It was your body's way of helping your mind sort through it. If it does not feel right, it is probably not. Simple.

The few times Daniel came down to my house, he

was so tired from working so hard all week he just wanted to sleep. If I wanted to do something I was monopolizing his time he told me. I tried not to cause any waves because I always thought things would get better. Whenever I spoke to him on the phone he would insult me and tell me there was something wrong with me, I was selfish and would not share. The verbal abuse escalated every time we spoke.

One of my garage doors had a wood section coming loose and needed to be replaced and I told him what I was going to do and he said absolutely not, we did not have the money to use for my house. There were a few things that needed updating on my house but I kept putting it off waiting for him to catch up financially. Instead every check I received was to cover for him at the ATM withdrawals. I finally told Daniel that I would just sell my house and there would be nothing to worry about. He begged me to keep it because he loved it there and wanted to stay there and it would be better soon. He explained it would be better if I just filed bankruptcy the way he told me earlier. I asked why because I had all the assets and equity and a good job and income. My only liability was him, only him. He was the one that should have filed for bankruptcy. He told me I was stupid for not doing and wanted to know what was wrong with me. He thought I was crazy and needed help. Then he told me he loved me enough to try and help me by going to see a shrink so our marriage could survive. I told him I was fine and did not need a shrink to tell me what I believed and showed Daniel in black and white, again, about our finances.

I did not like being broke and borrowed a little

money from my kids because I was sure I could replace it soon. Daniel thought I should borrow money from my parents when the next set of bills came due and there was still no money coming in on his end. He kept on me about selling Jas' doll collection, Cal's motorcycle and other antiques we had. He told me I had plenty and it was all just junk and we needed the money right now because I would not file bankruptcy to help out. So if I just borrowed the money now he would make plenty to pay me back. I told him he always said that and it never happened. He told me not to worry because he would never leave and he would never give me a divorce. If I would just do it the way he told me I would not have to worry. He was raised and taught by the best and no one could ever beat him. He would laugh and say yes I am. He told me I could never leave him and he would never leave me alone and there was no one to do anything about it. He was dead serious even as he laughed about it.

Daniel explained how he could access people's credit reports at work and was able to change them. He told me he had his fixed many times. If I were to do as he told me when I filed bankruptcy he could fix it for me and then we could start all over again together. All of these were scams. OPM, which he explained to me, meant other people's money and that was how everyone should live. He told me that is how you do it and the only way to get ahead. I could not understand the concept or how it worked. I knew it had to be another one of his deals. How could someone learn all theses scams, I will never know. He told me that is how he was taught to live and it worked well. It was all way beyond my comprehension since I obviously did not have the criminal mind. I knew

I would never be able to walk away from any of it. He would make sure of that.

My bills had always been paid before the due dates. He never cared when or if any bills were paid. It did not phase him at all when I started receiving late statements and charges on his bills that were sent to my house that he supposedly paid. His credit card balances were high and so were the late fees. He did not care when I told him that I could not pay any more. That was not how it was supposed to be originally, the way we agreed, but the bounced checks and ATM withdrawals kept coming. It was a joke to him but I took it very serious. That was the way he was raised he told me. He was raised and taught by the best, he was the best, and no one would ever beat him. That was his favorite saying. His mentor was Al Capone.

As my money ran out, next to nothing, he decided his money and checks were his own and he would do whatever he wanted with it because it was none of my business. This was someone who literally begged me to keep my house for us to live in since he loved me, wanted to retire here, and it would be perfect. Perfect for what? No matter what I confronted him with he snapped back a story without the blink of an eye. He was able to make me feel stupid for even questioning anything he said. Even if it was in front of me, in black and white, he would end up somehow turning it all around. By the end of the conversation he would end up questioning me about what I started the whole thing with. There was the hammering again. Then he would laugh and call me names. By the time he was done, his stories always covered the truth. He was trying to make me feel inferior

102

and unintelligent but I never realized that until after. He claimed that was how you taught someone a lesson. He said it was for my own good and the good of the marriage so we could get along then everything would work out. They were just lessons I needed to learn. I had no idea what I could do because he had gotten away with whatever he wanted, and from what I could tell no one had ever stopped him.

Whenever he called it usually began with a few nice sentences and then out of nowhere he would be screaming in the phone about something, anything, for no reason at all. He loved to start a fight. Then he would tell me if I really loved him and wanted this marriage to work I would put his name on everything I had, or it proved that I did not really love him and never planned on staying married to him. If I did not answer the cell every time he called he would tell me I was up to something when I did answer.

Suspicion

Daniel called to tell me he had good news. His ex girlfriend called him and told him his name was still on their condo in a town near him in the suburbs. As far as I knew they had not been together in years. I asked him what that was all about since I did not know why he called to tell me. He said they had met and been talking about her buying out his half so I would never be able to claim that as marital property. Where did the money come from for payments every month? He told me he was not paying anything, but I can't imagine that she would pay for it all for him? So the good news was he was going to have lots of money and we could get back to our original plan, apologizing that it had been rough during the beginning of the marriage but now things were sure to be better. He wanted to continue to try moving forward while he planned on helping me out.

He had forgotten his name was on this title and they did not owe much money on it. At the beginning of the marriage he told me he had money invested in this condo but she would not agree to remove his name so there was nothing he could do at the time. Now she was getting married and decided she would pay him. It seemed odd but that was the story. I did not believe him this time either, so time would tell how that was going to play out. She realized that since he was married I would have an interest in the property so they were going to meet the next day. I told him I was coming up if it was really going to happen to meet with them and he told me it was not necessary. I knew that but I wanted to see what was really going on. Maybe I could recoup some of my money he owed me. Two minutes later he called me back and told me she had changed her mind and they were not going to meet. Maybe later, she had said. That was all he knew and then told me he would let me know if there were any changes but since they had two mortgages out on it now there would not be much equity anyway so it was no big deal. That was not the story he told me when we started. This was his last girlfriend that he lived with who spent and took everything he had. Suspicion was the only word I could think of since all that had taken place was negative. Something positive did not seem to fit my life any more and I could feel that intuition coming over me and learned to trust it.

Was Daniel trying to con me or try another scam or what? I could not keep up. Now that this deal with his sale of half the condo fell through, he had no money. If I would not file bankruptcy or do what he asked it would be a long time before he would be able to move down

A Burden of Proof

with me and help. There was never an occasion that he was able to help me anyway. No matter what, he had an excuse. But now it was my fault and he wanted to let me know that it would be about eight years before he could move down with me. He had done the math and would show me on paper the next time he saw me. He sounded so sad. This marriage had fallen apart so quickly. Now it would be eight years before he moved here and before it was this month, next month, then next quarter. It would never end. I could not feel sorry for him after all he had put me and my kids through. My life looked like a disaster and it happened in just weeks. How could so much go so wrong, so quick? Obviously I had allowed it.

The story was always the same, just a different day. One time he called to tell me he had broken his leg after work at a baseball game and was suing the dealership because it was for work. It would not be long; he said he would be getting a settlement. Once again he was going to have some money coming. If I could keep paying and keep up until it came, I would see. It was the same as all his other stories about next payday and the next something. It never happened and it never would. That was how he got by. He played on a person's sympathy and he was good at it.

He wanted everyone to feel sorry for him because everything was someone else's fault and that was why he had nothing and was broke. I always heard if "I really loved him and wanted to stay married, I would put his name on everything I owned". I could not understand why he was so obsessed with that.

My solutions would not work for Daniel. I tried to

106

talk him into downsizing and sell the additional thirty acres, trade vehicles for lower payments, among many other options. Absolutely no way would he have anything to do with that. His resolution was the usual story that I file bankruptcy, take out a home equity loan, borrow money, and so on. He would never sell the property under any circumstances. He tried one deal after another with me. If I would keep my house and all the property he would pay the payments, but he needed his name on it. That was all. I asked him how he would ever be able to pay for it since he was broke and could not help at all now. What was going to change that? That way he told me he could pay off all his credit cards and his kid's cars and catch up with his finances. It was too much of a strain on him and that would fix it. His kids, at twenty-one and twenty-three, had as many excuses for their lives as he had. I should not have to be responsible for their vehicles and their insurance. They came by it honest enough, another generation. He carried their auto insurance because they could not work, that was not my problem. My kids worked and they were in high school. It was his obsession and always presented some kind of a deal so I would put his name on my house. When I would no go for his newest deal he decided I was nuts, selfish, and needed help. Anyone would take that deal according to him, but he had no money and I could no longer support him and his family. It would only get me in deeper than I already was. Nothing was going to fix the marriage and none of his deals would help, even though he continued to try to talk me into one whenever we spoke.

Every month I attended the same political meetings as

I had done for 14 years. I was still working many hours. I tried to keep some of my paycheck out of the joint account but Daniel continued to overdraw that account. I drove to his apartment a couple more times and tried to resolve the mess. He would just hand me a stack of cash withdrawal receipts from many ATM machines and laugh. I checked and legally I was responsible for the ATM withdrawals made by him and all the checks written. I told him I wanted to close that account because I could not deposit any more money and still pay my own bills and ask that he return the debit card. Absolutely not was his reply. I explained, as I did in the beginning of the marriage, that I never lived like that before and would not now that I was married. He informed me that he had also opened an account in the suburbs but still needed our joint account to show he was married. He had a few bills and auto insurance bills that were mailed to my address. But all the payments continued to come out of the joint account. Since the money I had saved was about gone he told me it was all my fault that I was about broke and he could not help because I would not do what he told me. The solutions he had for me was to file bankruptcy, take out a second mortgage on my house, borrow money, sell my kids things, antiques, and keep only one of my vehicles because I could take my kids to school and work, and keep only the house and property. He continued to tell me I was nuts and needed help so he made an appointment with a shrink that he knew. The shrink he spoke with had told him I should be locked up. They must have had quite the conversation, if any of that were true. With Daniel nothing would have been a surprise anymore. The reason Daniel did these things, he explained, was because it is the only way to teach me a lesson and I had to learn.

Wake Up Call

I realized no matter what I did I had absolutely no control. It hit me like a ton of bricks. I tried to sort through everything from front to back and beginning to present. Each day that went by became stressful because the more I checked into these issues the more I found that my life was in someone else's control and tied all together into one big disaster. I wanted to slip out of it. Even though it would be a messy divorce I would be much better off and my kids and I could have our lives back. I was in financial ruin. I did not know where to start so I went to an lawyer friend's house and explained some of the situation while he and his wife listened in amazement. They were shocked and did not know what to say. This was only the tip of the iceberg, I told them, but I had to start somewhere. The lawyer, Nate, said get out now because it would never get any better and could only get worse. In explaining only part of the financial situation my friend could only tell me to "get out and get out now". He repeated it and it began to sink in. It was my wake up call. I simply wanted to cut my losses financially and emotionally.

A couple of times he drove to my house and came storming in and yelling at me about how he could not stay with me if I could not help him and his kids financially and stop being so selfish. He would yell and just talk off the wall, like whatever popped into his head and it was all my fault. Some of it did not even pertain to me in any way. My kids were there once and I returned the argument and told him to stop taking everything out on me and that it was bad enough I had to pay financially. I also told him I could no longer believe the stories he was telling me. They changed way too often and never fit the circumstances. I told him I would not allow him to do this to my kids since they did not deserve to listen to it and he had no right. Was he on drugs or what could always make him so abusive over nothing? Yet he would tell me there was something wrong with me and he would have to leave me if I would not straighten up and do what he said. Every time I was around him he seemed so unstable after the marriage. How could I have trusted and believed him?

One night, when my kids were not home, Daniel made a trip down to my house again to see me. He was acting all crazy and told me he could not stay with me since I had not done what he asked of me so we could be financially well off. The purpose of his trip was to let me know I would have to move out of my house. It would be his and he did not want me there. I told him he was

111

crazy and needed to leave. He refused to leave and stood at my door telling me I had to get out, that it was his house now and no one could make him leave. I went for the phone and he knocked it out of my hand. He told me I would not call anyone and laughed at me saying this house was his now no matter what I tried to do. He was crazy. I told him he left me no choice but to call and I grabbed the phone and dialed a person that lived close by. That person came to the door while Daniel was still standing there screaming that I needed to get out of his house. Why would he even try that and did he think I would leave my house of twenty-four years that I built? Daniel had never lived there and probably never planned on it. It was the first time I threatened to call the Sheriff's Department if he did not leave. Only when my neighbor and I told him we would have to call the Sheriff did he leave, screeching his tires and speeding down my lane. I knew from then on it would be a whole new ballgame. It was a game Daniel was playing and I had no choice, like it or not. I needed to find a way out but the web was tangled and I was stuck.

Sometimes he would call me in the middle of the night and wake me up to start an argument after he had been 'out'. Of course, it was always work or business meetings and dinners with customers. At that time the phone company did not have caller id available, so I felt I should answer in case of emergency. I explained many times to him that I was not a fighter and there was no need to argue if we could not have a conversation. It was always about me being nuts and needing help so the marriage would work. He did not understand why I could not grasp the concept that the number one argument between married couples was money. And that was the only problem; I just needed to understand it because when I did, everything would work out. Sometimes I could hear women or girls in the background with him. Sometimes when I called his apartment there was a party going on but he always explained that they were there with his brother, even when it was in his bedroom and he thought it was funny. The conversations were short.

What was there to work out? How could we work this out as two adults? I was beginning to realize that Daniel had more issues than a shortage of finances and it was far more serious than I wanted to admit. That meant I would have to admit I should have caught on to any one of these situations. There was a deep, dark past that I had become involved in and it was unfamiliar territory. No where to turn and no extra money to spend to continue making trips to the suburbs to try to get to the bottom. Where would I start? There was too much to fix now that it had gone so far.

Even after all of this Daniel continued to call and, under the pretext of trying to fix the marriage, ask for my social security benefit statement, tax return, pay stub, account balances, and other documents and information to be faxed to him at the dealership where he worked. Now he was trying to help me and he had a sympathetic tone. I knew it was for something else than just to help me. He was up to something again. I told him I did not have the time to put all of that together and send. He had never helped anyone unless it directly helped himself. When I did not do what he asked the calls would multiply. On occasion the call would remain under a calm tone, like a real, normal conversation. I tried to keep them short so the abusive undertone had no chance to arise. He just needed me to understand that he had to 'hammer' me when he called so that he could help me. He kept repeating that it was a proven fact that the only way people learn is by repetition and I should have learned by now.

The Twilight Zone

My life seemed like it had entered the twilight zone. It reminded me of the song about Hotel California. You can check in but you can never leave. It could not really be happening to me, it was not real. Even after a few people started to warn me to get out, I did not know how. I just could not believe someone would really do all this. I tried to get a grip on reality and the big picture. Maybe I needed a new perspective. It seemed so unfair. How could one human being do that to another on purpose, even kids, without remorse? That would be like a universal sin.

A couple more times I drove to the suburbs to try to sort and separate our lives. I called to meet him for dinner in a public place. Some days he wanted no separation and begged me to continue the marriage, and the next day he accused me of not helping him and that he was leaving me for good. Usually at dinner, places where he knew people, he would treat me very cruel in front of others but told me I could not lead on that anything was wrong. If I tried to talk about something negative, even though it were true, he would cut me down and say I was nuts. I could only say what he allowed me to say. I was supposed to pretend he lived with me at my house and stayed at "his other house" a couple of nights a week when he was overworked. His apartment was supposed to be called a house and no one was to know where it was located. Why? Who cared? No one was to know he lived with his brother in a rented apartment. Maybe he really did not stay there. He would tell people he spoiled me and gave me anything wanted and I was always shopping and buying, which was the total opposite of the truth. It was still embarrassing even though his actions and abusive words had become commonplace. The sad part was that I had become used to it in such a short time.

One of the problems I had to resolve was regarding the auto insurance policy Daniel kept for his kids. Without my knowledge, he had changed it to reflect me as the policyholder. I found this out when I received a bill in the mail. I told him I did not want any part of it. He kept promising to have it changed back into his own name but every time I received a bill, it was still in mine. Every time I called the agent, they would tell me it had been taken care of. I spoke with the secretary many times but when it did not change, I demanded that I speak with the insurance agent. At first he explained that the policy should be written that way so that I could help Daniel out and lower their rates. He explained Daniel had told him the policy was to be set up that way and remain that way. I told him I refused to do that and he asked for my driver's license number to see if I was currently on the policy. I told him I had my own insurance and my own vehicles through a company I had used for years and did not need another. It would not make sense for me to carry insurance on someone else's vehicles I had never seen that were in another state. I also told him these two kids were adults now. Also on one of the statements I found his mother's name listed with her car. About every two weeks a policy change or bill would be would be mailed to my house. The agent told me it would do no harm to use my name and address but he could not convince me. I refused again and he still would not do anything. One time when I spoke with him, he asked for my personal information like social security number and such. I refused to give it to him and I questioned as to why he was asking for that when I was trying to be removed. They were ignoring me and I feared nothing good could come out of it. Finally one time I called he said if I insisted he would totally remove my information. From that time on the secretary would never transfer me to the agent, she just took messages. Each time I would call it was the same story. I had written letters and received no response so it seemed I had to call on the phone. The secretary kept telling me that it had been taken care of and I told her it had not because I was still receiving statements. This had been going on for months. Then all of a sudden I received no more statements for billing and policy changes. I called to make sure and the secretary told me it was all changed now and I had been removed from the policy. I was relieved that one issue was resolved. I was buried in so many messes I had to decide where to start next.

If I had about ten more hours a day I could catch up and try to put my life back together. Every time I tried, I hit a roadblock because one thing led to another and it was all somehow connected. He was not just an irresponsible bookkeeper with his bills and credit cards, no way. No matter which way I turned, I could not make any headway. It was too slow. I decided I would continue to separate and sort through the last few months which was like a normal person's lifetime. How could so much damage be done in such a short time? It did not seem possible but there in front of me were all the papers and proof in black and white. It was like a bad dream which had become reality. I was awake and needed to do whatever it took.

My job took up most of the hours in my day. I would spend as much time with my kids doing whatever we could. It was very hard to explain the situation to them because I had no comprehension of how it all happened or why. We talked about what I was going to try to do and how I had messed up by believing Daniel. That was my fault and there was no denying it. I trusted and believed people too easily. This time it would cost me for that mistake. My kids were wonderful and helped out by paying for a lot of things. I could always depend on them and I let them help me because they wanted to, not because they had to. Maybe that was why we were a close family. They know I would do anything for them and they would do the same for me. They worked while in high school and I was proud of them.

No one knew what was going on except for a few of

my friends. It was hard to tell someone something you could not explain yourself. I would never understand why Daniel had come into our lives and turned it upside down. We had such a good life and everything going for us. Now it was a struggle to get through the next day. It was something that a person could never understand unless they had been in your shoes. My friends tried to help but there was nothing anyone could do for me. I knew I had to do it myself since I had gotten myself into it.

Nate and I continued to talk and he gave me guidance on legal matters and gave me a direction I could work towards. I was lost on the legal matters so any information helped because the money I had saved was gone and I was living from one payday to another. That was all I had left. Some days I did not think I could go on. At least I had a great paying job even though it was a lot of hours. Anything I could fall back on. My head would hurt some days as I sorted through what remained of my last forty-two years. It had all just disappeared before my eyes in a matter of weeks and I let it happen. Something like: you cannot see the forest for the trees. That was why Daniel had kept everything in turmoil emotionally and financially so I had no opportunity to stop and see what was really going on. I had no time to think it through because his messes all piled up so quickly and one on top of the other, never trying to resolve any of it before the next layer started. It became so deep no one could ever sort it out.

If You Loved Me

All of our conversations ended up the same. Daniel had become obsessed. There was no other way to describe it. We had been married for over three months now and I believed that I had made a very big mistake. No one could be so extreme in their life and have so many negative and drastic complications. Daniel was always trying to make a deal with me to add his name to everything I owned, which was becoming less by the day. I do not think we ever had a conversation after marriage that did not include that subject, always ending with him telling me, "if you really loved me you would share". Since he had nothing to 'share', it was a one sided request. What was the big deal if we were going to remain married, I asked him? The same reply as always: "if you really loved me....". When I tried to make sense of it all, I thought I was missing something and soon it would fall together and then be okay. What else could it be and why? That was a definite red flag and I proceeded with caution even though I had no idea where I was proceeding.

The rest of my life was being affected by now. I was worn down and tired and continued to work all the hours at the Resort as Director and share rides with my kids whenever possible and keep up with the ranch and animals. I enjoyed the time working the ranch even when it was by myself. Jas and Cal helped whenever they could and we had fun. Our animals were spoiled. During hay season, rain or shine, they helped me with baling hay and putting it up for winter and all the other chores that go along with the ranch. Everyone wanted to know why Daniel was never around and never helped me with anything. Daniel never once helped or even offered to help because he was always too busy at work and entertaining when he was off. He always explained he was trying to make more money so he could catch up and move here. I no longer believed that would happen and under any circumstances and that was a good thing.

The kids were growing up and we were still a close family even though Daniel continued to put a lot of strain on us financially and emotionally. Most of my money I had saved was gone, like a blink of an eye. We were only able to spend small amounts these days to keep everything updated and working if something broke. I tried to keep a normal, or what was normal for us, kind of life. That was almost impossible. In the back of my mind I knew there would never be a split between Daniel and me because he would not settle for it. He was in it for all he could get. Literally. It did not seem to matter what the cost was, as long as could run the well dry.

I would drive Cal back and forth to school, football, and work when I could and Jas did it when I could not. Daniel demanded that I keep my cell phone on at all times because he did not want me to stop and have breakfast with my kids before school because 'we' could not afford it. I was not to stop at any of the local coffee shops for even a couple of cups of coffee with my friends that I had known my whole life. I was just blowing money. A few times I took my kids to breakfast before school when I got paid. I even 'snuck' them to McDonalds a few times and he flipped when he found out because I did not answer the phone. When I told him I did it, he claimed I was nuts and that was why we had a bad marriage and no money. That was all I could afford to do now, not like the old days. Wait, I meant not like our lives were before Daniel entered the picture just a few months ago. He was very jealous of my kids, parents, friends, or anyone I spoke to. He felt now that I was married I did not need any contact with anyone. Since he was not at all close to his adult kids, my school age teens should not have much to do with me, Daniel claimed. That was how it should be when you are married. Jas and Cal were always very responsible and helped out financially and physically and emotionally. They were as unsure of what had happened and what was going to happen, as I was. Luckily, my kids did not have to witness or listen to Daniel's emotional and verbal abuse because it was usually on the phone or they were not home on those few occasions he drove to my house.

On those few occasions that one or both of my kids witnessed Daniel's irrational behavior I was mortified, embarrassed, and ashamed because I was now married to him and that they did not deserve to see or hear him in that condition or to treat me that way. I found that the only thing I could do was ignore him and tell him to stop or it would escalate into a huge storm. And then ask him to leave because of that. A couple of those times he left my house before it became too disastrous. I had to stay low key and keep things somewhat calm. No big waves so as to tip the boat or even rock it.

Once again I suggested selling the additional property because the market was still good for rural timber and pasture acreage. Absolutely not, was his usual reply. He loved it and wanted to retire there. I was not being fair because he was trying to move down here but I would not help out. We would have it made and it would all be bigger and better than what I had. There was still no resolution between us financially. As the days passed I realized that he was financially drained and sunk prior to meeting me. I had a ton of bricks around my neck and an anchor on my feet and I had been thrown in. The bricks and anchor had a name and it was Daniel, the one I married. Why had I not seen this or why had no one told me?

Daniel had been going a couple of days without calling me. Whenever this happened it was a relief not to deal with any of the problems although I knew in the back of my mind it was hanging over my head at all times. Ignoring the situation would not make it disappear but sometimes I think maybe it would if I ignored it long enough. I could not remove the bricks or anchor no matter how hard I tried. It was like they had grown on me permanently. That was a feeling I had never known and did not want to know.

If you loved someone, and really loved them, there would be no need to be abusive in any way. Everyone argues and disagrees and that is part of human nature. It makes the world go around. I was raised in a home where my parents did not raise their voices in front of us and I never saw anything thrown or broken and never heard any name calling of any kind. Was that rare? There had been no reason to scream and yell, we knew what was right and what was wrong. My friends all seemed to have the same mild mannered families. Nothing out of the ordinary. I guess that was not always the case with others. How else would people become so evil, I wondered. I tried to raise my kids in the same mild mannered and happy home.

Daniel continued to call me at work and he continued to be abusive to my employees, especially on paydays. There were thirteen people in my department that would take the calls if my assistant was not available. Daniel would yell at them for no reason if they did not get me on the phone immediately. Those conversations were about them covering for me and he knew what was going on and so on. They thought he was nuts. It was too much for me at work to keep the department running smooth and all the sales and money straight.

Three Strikes, You Are Out

The roller coaster ride was out of control and headed for a brick wall. I was way past the joke of his three strikes and you are out. Nothing I said had any meaning to him and that was why it was so hard to comprehend. Like he was not a real person, just a piece of body mass and skin that acted like a person sometimes and other times there was no soul. Missing the human element.

The marriage had drained me emotionally and financially in just a few short months because it was comparable to about fifty years in real, normal life. As real and normal as my life had been a few months ago.

One time Daniel bought binoculars and showed them to me. He told me it was to watch me when he was down here and thought it was funny. He was serious and I told him he was sick. I had nothing to hide, but maybe I should have thought more of it.

On that trip he came to my house and wanted to talk about my house. So we talked and I refused, as usual, to do what he asked. He still wanted to retire here and it was perfect, just what he always wanted. I explained again that it needed to be all sold now, not just the additional acreage so that there would be nothing to argue over. That way I did not have the upkeep nor have the expense of updating my house as I planned before he was in the picture. He told me I had moved up in the world now that I married him. I was beginning to think Daniel meant he wanted to retire here and it was perfect….perfect for him and that meant without me. He did not say perfect for us or we, but it was what he wanted and it had nothing to do with me. It was an eerie feeling and it stuck in my mind unlike some of the other things he did and said. Or maybe it was just filling in a bigger picture. Are the pieces in the puzzle coming together? Was I being paranoid? Because I knew it was not part of being crazy like he claimed I was. This was different but I could not put my finger on it yet. I was slow to comprehend how deceiving people are and I think it is because I believe everyone has a good side.

This time Daniel had new terms for me to come up with some money. Not a way for him to come up with anything or to help pay for anything, but for me to come up with it. His father and mother were moving to another state and Daniel was going to be taking over the used car business for him and he would need someone to help out with the accounting and books in that office. Daniel had a new addition to that business and wanted to show me on paper what he had come up with. He told me it was a win, win situation and I could not pass it up. He would be able to move down here sooner, of course, but I would have to handle some of it for him. The location of that business was about twenty-four miles north of me and about an hour from where he and his brother lived. The graphs and business plan he had made on the computer showed I would make more than what I was making now, and that was a lot. It absolutely looked and sounded too good to be true. If something sounds too good to be true, it probably is just that. I studied the plan but did not take it serious because I knew Daniel; I had seen how he lived and what he did for a living. I knew enough to be careful. What the plan all came down to was my signature and name ended up on everything which held me responsible. Not good for me and I really did not think I would ever see a penny. From what I had seen there was always a scam if you dug deep enough. It was just what we needed to help our finances and marriage he explained.

That was the same business that his father had been sentenced to prison for. He had run an illegal embezzlement and title scam out of a used car lot. Only after I was married did I find out about all that. So we discussed it. The story was that his father could not have his name on anything as a convicted felon, so the family took turns 'owning the business' on paper. He wanted me to quit my great paying job to do it and I let it go at that. But he wanted me to quit now and start that for him immediately and I said I could not do that because I had too much to pay for and he was not helping with anything. When he needed something he could be very persuasive and even nice. I was becoming accustomed to his antics and knew how it would end up. Another day of verbal abuse and how women were all alike, arrogant b------ and how he could get them to do anything for him and if I would not, he could get someone else to do it. It was probably true that he could get any female to do what he wanted because he had so much practice and would brag to me about it. He would tell of some instances and that he had it down to perfection.

Daniel used to think it was such a joke about how they got by with running the business, owned by his father, illegally and scamming everyone including the bank. All I knew was by what he would tell me. It was hard to understand why and how his father was able to get out of prison and turn around and do it all over again. I asked Daniel about that and he never answered and told me about how they would scam people and businesses and that he got away with it, laughing and bragging about how good he was. He thought I was stupid because I could not understand how and why they did it. My mind could not comprehend but I still tried very hard to understand. I saw no humor in any of it and wished I had known about it earlier, like before I got married. Many times Daniel told me the part about the day his father was sentenced and he was there in court to hear the verdict. He told me the judge asked Mr. Smith if he trusted Daniel's father to carry an envelope with money in it to the bank. Mr. Smith replied "absolutely". Then the judge announced that it was exactly what made Mr. Mohy so dangerous. Even after all the incriminating evidence and testimonies were presented there were still people in court that would trust him with their money. My guess was Daniel thought it so funny because he himself had gotten away with it and eluded the law while someone else took the fall. The Mohy's had no guilt, remorse, or shame for what they did. Their only shame was that they had gotten caught by someone that did not allow it to continue. Then I began to understand his claim that he "was raised by the best and taught by the best and no one could beat him".

I wondered why Daniel's father and mother left so abruptly but no one said anything out of the ordinary. Daniel made many trips with, and without me usually, to his father's business. If I was there they would have to leave and go to the office and speak in private even though I was paying the cash weekly payment for the business. It was only a few days before I received a couple of calls from his cousin looking for Daniel. His cousin wanted to know where to find Daniel's father or Daniel because he had taken off with money from the business. Daniel claimed his cousin owned part of that business, but only on paper. The money was gone and his cousin wanted it back. I asked why he would be calling me and he said he had no other way to contact them. I knew nothing.

There was a reason that I was only able to write checks for certain things. Any thing dealing with his father's business and auto titles from the dealerships Daniel worked with, were always cash no matter the amount. They all shared dealer plates and Daniel's name was on them but maybe just as agent and not business owner. That made sense. Daniel's father paid him cash per title and I paid his father cash every week for the business.

I knew there had to be more to this story too. Nothing was ever what it seemed with them.

At the same time all of this was going on Daniel's

sister, Amy had disappeared and everyone was frantically looking for her. Amy managed a gas station and money was missing and she had claimed a large man entered the station and robbed her when she was alone. The authorities and company went through the surveillance camera and all the details and could find nothing and no one else around. I never knew where or any other details other than the company claimed no one else was involved in the theft and she was fired and told she would never work for that corporation or any subsidiary again. Daniel thought she did it and no one ever spoke about it again. I did not know her and her husband very well and I thought she was an honest person but nothing fit, the story, the money, nothing. None of the money was found. No arrests were made. Was the whole family the same? Were they all raised to be criminals?

For Your Own Good

I ran into an old friend that I had not seen in years who also knew Daniel from a mutual friend. She asked how married life was going with Daniel and my reply was evasive. It was not something I wanted to discuss with someone I had not seen in years. She seemed to know him quite well and laughed at my change of subject. It did not seem to work because she asked me if Daniel was still scamming his way through life and it blew me away. I was speechless and did not know what to say. So there are other people that know what was going on and it seemed to be nothing new for him. His tactics were both his old way of life and his new way of life. It was not just me or my imagination. When in public with Daniel I would be quiet even when he would lie so he would not embarrass me in some way.

In passing during a conversation with Daniel I

mentioned what my friend asked me and he told me she was just jealous. In a snap he could come up with a story or excuse and full explanation without ever blinking an eye or taking a breath. It came that natural for him. So much practice I believed, I was caught dead in the middle.

Cindy, his daughter, called my house once looking for Daniel and could not get hold of him. It was the only time she had ever called. She tried his work and apartment many times and finally got my number from his brother. I thought it must have been an emergency but what she needed was a sticker for her car. A yearly renewal for seventy-eight dollars for the car plate. Since she lived a couple of thousand miles away he would need to get that for her right away. Why was she getting a sticker from this state? Where was her car registered? Why did she have to spend days and many, many phone calls tracking down Daniel to buy this for her and send it in the mail? Daniel's explanation was she did no know how to do anything like that and had no money so he had to take care of those things. She was twenty-one. He explained if he did not do these things his kids would not speak to him. I told him that was not right and he told me that was how it had always been. That check I had to cover to keep the joint account from overdrawing. It was always that close now.

The way I understood, his son had a hard time in college because he was a bit slow and not able to work. His degree in theology was what he wanted but school was a struggle for him so he had to spend all his time after school studying and trying to play basketball. Daniel Jr. was twenty-three years old and had tried to play basketball but lost three scholarships already. A few months into the marriage I found that Daniel had to pay for all of his school, groceries, vehicles and maintenance, insurance, and vacations and credit cards. Vacations and credit cards! He was perfectly named after Daniel. Daniel showed me a credit card statement mailed to his apartment that I was never aware of. Another surprise. I think his daughter probably had one or more too. It seemed he had to come up with more money on more credit cards that I never knew about before. All of it paid out of the joint account. He had to pay financially so his kids would speak to him, but did I because I married him?

Daniel told me it was his ex-wife's fault that his kids treated him that way but I know now that was not true. I had seen the other side of the story: the control, deceit, abuse, and sickness. It was probably why they lived so far away and did not see much of him.

There were a few times his credit cards were maxed out and he called me to get my number to use since my credit cards had excess credit to use. If I was not going to let him use my credit cards he thought it was only fair that I take out a home equity loan on my house because I had so much equity and it should be used. I was being selfish again. His kids needed help and if he had the money he would help my kids and me but it would be a while before he could do that. He always had a smooth, sympathetic explanation and never blinked an eye. It just rolled right off his tongue and I had not seen anyone that could come up with such a story line in my whole life. I had not been around people like that. It would make you think he was so sincere and in need and if you did not help him, it made you a bad person. That was an expert with many years of experience. I was catching on to all the patterns since it became an almost everyday occurrence.

It was not much of a surprise that I received a call one day from Daniel telling me that he had made another appointment for me with a psychiatrist friend of his. I would need to come up there close to where he lived and this psychiatrist told him I needed to be committed. I would need to stay in the hospital for a while. I told him he was the one that needed help. It was not an argument because I knew there was something very wrong and that something bad was in the very near future. Daniel was insistent that I make the appointment because that was the only problem with the marriage. That way we could stay together and make the marriage work. I was upset that he had taken everything that far. He explained how he was only trying to help me. If I would do that for him everything would be great and work out as we had planned when we were married. That was all I had to do to make it work. I refused as usual and tried to get him off the phone without too much drama. My nerves were shot and I had no energy left to argue with him. He continued to call me about that again and again. The calls would not stop. They were always the same and it was too much. Maybe he would drop the whole idea and move on to something else. Some other financial crisis.

Another time, Daniel stood at my door and called me every name in the book because I refused his appointment. If he needed something he would show up at my door, not to see me or help with anything. After about an hour of verbal abuse from Daniel I begged him to leave. Again he explained he was only trying to teach me a lesson and I told him he had to leave immediately. Apparently his lessons worked on some people but it did not work for me or for 'us' as he said. He continued that I was nuts and needed to see a shrink because I was a selfish, arrogant b---- like all the others and did not know how to share and I could not make it without him. I was nothing without him. That was what they had to do with his mother, put her in a psych facility. They had to commit her because she refused to go along with them and could not take it anymore. That was how they treated anyone that did not submit to their 'way of life'. They believed that their lifestyle was the proper way to live and they had the right to coerce others to follow no matter what it took. It was my fault that I made him verbally abuse me and act the way he did. He told me all of his friends up there believed him that I was nuts, evil, selfish, and need to be committed. I did not know if that was what he was telling them or if it was another story. Fear and sympathy games.

Now that I had moved up in the world by marrying him I would have to learn to act like it. His constant hammering was for my own good and the good of the marriage. If I had really loved him and planned on staying married, I would go. I was the only problem in the marriage. They could get me right into the hospital and I would not have to stay long and he would take care of everything for me. He had it all arranged. It was a nightmare and I was going to wake up. I did not know this person. Who was he and where did he come from? He explained further that now no one would ever want me because I was trash and a three time loser and I would have nothing because if he divorced me, he would take everything. My kids and I would be forced to live out on the streets. He would see to it that that would happen. He told me I had no friends because they all thought I was crazy and they agreed with him. I was nothing without him and I had no way out except to do what he asked. I think I started to believe him in some ways. He exploited and used the fact that I said I would never divorce again. It was the same over and over.

The exhaustion was taking its toll and since I worked so many hours I felt like taking some time off and try to deal with the situation head on. I needed facts and did not have the time to do the investigating and still spend time with my kids. Something had to give. I tried to attend all of the meetings for the political organization for which I was now the Vice-chairperson. The stress from Daniel was more than I could take and then it spilled into my work performance. I was still making good money and paying for everything. I could pay my bills, but now it had ended up that I paid for Daniel's which were way more than I even made. Now I was going further into debt and Daniel worked and paid for nothing. I spoke with a couple of lawyers and a friend in a legal department and they all agreed I should get out and do it immediately. But none of them could tell me how because it was already getting too complicated with all my assets tied up.

No Way Out

It was time to put what little energy I had left into some problem solving and investigating. I needed to somehow figure out what to do next. I made some appointments and worked around my job so I could take off as little time as possible. My nerves were shot but I had to keep going because I had nothing left to fall back on with my savings gone and nothing left in my cash box or checking account. I had even borrowed from my kids savings for groceries a few times.

Jas had her senior class pictures ordered and the first down payment was due. I knew there would be no money in the checking account so I saved it out of my paycheck. I told Daniel about it and he told me I would have to cancel them and she could get some done later. Of course I paid it and told him I would be paying the balance out of my paycheck later that month. He was infuriated on the phone and yelled that we had no money for things like that right now and I was to cancel her order. I refused and explained I had nothing left because of him and his adult kids and it was not fair that my kids and I were not allowed to do anything or spend any money. That made him crazy. I hung up the phone because I was tired of hearing the same thing over and over. He kept trying to call back and I let it ring. Of course there would be repercussions. He must have sensed that I was at the end and was planning my own resolutions. He had to know I did not believe anything he told me and that something was very wrong. It could not go on any longer.

A couple of days went by and then I answered the phone. Daniel called to tell me how I would never make it without him and no one would want me so I could never leave him. He owned my house and it was all his and there was nothing I could do about it. I hung up the phone again.

One of my appointments with my bank president was informative but I needed an end result. I explained what was going on with the joint checking account and the ATM transactions and asked what legal right I had as far as the bank was concerned. The bank president was perplexed and looked up the account information and decided he would do some further research as to what I could do. I knew I was still liable for all the overdrafts he created. But I wanted to know the legal way to remove my name because I wanted no more problems to add to what I already had. He had known me since I was eighteen and decided to build my house on the property I had originally purchased. He gave me my original home loan and knew I was honest and paid my mortgage payments and bills. That was twenty-four years ago. That bank also had the loan on the additional acreage purchased so they had an interest in what was going on. I tried not to go into too much detail because I was embarrassed and could not possibly try to explain something I could not even understand. Part of it was I wanted no one to know I had been so naive about the whole marriage and my finances. I was too trusting and had no idea there were evil people like that out there that would go to such extreme for money. When he had more information available in a few days I could call back or come in. So I waited to get back to him for information on closing the account or removing my name. For the last time I asked Daniel to come with me and close the account to make things simpler because I could no longer continue to add my paycheck and pay all his bills and charges. He refused since it was the only account he had and he was getting caught up and he was going to help financially and so on. Same story as always.

Another appointment with a lawyer left me mind boggled to say the least. I tried to take as much information as possible. One letter I had in my hand from a large corporate financial advisor addressed to Daniel and Molly Mohy. I had no idea what it was or meant but by the end of my meeting I was sure it was very bad. Bad in a way that I was in too deep and had no way out before I even left his office. I realized there were many people involved in many scams and illegal activities and I wanted absolutely no part of any of it. The lawyer's suggestion was to get out now because it would only get worse. But I was going to lose a lot and that was a fact. It came down to how much was I going to lose? My name and everything I owned became entwined into a nightmare. Some of the things I showed him and explained was unfamiliar to him.

Over the next few weeks I did quite a bit of thinking about what I should do and how to go about it. There was no way to make a plan in my head because I could not find my way out and saw no light at the end of the tunnel. There was no where to start because every aspect of my whole life became involved. When Daniel would call I would speak in general conversation and tried not to talk about much and keep it short. It was like a person that you did not know but were stuck in a room with and carried on a general conversation about nothing personal. I was sure he knew something was up and I tried not to let it show in my voice because it would be dangerous.

The whole situation was making me nervous when I started to receive mail that made no sense. If I asked him questions he would become very mean and threaten me and turn it all around so I was the one defending myself for what he was doing. The mail I received at my house included auto insurance in my name and address for his son, daughter, mother, and father and none of them or their vehicles were even in this state. Everything was escalating. I continued to call that insurance company and demand that my name and address be removed immediately. Even when the secretary and agent agreed, it was not done. The three of them were in the scam together. Some mail was for Daniel and other women and other addresses and he denied any knowledge of who they were or their addresses. I received more bills that were due in his name that I did not know about. It had

140

become very clear now that Daniel was a chronic liar and great deceiver. I saw his financial history and it was a bottomless black pit. No, he was a whole bottomless black pit. Yet he continued to demand that I file bankruptcy and borrow money and use my home for an equity loan. I would explain and show him in black and white how much debt piled up on me since I married him. By that time I had been through sixty thousand dollars in a few months and told him I could not even save a dollar out of my paycheck because of his spending with our joint account. I had bought nothing, never shopped, went no where except with my kids to their events and barely bought groceries. My own original bills were few, thank God for helping me, and I scraped now to pay those. To Daniel money was just water, never ending and always found somewhere close by. He never had any assets, no home or furnishings, no vehicles, no savings, nothing. Before marriage he claimed he had no debt either. Now I found that was an enormous amount. How had he paid for all of this prior to marrying me? His debt was far more than his income. It did not happen overnight. I was close to broke in those few months but kept thinking he would at least try to make amends as a real man, even if it were to repay just part of my money he had used. I rewrote and added over and over and still came up with the same numbers. Daniel was out nothing and actually was making money from me.

Daniel still called because he always needed money and wanted to be sure I deposited my paycheck into the joint account and still needed to know the amount to the penny. He had so much that needed to be paid, but not to worry because he would pay me back later.

As usual, that was how the story went. But now I was unable to believe him. Everything I owned was now in control of someone else and no one could tell me how to stop the insanity. He continued to beg me to keep my house because I wanted to sell some of the property first, which he said would never happen because I needed his signature. Since my house was the collateral for the additional acreage, I had to keep that.

That was how it was with Daniel when he wanted something or needed money since he could not afford anything himself. He wanted the best as long as someone else was paying for it because he would always claim to have the money next week, next payday, next lawsuit, and so on. I had asked him on the phone what had happened to his father's business and the money I was paying in cash every week and he explained he did not have the time. He had been talking with him and they decided it was not a good idea and there was no money in it and now he would not be able to move down here. But I was already onto that story.

Daniel did not want me to work unless it was for him. He knew every move I made. I became more isolated because I could not explain what had happened or why. My dress and hair should be worn the way he liked. Everything I had on was supposed to be approved by him so I was happy he never ended up living with me. My kids wanted to know what was going on because we were no longer able to do the things we were used to and it was a different lifestyle. I tried to hide as much as possible because I was sure things would get better because how and why would it get worse? I was wrong. It was difficult to tell anyone about it. Everything I had saved and built my whole life was no longer mine. Each call seemed to become more viscous and demanding. Even when I attended political meetings he claimed I was seeing someone. I was to stop going because it was not right now that I was married. Many times my kids went with me. These people had been my friends growing up and I had been in politics for about fourteen years already.

I tried to persuade Daniel it would be best financially if we were to sell the additional acreage and, or the house but he only became angrier. He refused to do anything to help the financial situation even though it was going downhill fast. What did he expect when I ran out of money to pay for all that he needed, I had my own bills like utilities and house payments. Groceries were becoming a luxury at my house while Daniel went out almost every night to wine and dine "clients" and use the ATM debit card to pay. Then he would call me later that night or the next morning to let me know I needed to be sure that amount of money was deposited. The terrible part was that legally I was responsible in the end because I knew he would not cover it. No matter how I presented the fact that all would be okay once I was able to sell part or all of the acreage and have some money left from my paycheck, he disagreed and simply told me absolutely not. He knew I needed his signature now to do anything. Sometimes he laughed and other times he would tell me it was all his anyway and then the next time he claimed he had lots of money and would start to help me with some of it. I never saw any help from him and knew I never would.

On a trip to see Daniel at their apartment, I watched

while he finished what he was doing on the computer, before he could talk with me. I wanted a resolution to the mess and thought if I drove there and confronted him with some ideas on how to sell, he would at least think about accepting my idea. Instead I was in for another roller coaster ride that I could not handle. Daniel proceeded to show me what all his constituents did for a past time. I thought he must be joking. He would get on-line with under aged girls and call them, meet, and have them over. He told me that was what everyone did and I just did not know any better because I was isolated and from a little town in the middle of no where. We were behind the times. I told him he was sick and so were his friends. He explained that there was something wrong with me because everyone did it. I told him it was not right but he objected because it was not his fault that these boys and girls were on line since that was what they wanted or they would not be involved. It was not his fault these kids were under aged so no one could do anything to him anyway. I told him he was missing the point and would be caught and he said it was just sex. What was the big deal? To me it was more than a big deal. Over the next week I cut out every article I could find about this kind of thing which were few because it was new and not much publicity yet. The Federal government was involved with the internet porn and trying to get a handle on something that was so out of control already that they had no idea. I drove those articles to him so he could see I was not the crazy one in the marriage. I told him to read them and wanted him to know he would be rightfully caught when he had these kids came to his apartment. He laughed and thought it was funny because no one would touch him. I hoped they would lock him up. Of course I turned him in but authorities did not know where to start and since I was married to him I was not a credible witness. That was the first time I had heard a spouse cannot testify against the other in court. Not a valid testimony. I had kids and so did my friends. My conscience would see to it I did all I could to keep him from continuing this evil crime and hurting children. I did not believe as he did, that these kids knew what they were doing and that they really wanted to be in that situation. Children are innocent and it is the evil people in our world that ruin them. I told him he could not get away with his kind of lifestyle where I lived and that was why he had to live in the city where no one knew him. That was part of the reason I think he and his brother moved around so much. I found that Daniel was smarter than those in our legal system. True criminals know the system inside and out better than those trying to stop them.

Being by myself with my kids was a blessing. We had always had such a good life and were happy. Our lives had changed drastically and we talked about it but I was still searching for a resolution. A smooth, quiet move to return to my old life. It seemed to be all dead ends and me losing everything.

The craziness continued daily and the calls would not stop. Daniel knew I was checking on things because I would ask questions about things he had not told me and it was on purpose. Though he did not know how I began to find out what he was hiding. He needed money and would tell me I could never leave him and could not survive without him. If I would not stay with him

I would have an accident and it would all be his and he would not allow my kids anything. He knew legally he could do that. He did not care where Jas and Cal went or how they would get by. He had made copies of my social security benefits statement for 'our budget'. He knew how much life insurance I had and with who but he also thought it had been changed to his name because that was what he told me to do right after we were married, but I never got around to it. It was not a priority at the time and then everything got so crazy I just forgot. I would never change any of it now anyway but I never said a word about it. This was no marriage and he had other plans. It was like watching a movie except I could not turn it off and walk away. I was sad and isolated and felt guilty about putting my kids in that situation. He harassed me at work and at home, day and night.

I continued to work and attend my political meetings and Jas and Cal's activities. Daniel and I no longer met for dinners or anything that cost money as we used to and spoke on the the phone only. The conversation always ended up the same. The whole marriage picture was a little fishy and all that was planned prior to the marriage was nothing more than talk. Just words and no meaning on Daniel's side. He never intended to follow through with any of those plans, but just agreed with whatever I said and wanted. I took the time to write down all my assets and liabilities and shocked myself. I had not realized what I had all the years I kept adding and paying off and the end result was great. Is that why he married me? If I had an accident and died what would happen? My kids deserved all of what we had before Daniel came into our lives. But now I had Daniel who wanted everything just because he could demand it. I was certain as to what was going on now. An ulterior motive was evident and I had to be careful. I was very careful when my kids went out or to work. Now I know why he tried making me deals to get his name on my house and why it was so important and he demanded it. That was starting to make sense. His story of "if I did not do it I really did not love him and plan on staying married, or everything I owned would have his name on it". All the stories and promises were words to him and nothing else. A true con artist.

Daniel now constantly threatened me and promised me no way out. Jas and Cal had no way out because they were still in school. That was my fault. A few times Daniel called and I did not answer, so he came down to stalk me. My friends would ask where he was because they had just seen him. What could I say except that I did not know he was here and I had not seen him. Since I had not changed my assets to his name he threatened to have me killed and my house burned down. He told me if my house and contents burnt down he would automatically be entitled to half of everything and it would not matter what I said. He claimed I needed to be committed and everyone agreed with him. He would never divorce me and I could never get away and he could kick me and my kids out of the house whenever he wanted and there was nothing I could do about it. It was for my own good. No one would ever want me because I would have nothing, I was too old, and a three time loser. Deep down I wondered if he were right about some of it. Married three times and lost it all did not sound good to me. I wondered what was wrong with me for putting myself in this situation and being so trusting. He exploited my biggest fear about marriage, which was divorce. He used it repeatedly.

Daniel would continue to call me at work and leave nasty messages with my secretary or employees. There was nothing I could do about it because when I asked him not to, he laughed and said he did not care if I was fired. It would be my fault for not being available to talk to him every time he called. It became too much for me to try to keep up with work and my kids and the ranch. Everyone thought I looked terrible and wondered what was wrong. I explained I was tired and had too much going on. Well, I did. It was almost full time just to figure out how I could get out of the marriage. I was not going to let it interfere with my time for Jas and Cal. They were always first on the list of priorities and that was how it would remain.

One day at work I found that the corporate office had increased my client's dues and I had promised them it could not happen when they signed their contracts. The corporate office then allowed changes on those contracts after my signature finalized the paperwork. I disagreed with the whole mess but they claimed that was how it would now be done. I quit because I did not want to be the responsible person for those changes which created havoc when the clients found out. Another mess I could not be involved in and chose to walk away from a company that would in no way stand behind what was right. They could have increased the future sales but not all those clients that had previously purchased and signed. That would have been okay. Now I was not working and would only have unemployment checks for a short time.

It bothered me but I knew I had done what was right. In some ways I was relieved. Was it subconscious? I truly had a full time job just trying to get out of the marriage.

Daniel wanted me to talk to no one and when I told him I had quit on the phone he was upset and told me we could not make it anymore and he was leaving me. I was making more money than he was and now my income was gone. It was not a shock to hear that but the next day he called to let me know I could work for him. I just let that one ride quietly and decided to use that time wisely and put my life back in order by doing whatever it took. I knew my time was limited but I had a goal. My goal was to clean up the disaster that was created when I married Daniel.

One job a person can always go back to is a bartender or waitress and make whatever hours or days fit your schedule. Those skills were easy to remember.

Daniel had obsessions and it was true stories. The 'clubs' he and his friends frequented were not party places and not meeting after work for drinks at the local dinner establishment like I thought. He explained that everyone that is anyone belongs such as doctors, lawyers, politicians, corporate CEO's, and business owners, and all of those kinds of people. It was child porn and internet sex sites where they would meet through chat rooms and go to these 'clubs'. Everyone belonged and it was common but I was from a small county and backwards area. He would not believe I would pass up an opportunity to be a part of his prominent crowd, as he called them. I had no interest whatsoever in their crowd. I told him I could not understand and did not want to. He claimed there was something wrong with me and I needed help.

It was part of his GA, which I learned meant gamblers anonymous, but I never knew he had a gambling problem. He explained he went to their meetings all the time. I had never been involved or knew anyone that went. He claimed it was not his fault that he did these things because it was a 'monster' that was always there and it just moved around but it never goes away. Daniel said it was all part of it, the GA, AA, SA. Now I know what the rest meant. Alcoholics Anonymous and sex anonymous were the other meetings he attended because it was always there and will never go away, so if he was not involved with one he had to be involved with the other. If I would only attend his meetings I could understand his dilemma and why he had all these problems. It would help us and the marriage and it was something you have to learn to live with. He was never nice when he drank more than a couple, which I saw only after marriage. I would learn his addiction went from alcohol to gambling to sex. Everyone at his meetings had the same addictions. He explained that was why sex was on the internet, so people could meet for sex in two's, three's, and groups, and swinger clubs like the one there in his city.

One time Daniel called to tell me to turn on a channel on TV. It was about swingers and sex clubs and all the upper class people involved like he told me. It was supposed to reinforce the morality of his lifestyle but it did not work for me. I thought it was pathetic when I turned it on. At first I did not believe him. I told him he would get caught with the under aged kids and it was not their fault.

The Used Car Salesman

After being married for these few months, which seemed like a lifetime, I entered a whole new life. It was not one I would have chosen if I had known the facts. The truth seemed to matter less everyday. Now I understood the "used car salesman" mentality. Tell anyone anything as long as you can get what you want, the money, no matter what it takes. That sums up the whole philosophy and life with someone like Daniel. The scary part is just how far will someone go to get what they want? Where will they stop? Or will they stop at all? It seemed to be easier and non existent if their crimes were not acknowledged by authorities.

I had to find the answers to many questions soon. There were no longer any choices in the matter but for me to dig and find a direction. I could see no way to fix the marriage but a smooth transition back to my life would be wonderful. I knew I had to take my losses but why should I give Daniel everything I had only a few months ago? After forty-two years of hard work and saving? I was unable to ignore the mess and no matter how much I wished, it would not go away. Days were slipping by as I tried to find the answers. Daniel's calls did not stop. Sometimes we would have a conversation but most would end in his need for my financial help and his promises. Broken promises and threats would not go together unless it was the mind of a sociopath. People that lived by the basic rules of life and laws would be overwhelmed and lost, like I was.

Lost

I had no idea where to start and no one was able to give me any guidance. It seemed there were no laws out there for what I was dealing with. No one had a clue as to what it all meant or how it was done. I was surprised at the people I spoke with because they were very knowledgeable in the law.

Receiving unemployment was a great help, but it would not go far with the payments I was left with. Daniel's sister had called and wanted to meet with me and a friend she worked with in a sales commission type job. It sounded good because I could work from home and it fit at the time. I checked to see if it was a reputable company before the meeting and found it to be legitimate. I would have no ties to her.

The next time I spoke to Daniel I explained what I was doing and he did not have much to say about it other than I should be working for him, where the money was. After the meeting with his sister and the woman that signed her on, I wrote a check to start the business with a well known communications company. I did not mind working for commissions and knew it would take many hours to earn a comfortable paycheck. The fee included all books and materials needed and I immediately began to study.

A few days later Daniel called and said he had talked to his sister and I was to cancel everything including getting my check back. That money needed to remain in the account because he was behind with his credit card payments and I was not to spend any of it. I asked if that was what he told her and he said no but I needed to do it right away. I was to return all the materials and have nothing more to do with them. We had no money and if I wanted to work, I would work for him only. During that conversation Daniel informed me that working for him with the business he wanted to run on the side would of course, require me to come up with some cash. His niece had read all his reports and income forecast and had paid to get in on it because it was such a perfect business with extremely large profits. With only a few thousand dollars and my credit card I would be able to get in on that 'business' with them and make so much money I would not need to work any where else. He expected to make over a million dollars right at the start and then he would pay me back the money he owed me. He brought me a set of papers detailing what I would need to do. I read through the ten pages. This one was a car sales program on a website relating to his work at the dealership. He complained I was not making the money I made when we were married and that would help.

When I contacted the manager from the communications company, I explained how irate Daniel was over the fact that I wrote that check and needed to cancel everything. She said Daniels' sister had already contacted her for me to cancel and understood he was not being very nice about it. That was helpful. I apologized and she asked that if I ever changed my mind to call her back.

As far as I knew all his credit cards were paid to date but then he admitted to other cards past due that I did not know about. Once again I was surprised with more stories and more debt. I did not even know what he was charging all the time on these cards. My name was on none of them and I had not seen any statements so what was going on? When I checked on the laws I was told by more than one lawyer the charges were accumulated during marriage and I had the burden of proof to prove otherwise. The burden of proof was a new term to me but I would soon become very familiar with it.

That burden of proof included everything he had done since the marriage. The knowledge, the charges, the signatures, everything. That was nearly impossible from what I had tracked down so far. When I asked specifically how to prove what was going on and to try to separate his and mine and to prove I had no knowledge of these transactions or purchases, I was told it would be extremely expensive and almost impossible because when it was over all I had was his word against mine. I know how persuasive he was and always got away with everything by talking his way out of it. I would not stand a chance in court because I was not a liar and I knew how he worked everyone. He was a pro and when he told me how no one would ever touch him because he was the best, taught by the best, and I would see if I ever tried to divorce him. No one would go against him and I had seen that was a fact. Why, I would never know. All the evidence of his crimes were there in black and white and over the years they involved large corporations and businesses and people from all over. Why was everyone scared of him?

One day Daniel would call and tell me I needed to get a job so we would have money and the next day he would have one business or another for me to run. Of course he needed me to start the business because he was too busy and I was the one with the money. When an option for a state job came up that I had some interest in he threw a fit and told me I was not taking a state job and needed to get out of politics. I needed to follow his notes he had given and start his business for him. He knew I had access to a few thousand dollars so if I would not contribute like his brother and nieces, he would have someone else do it. It was simple, but I was stalling.

I became so worn out physically and mentally. There was no light in sight and no one could help and I had nowhere to turn. All I could do was keep digging and come up with a solution. The more I investigated, the more I found. What was I supposed to do with more information and more links in the chain? I could not do anything with what I already had and did not want more. But each time I tried to sort out one problem or question, ten more would pop up. Another link and more messes. Unfortunately, I was right in the middle of the well woven web and so was everything I owned.

I wanted out and I wanted to forget the last few months like it was just a nightmare. I wanted to wake up so I could live my good life that I had with my kids before Daniel.

Daniel called me on the phone to let me know he quit his job. He had another dealership he thought about working for, but it was no big deal. I was not to call his old work number. He had no money now, again, or as always. I was not sure if I should be worried or relieved because maybe he would move out of state and forget about me. I tried to figure out what to do but at that point it was too late because nothing could have been separated unless I gave everything I owned to him to get out. Then I could have walked away but I knew it would all follow me anyway. There was something very wrong in the big picture.

That also meant his brother would be quitting and as always they would work at the same dealership. Once in a while I would get someone new at the dealership and a different story each time. No one told the truth or did they know? Daniel would tell me he was working early and staying late but when I called it was a different story or he never showed that day, or he had a funeral, and would be off a couple days or sick because he was driving so many miles back and forth to my house every day. Then when I asked him he would tell me a different story even after I told him what his co-workers said. Daniel never told the truth. It used to embarrass me because it sounded silly that I did not know he had a funeral or was sick or whatever, but after I realized it was a game to him and a way of life. It did not take long for me to realize I was better off not calling at all. He did not want to take the chance I would call and someone would tell the truth.

I was collecting unemployment and trying to find a job to work around my kids and the time I needed to sort. Sorting meant calls and letters and waiting for responses and follow ups and more calls and messages. I wanted black and white and originals and names and dates so I knew what I was talking about and could piece the puzzle together as best I knew how. I became self taught in investigative and legal procedures. I wanted a very clear picture and paper trail to prove to myself that this was really happening to me. Daniel could claim I was crazy and should have been committed all he wanted, but I was going to prove to myself and anyone that cared what the facts were and what was going on.

Now that Daniel was not working and I was on unemployment he called and asked for my credit card again insisting his son had another emergency. I refused and he told me he would again leave me, whatever that meant. I told him I would not go any further in debt for him. He claimed his son needed another flight to a few states and we needed to buy it for him because he needed a vacation. I told him 'we' needed to sell the acreage because there was no money and I was broke. There would be no vacation for his son paid for by me. No it was not some kind of joke. I explained the options I had come up with and none of them included me paying for his adult kid's vacations. I explained something had to be done and there was no need to put it off any more. His credit cards were always over the limit and if I did not let him use mine I would be dead. No one would blame him because they knew how I was since he told them all about it. I was a selfish b---- and would not share or help out his kids. He would never leave. He could take everything from my kids and no one would stop him because they never had. It was very believable from what I had seen. The thirty acres…. He told me why would he have to sell anything because it was already all his and he would never have to pay for it. He had plans and laughed and explained how easy it was for my kids or myself to have an accident or to have me committed. I would be out of the way one way or another. He would win no matter and it would all be his. It was always the same claims. After you hear it continually on a steady basis it becomes common and desensitizing. One cannot see the forest for the trees. I know.

Stuck on a speeding roller coaster ride that broke and there is no way off. What do you do? The stress will kill you when it is twenty-four seven. I was not sleeping because I worried and had so much on my mind all the time. Weeks went by and Daniel would call and threaten me if I would answer the phone. Once in a while he would carry on a brief conversation as long as I never brought up the fact that I had no money left to continue paying for everything. He never cared if I could buy a gallon of milk because it was not for him. He only cared that I continued to pay off his bills and loans and debit charges. Then one time he told me he had moved further north and was working at another dealership with his brother. I did not know when or where. That was what the 'marriage' was like. What he did was none of my business. His finances were none of my business. It was an arrangement for him at my expense. I believe the last dealership was catching on to some of his scams he was running on the side and they fired him. He was out of work for about a month. Once again he was living in the same apartment as his brother. That was no surprise. I often wondered if Daniel was capable of living on his own because he never had.

The next call I had received was about the fact that Daniel had so much money he did not know what to do with it. I was a fool not to work for him and make all that money, too. He would love to help me with my house and property. I thought it was another episode, another day, another deal. I did want help financially from him since most of the debt was his that I ended up paying. If I was not going to work for him I needed to find a high paying job. There was a different plan every day. I never knew which end was up.

My kids were worried about the direction everything was going. Cal's grades were dropping; he was unable to concentrate at school and was not himself. He did not smile anymore. Something was bothering him. I went to his school and spoke with the administrator. He assured me it was not a behavioral problem and I explained, in general, what had recently transpired at home. I knew Cal did not want anyone to know what had happened. I was embarrassed about what I had done to our lives and I deep down hoped our lives would reappear soon. I was pretending so I could get through each day and be there for my kids.

Jas was older and the situation seemed to have a lesser effect on her. Maybe because she was a female and older, I was not sure. She was not around as much because she worked and had a boyfriend. We talked about what was happening and what I had tried to do to fix the situation. I told them both it would be okay and it was just a temporary problem. Our business plans with the cabins and horse riding on the property would still have to be put on hold until I could straighten out the problems and recoup some of my money. I promised my kids we would get our lives back. They were very concerned for me. It had to get better, I thought, how much worse could it be? I did not let on that things were so bad and I was going into debt and could not get out. There had to be hope, but it would have to be soon. They thought I should get out of the mess quick.

I would not go far if I went for groceries or anything. I was not out shopping for new furniture for the new ranch he was building for me, and clothes, maxing out his credit cards while he worked, as he told everyone. I had no need or room for any furniture or clothes and I had never used his credit cards. My friends knew the truth and that was all that mattered.

Daniel continued on with his life up north and if he felt like calling he would. It was better when he did not have contact with me. He did send part of a monthly payment to me in the mail once and when I opened it I was shocked. It was like bait to see if I could wait for the next bite. I should be grateful? The print outs he gave me showed 'the budget' so I could see how he would move down here with me in about eight years and the more I helped him financially, the sooner he could move in with me. I knew it would never work out the way he printed and I do not know if he ever thought I believed him. His stories and plans were all so far out there and different by the day that I do not think he knew himself and could not keep track. I wanted to believe and trust but the past few months were a disaster and I was losing and he was gaining from me. Why was it such a big deal to tell someone where you really lived?

Daniel's mother had called my house a few times and the last time she called for him I told her he did not come down to see me much any more. She explained "I will tell you the same thing I told the last one because I knew something was going on". Deja-vu for her. Then I understood that was his way of life in the past, present, and future. The only way of life he knew. It was not my imagination like he told me over and over. I should have caught on when we first talked about getting married with his parents and sister. They would joke about Daniel's problems and not staying out of trouble, though no one was ever specific. I did not realize they were serious and it was mental and financial. I really never knew those people existed so I had no idea what to look for. The red flags.

The End Of Summer

It was fall and seemed like a lifetime during the last few months. I tried to keep everything together and pay bills and keep my sanity. I had taken a bartender and waitress job for a friend at her establishment. I could not have handled much more but being around friends I had known my whole life kept me going. Some of them were very good people and will always be special to me with all the help and support they gave. The hours were flexible enough so I could spend time with my kids while they were still at home. We did a lot around our property and house. Trails were kept cleared through the creek so we could ride the horses or hike, but nothing as far as building as we had planned when we purchased the property. It was a beautiful ride on horseback. There was always something to do and I loved being outside.

Summer was almost over. As each day went by the bad feelings and dark aura became stronger.

Jas and Cal worked during the summer when school was out. I worked as many hours as I could because financially the only thing I had left was my paychecks and equity in my house. I had no plans on living on the equity I had built in my home over all those years. I felt safer when I worked around friends and decided he could not do anything if people were always around. My kids kept close contact and we always knew where each of us was. I thought my kids were safe since there was no financial gain by bothering them.

Daniel would call me at work many times when he had nothing else to do. I never thought he would harass me at that job, too. My friend that owned the bar and restaurant finally told him I could not come to the phone because he would threaten me and scream into the phone and would not hang up. After she told him and he got the hint he would drive down and sit at the bar and make a scene in front of everyone. But when he was there in person he had a different story. Then the story was how much he loved me and did not want me to work because he would take care of everything financially since he had so much money. He could not figure out why I wanted to work when I did not have to. Daniel told them he could not understand why I was doing that to him. He would order his drink and throw out lots of money on the bar. My friends did not know what to think of him but they knew me and that I was not lying. A few times he begged me to leave with him and stop working because he gave me everything I could ever need. There was obviously something wrong with me, he would comment. That was his story when I was at work. Those were the stories he told and he made sure everyone could hear. Daniel was quite the actor and so believable. I knew first hand because I fell for it all and had the full understanding of how he would manipulate people to do and get what he wanted. He was raised that way and that was what made him so good at it.

My friends wanted to know why I did not leave him and I told them I had no way out. I tried. I was all tied up in this mess and wanted to keep my vehicles and house. None of them believed he was able to get away with all that he had already. It all happened so quickly. They offered help but everything we tried ran into a dead end. I learned more each day about our laws and gray areas. I say gray areas because he proved that laws did not apply to everyone.

Another lawyer advised me to be sure to keep everything I was able to separate and not, under any circumstances, sign any type of IRS forms or tax returns with him. Daniel threw a fit again, screaming at me on the phone that I could not have my taxes done separately and I needed to cancel everything I had done already. He would go to the IRS and have it stopped because we were married and they had to be done together. He told me he knew the ropes and had it done to his last one and he would do it again and I would go to jail. Legally, lawyers told me it was the right thing to do. He informed me he had called my bank and used all my home mortgage and deductions and was claiming it as all his. I was not to use any of my deductions because those were now his and I would not need any. If I did not immediately cancel mine, he would see to it I went to jail. I told him I would not make any changes since I was paying and all assets were mine previously, built my house, used my cash down payment, and used that for equity to purchase the additional acreage. I did not feel I owed him everything I had after a few months of 'marriage'. He had never lived with me or helped with anything and I could prove it. I told him he was lucky his name was added to the additional property I purchased and that was a mistake. There was nothing fair about it but that was after the fact. Daniel never had a next payday. Like always it was another story to get me to do something. He never paused when he came up with these stories; it rolled right out of his mouth without hesitation. I paid close attention to details then because I had to know. Only someone with evil thoughts could stare you straight in the eyes and say the things he knew were complete lies and stories and not blink.

Daniel needed the money from his tax return for his son, again, to purchase another airline ticket so he could visit friends in a few states. If I would not let him charge it on my credit card he was leaving me for good. I told him that was sad. He has to work early and stay late at his job because he has no money and I would not try to help. I should understand that was why the marriage did not work. That was an example of what he was talking about. I was paranoid, selfish, and would not share my money and possessions as he explained. It was for my own good. I heard this all the time and it was not phasing me at all anymore. Look what happened in one day, and I did it, no one else for me to blame. I ended up on the losing end with Daniel. After hearing it all the time a person will begin to doubt their own judgment and decisions. I tried to tread lightly while I unraveled the thick web. If it were up to Daniel, my kids and I would disappear and solve his problem which was like a thorn in his side and slowed down his plan. I began to believe he would go to any extreme to get us out of the way. As long as all my assets were left to him.

The chance came for me to take my final tests for a state job. There were some openings coming soon and it was a long process because I was not sure which position would be best. I proceeded with an open mind because I needed insurance again for my kids and a steady paycheck. The best part of that job, Daniel would not be able to harass me and show up at my workplace without consequences. It would be a relief for me to work without that pressure.

Property tax bills were late coming out that year and I was in for yet another surprise. I had five separate tax bills and three were from the thirty acres recently purchased. Daniel's name, unfortunately, was on those but the problem on the remaining two for my house and buildings also came in his name first and mine second. He had no claim to any of that and his name was never added to my home or other property. God was watching over me for that. I was infuriated to say the least when I drove ten miles with the payment invoices to the county assessor's office and asked that they check their records because there was a serious error. I knew to watch everything in the mail and was warned to be very thorough no matter what might seem unimportant at the time. They were right. I asked how Daniel's name could have been on my house and they had no explanation as they searched their records. It did not appear that way one day without someone specifically making sure it was added to my taxes. His name was not on my house or any other part of my property so I had to investigate and keep my cool. I did my research and wanted the assessor to show me how and when that had been changed without my knowledge and any signatures. Were there any property title changes? No one knew, but I left asking them to find out because I would be back for the information. A week went by and I returned to the courthouse. No one had any idea how something like that could have happened after twenty-four years in my name some one just decided to add Daniel's name to not only one tax bill, but two. I was not buying the story and kept very good notes. They decided they could fix it and I told them it needed to be corrected immediately. No one said a word but they corrected it and I made sure there were no other surprises with my house and taxes. I was not happy with that office and let them know. How and who did it illegally? No one ever gave me an explanation. Was that being paranoid? That was a fact in black and white.

Once again there was a calm and it became quiet. I could not tell if that was good or bad. Daniel always told me it was just the money that caused problems in our 'marriage' and that statistics showed it was the main reason for divorces. Now I believed it was all much deeper and if I kept digging I would find more than I cared to, but I knew of no other way to get my life back.

My last unemployment check came and my kids and I kept everything paid. Daniel would continue to call to be sure the payments were being made and to let me know he would send some money 'next payday' when he thought he could spare the extra.

I made a trip to our Capitol to test for State employment because they would be hiring. I tested twice and met with friends for lunches. When I told Daniel he flipped that I would go to test for a job instead of working for him, and that I was around friends he did not know.

Another call was to inform me that a friend of his had done an appraisal on my house and property and he had a deal for me to help me out financially. He would pay me half of his friends appraisal if I were to put his name on everything I had. It was his win-win situation. Or so he thought. I had a feel for what was going on but could not put all the pieces to the puzzle together yet. There was too much. I refused to have any part of it and told him to keep his friend away from my property and I would not be making changes. I certainly would not add his name because he could never help with what I had already added his name. I was paying and adding equity and that part was half his to just take. Even though I showed I made the payments, legally he could claim half of that part of the property. Since I would not go along with this 'arrangement' he was offering me, he moved onto the next one. It only took a couple of weeks.

Daniel called again with a new story. Now the bank I had when I purchased the additional property was in collusion because he had done some checking and found that his name was not put on everything I owned when we were married. I explained that was true because there was no need or question at that time. Daniel was there for the whole transaction and knew what he signed and it was explained because I always asked lots of questions. He was well aware at that time. He told me he could have us all thrown in jail and automatically own everything of mine anyway. Now he wanted to sue the bank and me. I had to see what he meant by the bank being in collusion since I had never heard of it before. I wanted to know what he was talking about. I told him he was nuts and hung up and quickly called the bank to have them check clearly the names on the titles and loans hoping I was right that his name had not been added to everything I previously owned. The bank confirmed that my name was the only one on that which was originally mine. What a relief. He was trying everything he could and using everyone he could to have his name put on my house and the rest of my property. That was very obvious.

It felt like a hostile business takeover deal and no one knew what was going on under the table and behind the scenes.

I repeatedly tried to get Daniel to agree to sell the additional acreage because I could no longer afford the extra. I certainly would not be able to start a business and come up with more money and further my debt, as I had originally planned when I bought it. My kids and I had prepared the property for our original business plans but those plans were fading fast for building some cabins and a stable. I told him something had to be done immediately. His solution was to let him have it all and he would take care of it because he had his own plans. He told me I might as well give him everything now that I could not afford it because he was going to get it all anyway. He could not stay with me and was not going to let me have anything. When the money was gone, so was Daniel. He called to keep up on my status with payments I was making because he had no money and could not help or move with me. That story was old and meant nothing to me now. I was losing everything I owned right before my eyes and had no idea how to stop it.

Most if his mail goes to one of his addresses in the suburbs. I had no idea which apartment he was living in. One piece of mail I got from a major investment company in his name and another woman. Two different apartments in the same building. No account balance was listed so I had no idea how much money he was pouring into that account and I knew there were many more. I took it to a lawyer and they informed me the account was set up by Daniel for her and another woman. I called him and he claimed he knew of no such women. It was a mistake and not him. Someone must be using his name. I did more investigating and it became more piles of documents and notes. I became very good at it and found much of what I did not want to know. It was months of letters and phone calls and messages and follow ups and each avenue brought more files that I had not even touched on yet. More names and addresses all linked to him. Many people in other states and businesses, credit cards, banks linked to him or with the same last name. Not coincidences. Too much. There could be no such thing as that many in my little investigation. I had hardly any money so what I had for resources was scarce. Kerri helped with some of the research because there were so many questions each time I tracked one problem down ten more came up connected I told her. When she saw it all in black and white it was overwhelming. I showed Kerri what I had found so far and when I asked her questions she became more curious. She was shocked at what I found already. Even though she and Daniel had been friends she had no knowledge of his dark side. She truly felt bad that she had anything to do with Daniel and I meeting.

There were many accounts and illegal activities coming to the surface. I did everything I could to separate myself from Daniel's family and name. I asked him to discontinue his life insurance policy payment for his kids out of the joint account and also their credit cards. He refused to stop any of his payments from the joint account. I explored all avenues for me to proceed with the separation of everything because I had no choice and no money. I was sliding by on that job and making all those payments that were not even mine because I wanted to keep up my credit rating and make sure everyone was paid on time. I was afraid of what would happen if I did not. What did I get myself into? I had no idea where to go to figure it all out.

My mail was Daniel's unpaid doctor bills, insurance accounts, credit cards, loans, and mortgage applications. The mortgage applications were for him to take out a second mortgage on my house and property. I made many calls to all of them and some were not very nice claiming that I was responsible because I was married to him even though I explained we had never lived together and were separated. Many of his insurance statements mailed to my address were late and unpaid. I called when I received them but they were animate that I was fully responsible for these payments even if my name was in no way involved and on nothing. My address was listed as his apartment, so they claimed it had to be correct.

When I called Daniel to let him know he needed to make those payments and have his address changed to his and not mine because I would pay for no more, he would just laugh and say he had no money and I should help. I was upset with myself that I had let it get that far.

A good friend of mine asked me if I had checked my credit report since I was so worried about all that was going on and told me how to get a copy. That was an important piece of information because I found even more. They took a while to receive by mail and I do not believe the ID theft reports were taken seriously. They were general information and were many times not precise. So when I finally received my report it meant another pile and more leads. It was like a full time job just to try to remove myself from this person. I had to learn how to read these reports and put together the pieces of the puzzle with most parts missing. Most people have never seen their credit report and if they had they never picked it apart with a fine tooth comb. Well I had to. I had no idea what I was doing or where it would lead but what choice did I have? Hiring a private investigator would be very expensive since it was so extreme and included many other states and people. I tried to find the cheapest way to proceed.

I tried to summarize my 'new life' and how it had changed in the last few months. It was very hard to backtrack. As Daniel stated, why would he let me have anything because now he was entitled to it all. I noticed some of his bills and mail that used to come to my house now went to his apartment or one of his other addresses. The only one I knew about was his brother's apartment but as I did my research, I came up with too many addresses.

When we were married my income was more than Daniel's. All of his debts were being paid off and mine were rapidly building into a mountain. He was gaining everything and I was losing it. Daniel stayed in his apartment with his brother who paid too, I thought. They had a maid and Daniel came and went as he pleased. When nothing was going on there he would come to "his ranch" he built for me and be married, as he told all his co-workers. That sounded great. Nice arrangement. Play and live how and where he wanted whenever it was convenient. What a package, except that I was in the way. My trips to see him to work something out were a waste of time and gas. Nothing made any sense and it was much more than I could comprehend. It was not my imagination.

The few times Daniel came to my house and used my computer in the computer room, was questionable because I could never see what he was working on. He explained it was just work so when I came into that room, he was done or he would print out my new budget. That was a bizarre print out and so far from reality. I wanted to know how it was possible and asked him to explain where he came up with the numbers. I tried to find anything he might have been on in my computer but never could. I was not a computer whiz by any means so I let that slide. After all, what would he have possibly done on my computer that would affect me or my kids? I had bigger fish to catch that I felt was more important and life-changing.

My head was spinning and I had to stay focused on what I began to research because too many other people and places and businesses began to surface. I had to proceed with caution because Daniel had a terrible temper and I believed he had no conscience about what he did. It seemed that nothing mattered to him except how much money and assets he was able to scam from everyone. It was as though everyone owed him.

I had made a list of his payments that he owed and paid out of the joint account. It was staggering and more than my income. Now I was trying to put all the numbers together from what I found, not what he told me. If he owed and paid that much debt before he married me, how did he pay? He made less money than I and had at least ten times the debt or more. Nothing made sense. Adding and subtracting was not something that took a lot of intelligence. Even my calculator agreed with me. Daniel had no comments about my questions other than I was wrong.

I was still working whatever hours I could and tried to keep my hours so I had as much time as possible at home with my kids. I still tried to keep up the same relationship with them and do whatever we could together. The days flew by and it was difficult to be to work at five am and also work late nights if no one else could. My favorite was five in the morning because all the customers were laid back and happy and usually retired. Then I was home by the time the kids got home from school. Evenings were harder but at least they were able to come and see me and have dinner or pizza. I was not letting Daniel ruin my relationship with Jas and Cal. I needed them as much as they needed me. My employers were my friends also, so they understood.

What Happened

Summer was over and I was not even sure where it went. It was like a whole lifetime yet maybe it was a nightmare and I would wake up one morning and it would be my "old life" again. Deep down that is what I thought would happen. What was currently happening could not possibly be real. As I researched and investigated I was sure that it was all just a simple mistake on my part and there would be the whole explanation. All would go back to how I had planned my life. Once in a while I detected a positive note when speaking with Daniel and held on to it. That was not reality, but I believed it was a necessity at that time. Were there really people out there in this world like that? I had a hard time believing that and it would not sink in. That was only on TV.

Everything Daniel had told me became a lie as I investigated what little I could. None of it was good. None.

My address had been used for some kind of business with titles, cars, and insurance companies illegally. There were other women, men, businesses, social security numbers, and addresses associated very closely to him. I did not want any of this to come back on me for any reason. Is that why he never lived or worked in any city for long? Daniel's accounts seemed to change on a steady basis too. Why had I not seen any of this? Because he always had a great explanation for everything that sounded right and made me believe I should never have doubted him and that made me a bad person. I began to believe when his mother stopped him from pulling the trigger on himself, she did the world an injustice. My friend Kerri called him a waste of good oxygen. His kids knew well what he was doing and used that to their advantage. Why had they never been to my house since the day of the marriage? I wondered. Daniel always had a story. He used his mother in the same way whenever she would not go along with him and he needed her to do or say what he wanted. She was stuck too. It was like he truly hated all women and used them as he saw fit. They were there for him to use.

There was a new 'arrangement' with every conversation we had. Daniel would tell me how screwed up I was because he was not getting a divorce and he would pay only his bills. I explained we did not have a marriage. He told me it was my responsibility to take care of everything and pay for everything and when he had a chance to come to 'his' ranch he would. That was his plan in a nutshell. It was simple to him. He was married when it was convenient and I could pay for it all. Now when he told me to trust him because he had it all worked out, I knew what that was. I told him he was riding the fence and this was a marriage or arrangement of his convenience. Some days he told me he could not stay with me since I had not helped him financially and would not take out a second mortgage on my house to help him pay his bills. He assured me that I had more than enough equity to have a very large second mortgage after his friend appraised my home. That should never have been done without my knowledge and consent. But I could see what he was able to get away with. The next time the story was I had to work for him so we could do as planned in June and be wealthy. If I did not want in on his new business then it was all my fault because he was trying and I was not. With just three thousand dollars I could be a part of it with the rest of his family. It was a 'sales ad' this time and like his business with credit reports the money would roll in. Once again I explained my money was out. I did not fall for that deal he had either. Each time we had a conversation Daniel would turn everything I said around. That must have made him feel good or maybe that was his excuse to try to look like a real 'man'. I thought he was a psychopath and began to wonder how far he would go. Maybe there were people around so he needed it to sound like I was some crazy woman. I could not make sense of any of it.

One day Daniel would call and be verbally abusive and tell me it is my fault and the next he has a business venture for me to work for him so I can stop working my current job and make lots of money. I tried to not answer the phone but I could not avoid him. I had to keep things cool and not upset him too much until I had as much information as I could get my hands on so

I could get out. And I mean out. Whatever I was in, I wanted out! It was taking me a long time to figure it all out because there was so much and I was unfamiliar with all of it. I asked my friends so many out of the ordinary questions that they knew it was bad. At least I had some friends that were in the legal field, even though the little pieces I asked them about blew their minds. They could not believe there were people like that around and that it was so extreme. Well neither could I, but I seemed to be living it. I would explain to him that I could not do it anymore. We were beyond talking and figuring anything out. Even though he would not help to pay for the property, his name was still on it and I was advised legally to try to get him to remove his name. I tried many times and he refused telling me that he would be a fool to take his name off because it was half his anyway. It would all be his and he could wait. He planned on everything being turned over to him because he had a good job and the ability to pay whereas my income had declined and I used all my savings and extra cash to keep it all paid so my credit would not take a turn for the worse. Then what would I do? What would happen if I stopped paying on the property since my house was the equity to purchase it. Yet he continued to tell me I was stupid if I would not take his deal and take out a second mortgage because he had plenty of money and would make the payments. My house was in my name so I would have to take out the loan.

Once again I offered Daniel the option to pay for half of my house and we could use the excess to pay down some of his debt since I did not owe much on my house. His response was exactly as I and everyone expected it would be. He explained, why would he do that? He already had his own plan and I had gathered that by now, but I was slow putting it all together and connecting the dots because there were literally hundreds of dots. I was learning. Nothing sane seemed to apply. I kept running into a brick wall.

I received more overdue credit card statements and invoices in Daniel's name. He paid nothing. Did he think I would? It continued and I called to let him know these were still being mailed to my address and he needed to contact them to change his address. He asked if I could just pay them for now so he could catch up and he would pay me back next payday. I refused. I finally called and began to explain to them that he did not live there. Most of them were great about it. A few were not. One invoice came to my address in my name for an ad for auto loans. When I called I explained it was not mine and I had no such business. They were animate that it was a correct billing and it would have to be taken up with the supervisor to be resolved now. They told me I was responsible for the payments on these ads which ran continuously. I was livid. It took weeks but finally I spoke with someone and they were very evasive as to who was running that ad in my name. They could not answer anymore questions about the ads and never did stop sending me the bills.

Daniel denied his bills being late and any involvement in the auto scam ad. He claimed that it must have been someone else. He also denied that the home mortgage apps were from him or that he had any knowledge of why I received so many all of the sudden. He had no clue what any of it was about because he was paying his bills. His auto and life insurance policies were all up to date and he would call to be sure there were no problems. He could not understand what my concern was. I hoped he would take care of it now that I refused to pay and had contacted these companies. Now I know there were no mix ups or errors with Daniel. Everything was done specifically on purpose with full knowledge of a plan.

I was learning to shop at cheaper stores and buy only what I needed to use currently and not later. We bought what we could at dollar stores, which I had never been to before June. I realized we did not need as much as I thought. I was surprised to learn it was not that difficult to live on less. Only necessities were on my list because I did not want to lose my house. I continued to cut back on everything possible since there was no longer such a thing as a budget. The list I made to take to town became only bare necessities. It was a different kind of life but we were surviving. Jas and Cal were very confused and I tried to protect them and not discuss much of what the details were. They were still kids in school and in no way did I want to put any extra burden on their shoulders. In a way I thought maybe it would still all go away and we would have our life back. Maybe Daniel would leave us alone and go away because I had not given in to any of his requests. The whole scenario was bad and the long distance should have made it more difficult for him. What happened to everything? Where would Jas, Cal, and I live? Even worse, how would we live and how could we make it now?

Jas And Cal's Change

No matter how hard I tried to keep the disaster out of Jas and Cal's lives, it hung over everything we did. Like a severe storm above, I had no control. Would it be over soon and what would the outcome be? I did what I could. Their lives changed and I was responsible. That weighed heavy on my mind.

We were survivors and strong as a family. Jas was older and would soon be out of high school and would attend the local community college. Her goal was a business degree. She grew up helping me with our business and it came natural to her. She made good money as a waitress and was happy to work and help out. She continued to spend time with her friends and follow all the rules, except for one time. That time she stayed out with a couple of friends and did not call and check in with me. When I called there was no answer. It was past curfew and I contacted the parents of her friend because it was so unlike them. We were all very worried and of course the mind will play tricks on you and causes unnecessary thoughts. Then they were home and explained they just lost track of time and everything was okay. They were grounded. I was so relieved at first, then so upset with the fact that she did not follow the rules. That never happened again, thank goodness. She kept her grades up and remained well adjusted. Overall she handled our situation well and I answered all her questions during our conversations. Jas understood part of what had taken place but had questions about her father. Another subject which I could not explain. I kept the conversation and answers as positive as I could. I had no reason why Jeb had no contact with them. I would never tell them he did not like kids and decided after the fact he wanted none. That would have devastated them and they would never have forgotten it.

Cal was a tough kid and way ahead of his years. He caught on to what was going on and he had a gift into the soul of people. He could see things that I could not. He grew up faster than most kids his age and always tried to protect me. He hung out with his friends but never really got into any serious trouble. I prayed that God would get my kids through whatever seemed to be happening. Still, his grades seemed to slip and I tried to make him care. At the parent teacher conferences, his teachers were concerned that he was just sliding by and drifting along in class. They told me he was very intelligent and we needed to keep him on track. The school counselor and three teachers explained to me that it was not a behavior problem, it was his concentration and they all liked him and tried to help. The only thing that helped in school was football and I never missed a game. Jas and my parents came to those they were able to. He loved the game and it was everything to him and he was good at it. His grades had to be kept up to play. Cal also worked after school and on weekends. He helped to pay whenever he could without complaining because he knew I worked hard and tried to hold everything together. He saw into more than what I told him. During our discussions I tried to ease the overall situation and keep them looking ahead positively. That was very difficult in reality since I was having a tough time doing the same for myself. I was lucky Daniel was rarely around us and I think Daniel knew Cal could see through him. Jas dealt with it by ignoring it as much as possible. I knew what Cal saw was not good. Cal worked all the hours he could and still did his homework. He had to study hard for all of his tests because it never came easy. Cal tried to hide how upset and worried he was and I could see that, so I always reassured him it would all turn out okay and our lives would be like it had before I married Daniel. Maybe the fact that he was younger and male and he was more impressionable than Jas. I tried to pick it apart psychologically and read and study because teenagers had different needs and issues and had their own growing pains without all the extra drama to deal with. Not just that it was drama, but that it was evil which we were not familiar with. I felt I had let that evil person into our lives and he was destroying us relentlessly. Cal was needier than Jas and she helped me to keep him in a more positive light. She understood since they were close. Cal asked the same questions about his father. The three of us had many conversations about Jeb. I always tried to keep it light and positive but never gave Jeb total excuse for what he had done or why. There was no justification for Jeb to treat his kids the way he did. I told my kids it was their father's loss and hoped someday he would see that. Jas and Cal were together in that situation so they could talk to each other and help each other to understand and move on because dwelling on the non existent relationship with their father had no productive or positive outcome. Cal did not handle it as well as Jas and I knew that and tried to compensate for that loss in his life. He needed lots of positive support. Now that Daniel was in our lives it was another negative male figure. There were positive male figures in his life that I made sure had contact with him so he would not think all male adults were 'bad'. My father was involved with Cal as he grew up and taught him many things he needed to learn. It was different learning from a positive, stable male figure. It was nice that they lived across the pasture and trees.

Their Grandfather and Grandmother, my parents, were always there for my kids. Always. They were the best Grandparents they could have. Jeb's parents had nothing to do with helping them as they grew up in any way. Oh, they had received a few birthday cards when they were little, but ultimately had no interaction with their lives. I never considered them their grandparents and neither did they. My parents had conversations with Jas and Cal and were very close. I was blessed with great parents. They were always there to help and I needed it then. They attended school functions with us and took them on weekend trips and out to eat. They taught my kids how to work on indoor and outdoor things, right and wrong, church and life, and to lead a self supportive, Christian life. They were always there and stable in our lives.

My Aunt and Uncle, that we were very close to, spent lots of time with us. We did a lot together with them and my parents. They were a stable and good part of our lives also. We were lucky to have these decent, wonderful people close to us and permanently involved in our lives. More stability for my kids while they grew up.

When I had spoken with a male and female child counselor, they stressed that I should always keep a positive outlook in their minds about their father because they would grow up and see for themselves. That way I was not a negative influence in the matter. I think that also kept my kids and I close. They saw for themselves. I always did that and kept in the back of my mind that he would soon show his colors and they would understand when they were ready. The counselors told me that time would take care of it all and I would not have to be the one to open the wound. I do not know if time healed anything, but I do know they were right because I never had to be the bad person and explain his negative actions. Jeb showed them firsthand what he was all about and how he felt and what he did not want in his life. God helped me over the years to bite my tongue with what I really felt and wanted to say. But deep down I knew the type of person he was and that he would prove what I thought to be true. He just disappeared as they grew up even though they tried to keep contact with him, Jeb did not reciprocate. He was not about kids because that cramped his lifestyle. He never attended anything at their grade school when they called him and asked. Jas and Cal tried and Jeb never did. Not having a father in their lives as they grew up was sad, but that was something that was his choice. I did what I could to compensate and the counselors thought I had done an excellent job. They told me I had done all the right things and remained on the right track and should continue as I had. We had never moved and I made good money and took them to work with me when possible and our lives were positive. Something I felt great about. I guess that my kids never knew the difference with their father not being in their lives. Something that was not my choice.

When Jas and Cal were not home and I was off work, I would go out with my friends. Sometimes we would have dinner and sometimes drinks. It helped me to talk with my friends and keep my sanity. They were my support so I would get it out of my system and off my mind about all that happened. Everyone was so good to me during all the episodes and reassured me what was going on was not normal and it was not my imagination. I tried to keep to myself as much as possible because I was so embarrassed to be in that situation. I allowed myself to be abused and I had always thought a person was only abused if they allowed themselves to be. That was because I had never been there. It's like that saying about walking in some one else's shoes, now I fully understood the meaning. I was embarrassed to be in public and had a hard time explaining or even commenting on my marriage. People I had not seen would ask how I was doing and how married life was, or they would congratulate me. I was overwhelmed with everything. Some of the things that happened were too extreme to even tell most of my friends. I was afraid they would think I was crazy and making it up, it was that bad. I did not even feel it was reality. It was more like a nightmare so how could I explain it to someone else? Some of it had to remain unspoken. Sometimes when I would tell someone some of it they would get this look on their face and I knew not to go any further. After all it hurt my head and made me sick. Only I had to deal with it and fix it. It was all so hard to come to grips with and face the reality of the situation. I explained what I needed and tried not to involve too many people. Some people had known Daniel and made comments and I knew they knew what I was going through. They were sympathetic, which is not what I needed because I needed help and guidance, but no one knew the way out. They tried to help me and as usual it was a dead end.

I had my kids and they were healthy and the rest would just have to fall into place. The holidays were around the corner and days flew by. I tried to make our usual Thanksgiving Dinner plans same as always. Daniel had no need to celebrate which was great news because I did not want him around. After that Jas, Cal, and I planned our Christmas shopping to try and keep things our normal. We bought cheaper gifts that year but it was hardly noticeable. We planned the usual school break time off and spent time together even if it was cooking and baking or spending time with my mother and father. We all tried to forget the fact that Daniel was somehow still in the picture. It made our lives a little off balance.

We were still celebrating Christmas as a family and hoped
Daniel would be nowhere around. I knew Christmas was
the day we celebrated the birth of Christ so I tried not to
be negative in any way because it is a joyous Holiday.

Winter Already

Holiday planning was going well. I tried to keep control of what was normal for us. Daniel was going to have a Christmas meal at the apartment and asked that we come to see his kids who would be staying there for a few days. I told him I would call back. I certainly did not want to go. What would happen if I did not show? I thought about it and asked Jas and Cal what they thought. Jas did not want to go and Cal said he would go with me if I decided to do it. I had to keep things cool and not upset Daniel, yet I had no desire to spend time with him. At that point I had no problems with his kids. I felt it wrong to say I would not see them for their Christmas. After all, Daniel said they asked for us to come. But with Daniel everything was a set up for one reason or another. I thought I could keep the peace and show his kids I was not a crazy woman. I was still in this and hoped I would see that it was all a big mistake on my part. Maybe I missed something and that would be all it took to put it back together. Yes, I would go and see. I called Daniel to tell him we would come. Jas decided she would go with us since it was the holiday and we spent those times together. So that was on our list to do and I hoped we would slide through it smoothly. I did not look forward to it.

Daniel and I were living apart and did nothing as a couple. That was fine with me. Then he called me to come to the suburbs for his Company Christmas party. I liked the Manager and his wife and a couple others that worked there. Daniel was being cordial and even nice. He explained he had been under so much pressure and had no money and was trying to work on our marriage. We had brief conversations and they were calm. Nothing had changed except for the way he was talking and it was positive. I always kept in the back of my mind the other person Daniel could become at the blink of an eye. That scared me and I knew to be careful and tread lightly. He was an absolute pro at playing on my sympathy and fears, without me even noticing what was going on.

I had to keep the situation in some kind of balance until I found enough pieces to finish the puzzle. I hoped and prayed if I had all my ducks in a row and in black and white, Daniel would leave me alone and not continue to pursue 'my life'. Then he called to ask me for a favor. He and his co-workers were in a dilemma because they had to order fruit that day and, believe it or not, no one that worked at the dealership had a credit card. No one I asked, being cordial. No one. The order had to be in immediately so they could all have their fruit baskets for the holidays. I was the only person with a credit card they could think of to call. That was quite a story but I had no sympathy, if that was what he was looking for. At first I thought it was some kind of bad joke except that with Daniel that was the normal. Another story, another day, another scam. Any way he could to use O.P.M.

Daniel's credit cards were still maxed out and over the limit. He was not lying about that part because I still received those statements and letters from collections. I refused and told him I could not use mine. He told me he had access to the information on my credit card and knew I could charge the two hundred fifty dollars they needed. That should have surprised and upset me, but did not anymore. All his friends would be upset if I did not let him charge my credit card. I simply refused without much more explanation. Supposedly they were all in the room and waiting while we were on the phone. I did not care if they did or did not like it and were going to be upset. It was a bizarre request and I needed to stop allowing him to use me. Did he really think I believed him and would let him use my credit card again? He was going to pay me back after he collected the cash from everyone that day, so why was there a problem? The conversation went on and on and he pleaded his case. That was how it always went, same old thing. He had no idea what the big deal was and if I would not let them use my card the whole company would all have to go without their fruit order.

When he realized I was not going to let them, Daniel told me how I was being selfish, arrogant and would not share because now no one would have their fruit baskets. It would be my fault and he would have to tell them the bad news. I was nice and let the conversation drop because I was not paying. But I would not let myself feel sorry for any of them since I knew they all had credit cards and made good money. Later I wondered if that was all just a story and Daniel wanted my credit card information and approval so he could charge anything and everything on it. I no longer let him use anything I had left. Not that there was much left over, or so I thought. That was how all the stories went.

I went along with what I could and felt there was not much I could do yet because no matter which way I turned Daniel had a hold. I could not get around it. There were more names and addresses and businesses connected to him and each one of those had their own red flags.

Daniel had put my reservation in for his Christmas party and called to be sure I would drive up. I arrived with only enough time to go to the party. He and his brother were ready when I got there and the three of us had a couple of drinks while waiting for dinner to be served. We sat at a large table with others and had pleasant conversations. I said nothing that would cause Daniel to be upset. He was wearing his 'good' personality that evening. But that did not last long because he kicked me a couple of times under the table because I was talking about my house and that Daniel was so busy and unable to be there. He whispered that no one should know he was living up there at their apartment or that there were any problems. I refrained from any conversation that was not general knowledge, only small talk. That was all I was allowed to discuss. I knew how it would end up if I stepped outside his specific line. His instructions were clear. We were not even through with dinner when he continued with his 'bad' personality. Now it would not matter what I said or did. He told me I was being an arrogant b---- and I would have to leave. This time he had no problem being verbally abusive in front of anyone that could hear. He spoke loudly and continued to call me names and tell everyone what a terrible person I was. There were couples at our table and they sat there looking at me, not knowing what to say. Most of them got up and left while Daniel's brother tried to calm him down and tell him to stop. He only became more enraged. Those that did not leave immediately came by me and apologized for him. A couple of others asked him what was wrong with him and said he needed to quit and had no right to treat me that way. Daniel became louder and even yelled at them. His brother could not calm him down this time. Sometimes he could get Daniel under control. I sat there ready to cry and kept my composure and tried to plan the quickest way out in my head. One couple came to me and took me by the arm and asked to give me a ride to get away from him. Another woman stood between Daniel and me and told me to come with her. It was all too much and happened out of nowhere. My car was there and I told her I would rush out and take off. Thank God that I drove my car. I had to get directions to the interstate and then I could make it from there and everyone was very willing to help me escape. While Daniel's brother tried to calm him down and keep him occupied in another direction I slipped out, almost running. Deja-vu! This time I was one step ahead and would not be trapped. I do not know what he would have done had I stayed with him at the party. On my trip home I had a tough time focusing on the road. It was a long drive back, but I was happy to be going home, my home. I was more determined to complete my investigation and talk with as many legal professionals as I could, even if it meant a few days off work. It had to be done and as soon as possible. I would just cut back more and finish what I started. I never wanted to return to the suburbs again, but what about when his kids came for Christmas? I could not look ahead.

I wondered if that was an acceptable behavior pattern for people that lived in the suburbs. Daniel and his brother never knew their neighbors and moved around different areas within the suburbs, always changing addresses, bank accounts, different phone numbers, and so on. It seemed like they were sneaking around and no one was to know where they really lived. Why? They were very unstable and liked their lives that way. Some of the people that worked and lived there seemed decent enough when they tried to help me out of the bad situation. Are they the few small minority? Obviously someone could get away with more illegal activities and bad behavior because there are so many people there and no one seems to know their neighbors. They can blend into the whatever spot they are in at the moment and whatever kind of person they want to portray, then walk around the block and become another whole different person. Like a chameleon. In smaller communities and rural areas where people are more stable and do not move around on a steady basis, everyone knows their neighbors and local business owners and their families. They know what goes on and where and who. Not that they are nosey, but they are friendly and helpful if someone needs something. It is a network of friendly people.

The End Of The Year

December came quickly as did the last six months of my life. I did not want to spend another six months of the same so I worked as much as possible so our Christmas would be nice. It would not be like other years for us but it would be as close as I could make it. Jas, Cal, and I took some small shopping trips and ate out and enjoyed each others company like we used to. Lately we were not able to afford to do the things we always had in past years.

Besides my job, investigations, holidays, and spending as much time as possible with my kids, I was tired and confused. But I tried not to let on to anyone. Endurance. I kept going. I looked forward to the closure I would have once I put it all together and got out of the marriage.

It was almost Christmas and Daniel was animate

that we come to see his kids at his apartment. The three of us drove up there and we went out to eat with Daniel and his kids. I was surprised I did not have to pay. His kids were not very talkative which was fine with me, so our conversations were general. After dinner we went back to the apartment. It was late. What did his kids think? We watched a movie on TV and talked about sleeping and taking off as soon as the first one woke up. I would not dare take off and leave because he would be wild and probably drive down to my house.

Finally Daniel came over and announced that he figured out the sleeping arrangements. Did we need more blankets, he asked. He told me that my kids and I would have to sleep on the floor and sofa because his daughter would be sleeping in his bed with him. I looked at him, slowly let out a breath and said we would be fine right where we were. I had not planned on sleeping in his bed anyway, but it blew me away that he announced his daughter was sleeping in his bed with him. Half asleep and hoping my kids were fully asleep, the lights went out and it was quiet except for the TV. Then I turned that off so I could hurry and sleep and wake early with my kids and get out. I do not think anything sunk in or phased me anymore. Jas and Cal were there for the last time. I wanted no more to do with any of it. I was still stuck but I did not have to put up with his personal life. I would not allow my kids to be a part of any of it either. They deserved better and I tried to live a better life. I know I was not perfect. I tried to do the right thing and some things that I had done over the years was not, but I never deliberately did anything bad to anyone. Nothing I had ever done or

even thought of doing compared to what I had seen in
the last six months.

Six Months Later

The Holidays were over and it had been six months since the marriage took place. My investigation into Daniel's addresses, social security numbers, phone numbers, businesses past and present in his name, other women older and younger, auto insurance policies, life insurance policies, relatives in the same line of work, and the list goes on and on. I had gone through all of my bills, loans, and credit cards. I made up a form for my assets and liabilities. What a difference six months made with Daniel. We were not even a couple in any way, but now we were married and I was broke. Daniel was gaining financially and I was losing. In June he had nothing but a chair, bed, a few clothes to his name, no money, and a lot of debt. I had a great paying job, lots of clothes, a house full of antiques and collectables, a ranch with a large beautiful home, two new vehicles, money in the bank, not much debt, a John Deere tractor, horses, tack, dogs, and my best assets, Jas and Cal. I could go on and on with what I owned and had collected over the years. My kids had everything they could want within reason. Jas and Cal made it all worthwhile. They were my life.

The end of December brought me bad news with a total loss of sixty thousand dollars I had saved. I wrote the numbers down, over and over, forward and backward and still came up with the same amount. It was hard to believe that I had helped Daniel pay for so much of his 'life'. That did not even count my assets that were turning into liabilities. What choice did I have but to continue paying for everything and covering the checking account? I no longer had any savings and had borrowed from my kids savings. I refigured on paper over and over for weeks. No doubt about it. It must have been a mistake with an extra zero somewhere. There it was in black and white as I stared at it in disbelief. Money was like water to Daniel and it was never a big deal. It was to me because it was my money, not his. I could not work enough to replace what I had quickly lost. It was like a bet in Vegas, one signature and it was over and gone. I knew I had let my kids down. It was so hard to comprehend that I fell for the stories over and over. My files were still growing.

It was impossible for my friends to comprehend how that had happened and how I was stuck now. I talked with Kerri and Ken extensively to try to make sense of why Daniel was doing, what he was, and why his past was so extremely dark. What was he into? Kerri thought it was all in his past and that as far as she knew it was not that serious. I filled her in on how he had to still be involved in serious illegal activities, there were other women, he was psycho when he did not get his way, and I was losing everything I had my whole life. I continued telling her what I had found so far. She was unaware Daniel was the person I explained. She could not believe it. She thought maybe in his past while living in another state he had gotten into some scrapes. I do not think she fully understood the seriousness of the current situation even though she had considered herself a good friend of his. It made my head spin and it was difficult to tell someone that her friend was simply a bad person. No one wants to hear that their friend of many years is a con artist and uses people. That would be someone not to associate with and claim to be a good friend. How would anyone not know about the bad things he did? Kerri knew none of that. Ken had been a good friend of mine since school and he knew by what I told them, the guy was trouble.

I thought about the "why". Why did he do those things to people? I would never understand how he could come into the lives of a happy family and be so evil and try to destroy what they had. It made no sense to me. The more I tried to analyze the facts in my head, the more it hurt. No one could tell me why when I talked with my friends about it. I am sure they were all trying to figure it out too, but they had the luxury of not being involved directly. They listened to me and supported me as a friend. Surely they were weary of the stories which were like a movie on TV to them. It was difficult for anyone to understand my new life and even more difficult to explain it to someone. How had I made such an enormous mistake with my life?

I just wanted to find an end and closure. Daniel and

I were having brief conversations on the phone because I knew not to ask questions. It was best to let him talk and stay with only his subjects and agree with him. That was all he needed to keep the calm.

I was attempting to purchase the establishment where I was working while I still had some equity. I had spoken with a couple of bank officers and had made up a business plan. That was going well so I tried to keep it to myself and some friends. Daniel still wanted me to work for him. Then in a conversation I mentioned I should buy the place I was working and Daniel was all over it. He immediately picked up on it and ran. He had a friend at a bank and 'we' could get the loan through him. He would be down to make an appointment and take care of it. I knew he meant that I could get the loan. Then he would own half of that too, because he was married to me. Daniel knew the laws better than any lawyer I knew. Or I should say he knew how to get around any obstacle to get what he wanted. I went through the motions and a couple of appointments with Daniel. It seemed that his connection and friend would not approve it. This friend held a position in which he could approve or deny the loan. That banker simply told us they were unable to process the loan because Daniel's friend had called him to tell him not to write the loan. Daniel was furious and told me he was going to call him and ask what was going on. I never heard any more about it when I asked what happened. Daniel explained I should go ahead and try to obtain a loan and buy it and he would help me. The same old story. That told me something about his reputation with a lending institution. I already knew I was approved through two lending institutions because

I was in the process of deciding which one was the best deal with interest and collateral. My friend who owned the place had produced all the required documents for me. It was okay as long as I did not involve Daniel. That was where I was stuck. A friend of mine was the mayor and approved my liquor license under one condition. That condition was that I get my divorce so Daniel was not involved in any way. That was not a problem with me. I was all for it and thought I was on my way. After all, I had spent so much time working on it and my kids would help out.

Daniel decided it was time for him to write a new budget for 'us' again. He needed my social security statement, balances owed on my house and vehicles, bills, and anything else I had. Also he would need Jas and Cal's savings statements, insurance policies, and any I might have in my name too. It was not hard to figure I had always kept my kids protected in case something happened to me. Not that they would be rich but they would have a financial cushion. I had always made sure of that. Daniel told me he was trying. He might be able to move with me and help pay before his eight year decision. All I had to do was follow his plan and budget. Simple. I needed to remember that everything he did for me was so that I could learn and have a good marriage. We could have the life we planned when I stopped being crazy and selfish and made the appointment with that shrink he knew.

How long would I be able to go along with his plan? I knew many people had marriages that were far from perfect and went their own ways for what ever reason. Reasons that were between them and not common knowledge. Maybe I was justifying the fact that it was impossible to get out. It was not that I believed anything he said anymore. It was easier if I did not upset him. All his stories sounded so good and he justified everything. He was trying and I was not so if I really loved him and if I had ever planned on staying married..........same old story. Would he surprise me and help out or was that what a part of me wanted to believe? Then I would not have to deal with what was really going on. In my mind I think I was battling thoughts about some of what he would say and if he could be right, but in my gut I believed I was right. That happens when someone repeatedly and constantly hammers into a person what they want them to believe. Not that it would be true and factual, but the mind begins to doubt what they once believed to be true. They use a very extreme persuasion method playing on one's sympathy and fears. It becomes confusing and unclear. He reminded me I would be a three time loser (the marriages) and I could never leave him because he would never have to leave me alone and if I left I would lose everything to him. All the while, he continued to show me how trapped I was. Every where I turned I found legally he had that option and I would never be able to afford the battle in court financially or emotionally. I knew what he could do and get away with. I had seen firsthand. He made sure I understood the story about his friend who dealt with used cars. That friend had a network to be sure he received payments he set up for the cars he sold. They would take a gun and visit their customers. They were always paid one way or another.

Which ever door I opened, Daniel had the key. Some

days I really did want to give up. I thought it was the only way out. The only way my kids and I would remain safe.

It was going to be a long winter.

A New Year

Closure was my goal for the New Year. In one way it seemed like I had lived a whole lifetime in the last six months and another way it was only a few weeks. No matter how long it seemed it was not my life now. I wanted to step out of it the same way I had stepped into it quickly.

Daniel called to let me know not to call him at the dealership because he no longer worked there. I did not know when or how long he was out of work because he remained in the suburbs. He told me they screwed up and he quit, again. No details. I believed he got caught doing something illegal and they fired him. Daniel had nothing good to say about any of them all of a sudden. I was suspicious, but it had nothing to do with me so I never checked it out. I had plenty of problems and work to keep me busy already. I asked him what he was going to do. He was not sure, but he wanted me to know he would have to use the ATM card for the checking account because he had no money. He wanted to be sure that I continued to deposit my paycheck and asked how much that would be. I begged him not to empty the account and overdraw it because I could not keep up. I had no money to support him. I was already paying for everything so how much more would he need now. He demanded. I would not let it upset me because I was hardly sleeping as it was. I knew he would figure to the penny how much I had to deposit. I was never supposed to keep any cash out. All of my paychecks were to be deposited. My checks were not that much and I did slip out a few dollars on occasion.

Daniel's auto insurance agent called me one day to obtain my drivers license number and other personal information again. I did not understand what he was doing and what he wanted from me. I explained I had all my own insurance on my vehicles. The insurance agent explained to me that this was for Daniel. So why did he require my personal information? He continued to let me know Daniel's insurance would be so much cheaper using my name and address. I was shocked that an agent would even think of doing something like that again. What was going on? I told him something was wrong because Daniel owned no vehicle. My name should not be on any vehicles or insurance other than my own. The agent told me I would not be liable for anything and my name was on nothing. It was all just to keep Daniel's insurance rates lower. He wanted to know why I would not help Daniel, who was my husband? What business was any of that to him? That was an insurance agent and none of his concern, I thought. The whole conversation threw me off and I was not sure what more to say. The agent called a few more times to attempt to persuade me to help Daniel with his insurance and I refused. Why would a well known and nationally recognized insurance company allow their agent to pressure people to illegally use their personal information? Why was I going through that again? The first time I discussed that with them they promised to remove my information.

Daniel later called me to let me know I would have to put his kids insurance under my name and address because they could not afford to pay it. He claimed he would continue to pay it, or I should say 'I would'. Once more, his kids were unable to work and were in crisis because they had too many auto accidents. Daniel did not know what the big deal was and why I was so selfish. Why was I being like that with his kids? See, he told me, that was the problem with the marriage. Why could I not see that? I told him because they were older than my kids and my kids were working and still in school. Daniel always made me feel I had to defend myself and my kids. He called a few more times to try to persuade me to help him save money because it was really for us in the end. Oh, then we could have that life. The one we planned that was only some fantasy now that turned into a nightmare.

My parents were worried and thought I should be careful what I did. We all knew it was a deep black hole. Daniel was a deep black hole. I tried not to involve my parents and worry them, so I kept them updated without the evil details. They worried about what kind of people I was involved with. Like everyone else, they had no clue where else to turn. No one knew what to do. We all believed the laws would protect us if it went that far. As more weeks passed I was still lost.

I continued to receive questionable mail at my house. Daniel's credit cards that were over limit and overdue came to my address. My name was on none of them but he used my address. He had some type of life insurance policy using my address that had not been paid for quite a while; collection agencies, mortgage loan applications. He swore all the mortgage apps had nothing to do with him, but I received quite a few every week. I had been living there for twenty-four years and not seen any thing like it. His auto insurance policies were past due. I asked him to have them sent to his address where he lived. After some thought I wondered if he even lived with his brother.

I spoke with many lawyers to see what I could do each time something new came up. Whether it was mail I received or a lead or connection I found through my own primitive investigations, the answers were always the same. They had no knowledge and there were no such laws on the books to protect me. Our justice system was useless and it came down to how smart the criminal mind could be. Criminals know first hand how to skate around the laws. They were perplexed when I showed them what I had and thought it had to be a mistake or someone else. They could not all be the same person and not related. There are no such things as coincidences like I found. It was hard to believe that it was such a widespread tangled web. I needed to know if everything I found so far was true and factual. I could not get any assistance through any legal department so I went for an idea my friend had. It cost some money to do it, but I hired an investigator from another state. I explained what I had already found in detail of what looked to be a crazy mess I had gotten myself into and felt I was stuck. I told her there was so much to it and it was so extreme I had a hard time believing what I found. The woman was very helpful and knowledgeable and knew exactly what I would be looking for. She had experience and worked for a very large company in a very large city. I immediately sent her copies. They were way ahead of the Midwest in many ways. I was impressed for the first time that some one could help me with the facts and knew what I was talking about. She would get back to me shortly. There was light at the end of the tunnel and I was happy to hear someone familiar with my dilemma. Now I had to wait patiently. I had something to hold onto.

In the meantime I tried to continue everyday as though nothing was new. I could not let anyone know that I had done this. I had no where to turn and felt like I should not have been so sneaky about someone I was married to. I was left with no choice. Daniel was going to work for another dealership selling used cars further away. In a way that was a relief. I had no complaints and told him that was nice he found a job. I never knew where it was located and did not care. I asked him to send money to the joint account now so he could help to pay for his bills up there. Well now he and his brother were also moving and he would have to have money to open all new accounts and rental deposit. When we were first married he would deposit a small amount and then use the ATM for twice the amount he put in on top of his bills. I tried not to use the account because he always

used any money that was in it. It would be a while before
he had any extra money. I asked him to leave my money
I deposited for Jas senior pictures in the account to cover
that check. That did not happen. So I had to run and
deposit more money again after checking the balance.
He knew I would not let the account overdraft. I was
unable to use the account anymore except to continue
depositing my paychecks.

It was time to look for Cal's car for his sixteenth
birthday since he followed my rules the same as Jas. I
would do what I had to because that was a promise I
made to them. We looked for a while and he decided he
wanted to order a new Camaro. He wanted black inside
and out with the nice stereo and t-tops. I liked the car
too. I knew he would let me drive it once in a while.
Daniel knew my deal with my kids and called to tell me
not to look with any other dealer because he would find
out and be irate. So I told him what we were going to
purchase and if he found a better deal to let me know.
He called back to tell me he had a dark green Camaro
with t-tops and stereo like Cal wanted that just came in
on a trade. That was why he called me. It was supposed
to be a perfect car with only a few miles on it and mint
condition. The owner was older and did not like the
ride. Daniel gave me all the statistics and the price was
cheaper by a couple of thousand dollars. That meant a
lower payment for me. I told him we would be up to
check it out that weekend and if it was what he wanted
I would buy it there. Cal was so excited and could not
wait until the weekend. Daniel called back two days later
to tell me he made too much money from the deal not to
sell that Camaro to someone else. So I would not have

to come to look. Instead he would find a new one to order like he wanted. I hung up the phone and was very upset. I had to explain to Cal we would just order the new one he originally wanted. He was upset but knew I would not deny what I had promised. Daniel turned it all around as usual and was being verbally abusive saying I had to get the car from him because we were married. I was to look at no other car lots. He found another one he could order and have it there in a couple of weeks. Then he would drive it down so we would not have to make the trip up to look at it. I kept my cool and told Cal it would be okay. Cal was willing to wait a couple of weeks because I had a few months until his birthday to take care of it. I kept everything calm again.

I would have money coming from my tax return so I made the appointment and got my taxes taken care of. I filed them the same as always except that I was married filing separately. I did not tell Daniel I finished them. As everyone advised me, I did not file taxes jointly. No way. I did not know what the consequences would be if I did and I was not going to find out. I planned on keeping everything separate now because there was enough of a mess. He continued to remind me of the business he wanted me to help with. Now the deal had to do with titles delivered and ran through his father's used car business. If I would just do that for him he would be able to move sooner because there was so much money to be made and I could be rich too. It was for 'us' so we could get into the business when his father retired. I did not need to work where I was. I had taken a large envelope full of titles one time from Daniel's used car lot where he worked and dropped them off with his father. I asked questions when Daniel asked me to drop the envelope off, but he had no explanation and just wanted me to do the favor. I knew something was not right by the way he answered my questions. When he needed any more favors I would be unable and would have a good excuse ready. What would I find and what would come back to me later when I finally got out of the mess. I wanted to be sure my kids were in no way involved now or in the future. He hated the fact that I had some very close friends that supported me. He still wanted me to have no contact with anyone and not leave my house. I had to remember that someone was working on the mess and I had to keep it calm and running smoothly. When Daniel became abusive I would let it go and try to ignore him but not totally disagree.

My unemployment was done. I received my last check. Jas helped to pay for her Senior pictures because when the time came, as expected, the money I deposited was not in the checking account to cover them. Daniel's bills came to my address and I refused to pay and when I called the companies they claimed I was totally responsible and must pay immediately to avoid further legal action. One of them actually tried to inform me they would and could legally place a lien on my home. I explained to the insurance agent for his life insurance policy that I had no ties to the policy. I told them we were not together and Daniel lived in an apartment in the suburbs and he had never lived with me. The agent told me my address was his correct one and I was responsible for the full payment that was very late. My name was not on the policy anywhere. It had nothing to do with me but she did not care. They had probably checked and I was the closest one with assets and Daniel had none and his credit report showed all negative. Daniel set up a different angle for everything until he could find one of his schemes that worked. My nerves were shot and random people would start calling my house looking for Daniel's father because he owed them money. I knew there were no real records at his father's business, so if I tried to do anything about it, it was my word against theirs. They all used dealer plates from another dealership where none of them worked. Only titles were moved around but not the actual vehicles. Daniel's father was never able to own anything because of his prison record. I really did not know what was going on except that it was illegal scams. I had no idea how they worked it because there were too many pieces to the puzzle. I had enough to do to stay above the water that was over my head.

Then I found that my name was listed as driver on Daniel's mother's car. That was added to the auto insurance policy for which his insurance agent continued to call and request that I help with. The agent could not understand why I was not willing to help them all with a discount because all I had to do was give my drivers license number and social security. I still refused to give my information and yet my name was on the policy for all these people and their vehicles as policy holder. I did not know how they used my name and address since I had totally refused. When I asked the agent about it he just ignored me and told me how Daniel could not afford all his insurance without me on it. Finally the agent would not answer my calls. So I only spoke with his secretary and she promised over and over that it would all be taken care of and not to worry. I made many calls and she told me the same story each time. I tried to find someone to help me clear it up and remove my name from everything but no one could do anything. They told me to keep calling until it was fixed, but they had no idea what the bottom line was and how deep and dark it was. Most people could not comprehend one percent of what was going on. It actually made me feel a little better knowing that even law enforcement and officials had no clue. I had my insurance on all my vehicles and house as always, without any lapse. As we agreed when we married to leave my autos and house with my insurance and my kids. My insurance was fine.

My cash and paychecks were small as compared to what I was used to making. I had no insurance and if one of my kids or I needed a doctor or medicine I paid cash. We were lucky we were healthy. It enraged Daniel that I did not have the great paychecks anymore and since unemployment was done he became mean and abusive again. It was all just to teach me a lesson and it was for my own good, he would tell me. None of that helped my situation. When he spoke, I was not to speak and ask questions. Only listen and do what he told me to do so everything would be like we planned. When would I learn? I was only going to make it harder on myself.

Life On Hold

There was no such thing as a conversation with Daniel. When I asked about any of the insurance policies he had on the kids or his overdue bills, he would fly off the handle at any mention of it.. He would immediately turn everything around and reverse the situation like it was my fault. If I really loved him and planned on staying married why would I even question him? It was my problem and why we could not get along and have that happy marriage. Everything I ever said was turned completely around and it was so bizarre to me because he and everyone knew he was a liar. Flat out, plain and simple liar.

The problems with his bills and insurance companies continued. Daniel ran advertisements in local papers about auto purchases and loans using my name and address for the billings. That must be one of his family's scams. Daniel claimed it was not him and they made a mistake and he had no knowledge of any of it. As usual. It was almost impossible to find someone to help because all they wanted was payment. All of them claimed I was the person that owed the money. It was more than I could stand. I began to get physically sick and I had many sleepless nights. No matter what I did or who I spoke with, I could not resolve or remove myself from the situation.

I was still trying to find employment at the State level. I tested a couple of times and I had to do that without Daniel knowing because he accused me of sleeping with my friends to get the job. I knew it was just another turnaround story of his. What was he really doing? I was slow to realize what he was doing and why. He still wanted me to have no friends and no employment within the State. Daniel begged me to work for him and I kept making excuses and tried to be cordial. After all, if I worked for him it would only cost me a few thousand dollars and I would make that back plus so much more immediately. There was no need to look for any other job. At least I knew not to even attempt to get involved with him or his family. No matter what, that was not going to happen. The State was hiring and I crossed my fingers and waited impatiently.

The out of state Private Investigator called me and confirmed what I thought and had tried to piece together. That company had the resources and money that I did not to tie together what I could not. She began with "you need to get out and as far away from this guy as possible and as quick as possible". I really had hoped I was overreacting and my imagination was running wild because I was not familiar with these kinds of people. Deep down I knew it was a deep, dark abyss. It was pure evil. My stomach was one big knot and my heart skipped a couple of beats and I had to take some deep breaths. She told me to be very careful with everything I did. She explained how much came up with what information I had given her and how extensive it became. Many family members and friends and women and different states, different companies, addresses, social security numbers, name variations, and many, many delinquent and negative circumstances. There was a long list of bad situations and nothing was good or positive that she could find. She wanted to know which 'one' I thought I had married. Me too. I was not sure of anything anymore. Nothing seemed real. Maybe I would still wake up from the nightmare, right? There was too much to go over in detail on the phone and she would mail it to me. Then I could look through it and call her back with questions. It never ended and that is exactly what she found, too. The whole company jumped in to help her because the file was so extensive she could hardly keep up. That was one of the largest cities in the United States and they were shocked at what they found. What did that tell me? Nothing good could ever come from Daniel and the situation no matter what I did. I had to plan something to keep my kids safe. Too much was going on at the same time and I was running out of energy and time. My head would spin and it became normal to sleep only a few hours a night while I lie in bed wondering what to do next and how to do it. Still, I had to keep things calm and not let on what I knew. I would hide the report when I got it from the investigator. That way if he came to my house in one of his rages I would have one less problem to worry about.

Maybe Daniel was becoming suspicious or someone else was on his tail, since he had ripped off so many people. Daniel called me on the phone one day and my answering machine picked up. I refused to give up my cell phones as he demanded because I could no longer afford something like that. Besides he told me I was to be at work or at home by the phone when he called. I was outside working in the yard and rushed in to the house to grab the phone and Daniel told me he would have to call me back now that the answering machine picked up because he did not want that conversation to be recorded. I insisted I was not recording his conversation. He wanted me to look up some things on the internet for a business he had been working on and getting ready. He had ten pages written out but I needed to check on the web page and the phone and get some other information to set it up at my house 'for us'. I told him I did not know how to do any of that. He demanded I prepare the paperwork for him and I said I could not. He hung up. Another scam he was trying to draw me into using my name and house and address. Then he called back to beg me to use my name and address for his kids insurance so he could afford it. I should be nice and help him and his kids out. Why did I have to be like that? And then there were a few other names to add and if I loved him I would help out. Same old story which meant nothing. Another story and another scam and now in need of someone to take the fall if anything went wrong. I had that much figured out. He had someone with lots of equity, that if he could just manipulate enough, he could walk away with it before anyone knew what happened. I also knew he would have loved for me to get involved and get caught holding the bag and go to jail. I would be out of the way so he could inherit and handle everything I owned. Then if I ever got out and proved what they had done, my house, money and all would no longer exist. Daniel was very deceitful and cunning and would go to any extreme and use any one he could to get what he wanted. Daniel used everyone he could and had no remorse. He grew up learning to use people and that would never change because that was who he was. It was his way of life. Same story but different people as he continually moved around and changed identities. Daniel did whatever it took and never looked back except to laugh about how he got away with it.

Daniel called to let me know my income taxes needed to be done with his and he needed my W-2 and any other statements. Now I had to tell him I filed my own taxes as I had always done. He screamed and called me names and told me I was to cancel that immediately because I could not afford it. He asked when and who had done them. I was to call them and tell them it was a mistake. If I did not do that he would call the IRS and have me thrown in jail because what I had done was illegal and I would pay. Daniel would not allow it and he continued to scream and threaten me. He would see to it I lost everything to him while I was in jail. Before I filed, I checked that I could legally file separate and I could. But Daniel had a way of threatening and almost giving me a heart attack with worry even though I knew it was okay the way I did it. He claimed all my deductions on my house were his to take, with real estate taxes and interest and on and on.

I was to do what he told me and ask no questions. Why had I not learned that yet? Daniel informed me how he handled his 'last one', the last female he lived with. According to him they had done their taxes together even though they had never lived together. That was none of my business he claimed. She filed her taxes without him and his consent. Daniel told me he called the IRS and made her refile her taxes the way he thought they should have been done. He claimed she did not go to jail because she followed his orders that time. If she had not, he would have had to proceed with legal recourse. All I had to do was whatever he said. I told him I could not have my taxes cancelled and would not allow our taxes to be filed together. There was no reason for it. I could not do it. He slammed the phone and hung up on me. I was not sure what consequences would follow. He would either drive right down to my house and tear through it looking for my copies or come up with another angle. A nasty angle, like I would receive something in the mail from the IRS or a lawyer. I never knew what he would do next if things did not go his way. I waited to find out but did nothing. It was one more thing hanging over my head that I did not know the outcome. My files grew rapidly along with my notes. I was very good at keeping notes as each event took place. A phone call or piece of mail, everything that was done and said. The piles of papers looked like books. It had only been nine months and there on my table set what looked like a set of encyclopedias. More than a lifetime or many lifetimes in a few months. All of it was negative and illegal. All I wanted to do was escape, take my kids and run away.

Spring Time

It was almost spring but it was the same as one long nightmare. It was not like all other springs when I looked forward to getting out in the yard and working with the horses. Open windows, fresh air, and sun. It was like the sun would not shine anymore and it would not be nice outside.

After my friend, Kerri, gave me some copies of reports that she found about Daniel, she had no choice but to believe there was so much more to her old friend than she ever knew. There it was in black and white for everyone to see. It was no one's imagination or story. I received all the reports the investigator sent me and between the two I was able to fill in many spaces and answer many questions. Not all, but many. I was one hundred percent sure now. My investigator and her company had no ties, connections, family members, or business dealings with these people. I wanted to be sure there was no room for error. Only I had to put the puzzle together and find the answer to why. I needed to read the report but in a way I was in no hurry to get it because I knew it could not be good. Deep down I knew, but on the surface I wanted it to go away. There was always that chance that I was not right. The report showed Daniel used many variations of his name and had many addresses including other states. His name and addresses were connected to many other females and businesses including many other states. There were many credit cards, bank accounts, loan transactions, and debts. He used other social security numbers and dates of birth. Credit reports were altered and he listed a spouse with a business at my address. As the investigator stated, it was very extensive and negative and I needed to get out. My concern that Daniel, or someone involved with him, would use my house or equity to obtain money by placing a lien on it, was a fact. Daniel wanted my house and property and would go to any extreme to obtain it. It would take a lifetime for someone to sort through that mess. It would take thousands and thousands of dollars to start the process and there was no way to tell where it would end or if it would end. They all had advised me, including lawyers, to just get out because no one could afford to do anything about it. Many were actually afraid of him and refused to get involved except to give me advice. I never understood why. Maybe I should be worried now that I have all this information and know the facts. I would never let him know what I knew because that would be very dangerous. No one crosses Daniel and gets away with it. I have seen that for myself.

The whole situation was too much for me to handle and it became very difficult to sleep through the night because I was worried about the safety of Jas and Cal and if he would show up in one of his raging tempers. He was extremely unstable and would switch from one personality to another with a blink. It depended on the circumstances at that time and that was why I would never push an issue or totally disagree to a point that he would be upset. I did not understand why he had not been that way around me before we married. I never saw that side of him. The evil side of his personality. Daniel was good at what he did and how he did it. He was sure to have someone set up in line to take the fall for his illegal activities so he could not be touched. He knew how to cover his own tracks and set everyone else up around him. That was how he was taught to live. Then he realized the more extreme activities he was involved in, the more money he could make as long as he remained in the background. He was a wanna-be mobster boss. Following the paper trail, I had it was easy to see how advanced he was becoming. He was rapidly expanding with the help of the internet. The last few times he was at my house and tried to use my computer, I simply told him it was broke and the internet connection did not work so I was going to cancel it. That was a dark area and I do not know what he 'worked' on those few times he used it before. If I was good on the computer I would have been able to see and pull up the sites, but that was not my top priority. I really thought he had looked up some web sites he should not have and that was the extent of it. What harm could that do? There was nothing I could do about it. My kids used it for homework and on occasion I would look something up. I never had the time to surf the web.

My life was on hold. The real estate agent was waiting for the next step and I had to stall because I knew I had to be divorced to obtain the liquor license as I had promised the mayor. I was so thankful he had done that because I would have had that much more to lose. It would have been catastrophic for me to add a business. My friend, the mayor, knew what was going on and was smart enough and had the foresight to protect me and that business. Because I was still married at that time legally, anything I purchased was half his to claim. I knew Daniel would claim all of it since he knew all the ropes when it came to money. He would not even settle for half as he had already proven. It was all his because he felt that was what he was entitled to when I signed the marriage certificate. So it would not have mattered what I did for a business until I was legally divorced. I could not purchase a business, I could not build cabins at my home, and I could not offer trail rides with my horses. Daniel claimed he could claim all of what I had and get it in court because I had no "real and steady" employment and money now, but he did. That worried me because I was in a catch twenty-two with employment because the more I made, the more he took. I had no ability to pay because he was bleeding me dry. The joint checking account was still continually overdrawn and because my name was on it I still deposited all the money I made. Daniel continued to withdraw cash from the ATM from that account and I could not stop it. I was embarrassed to go to the bank and explain what was going on but I could not keep covering his withdrawals. I do not know where his money and paychecks were going and he refused to tell me. It was none of my business, he claimed.

While I was waiting on the State job, I was hired for a part time Federal position and jumped at the chance. I worked both jobs and put any business plans on hold. Most of my adult life I spent working two jobs at the same time and attended college in my mid thirties. With everything going on now, it was a real challenge. I met many nice people. The "Daniel file" was a full time job in itself. I continued to sort through my investigators file and mine. I matched up what I could and was not as concerned with the older stuff so I put that away in a separate file. I followed the trails and worked with the most current information and tried to follow up on leads I had.

In a conversation with Daniel, he admitted to stalking me to see where I went and what I did. Since he owned no vehicle, he used dealer vehicles or his friends so I would not see the dealer plates. He even used his insurance agent's vehicle and one was a female bartender's from where he frequented. To Daniel, it was a fun game. He laughed and told me I had not done anything but work and take my kids places. He thought it was a waste of his time, but he wanted to be sure of what I was doing. What did he think, I was like him? At least he was amused and let it go without a nasty confrontation.

Daniel kept up appearances so everything would 'look good'. He showed up for Jas graduation and was so pleasant to everyone. How could I have ever said anything negative about him, it appeared. I would not ruin Jas's high school graduation day and I made sure it was peaceful as I went along with his charade. Whatever

Daniel needed to get us through the day was worth it. He had to return to work, luckily. He had no interest in me, only in appearances and my assets. That was enough to handle. Everything had to 'look good' and appear to be a perfect life while he continued with his dark secrets. His other life. I should say his real life. At least it was a calmer atmosphere for now, though it was difficult for me to remain quiet and not ask too many questions.

The perfect car was produced in Detroit and Daniel happened to catch it on his computer. It was a brand new Camaro with T-tops and great stereo, all in black with nice wheels. If I could get the down payment to him he would bring it to me and all I would have to do was sign the paperwork. Did he just want to know if I could still come up with some cash? All he wanted was a chance to show me how much he wanted the marriage. He had been sidetracked with his new job and move to his new apartment further north. That was not what he planned but he had to take it since he was not working. I listened and made no comments. Could I give him one more chance, please. I knew there was a reason for him to be nice and do something for me. If I decided he had not changed, he would leave me alone. That was music to my ears. I knew nothing had or would ever change with him but I agreed. Then he would leave me alone!!! Would it be that easy? I had to think about it and check with Cal because his birthday was still a couple of months away. Daniel wanted to surprise me with the car and help with the payments. His insurance checks received on the side for over four hundred fifty dollars each month would cover my monthly payment in full so I would not have to worry. I knew I would never see any help from him and made sure Cal and I could make the payments. Daniel wanted to surprise me with the gift but he needed my signature because he could not find a bank to give him a loan. Why could I get the loan and he could not? How did he already know I could get the loan? I decided the car should be only in my name because I knew I would be paying for it all. I did not believe any of that story either. I fell for his stories too many times. Everything he told me was the opposite. I wanted no more ties with him. Daniel agreed to put the vehicle in my name and swore to make the payments and the marriage work. I trusted nothing he did or said. The car was his peace offering because he realized all he ever wanted was me and my place. He promised once again to change his ways for me because he did not want to split up. I was everything he ever wanted and so stable. We decided to get it if the paperwork was right and the price he quoted me was correct. I asked many details and it sounded like a good deal since we had been looking around. Of course Daniel did not know we had been looking elsewhere. I told him he could bring the car down with the papers and then we would decide. When it arrived it was Cal's dream car. I went through the papers with a fine tooth comb and knew most of what to look for, I thought. I made sure they did not slip in the page for additional insurance that was not even usable on a new vehicle, but paid the salesman very well. Daniel bragged about that steady income he received separate from the insurance company at his apartment. I suspected it was not legal, but no one would do anything anyway so why would I explore that avenue? He gladly left the Camaro and took the money and paperwork I signed. It was a smooth and uneventful transaction and he was gone. Even though I purchased the car earlier than I planned, it was a good deal and I would drive it those few weeks before Cal turned sixteen. Then it would be his and both of my kids would have what I had promised them. That would be a relief to know it was done and out of the way. Cal would be able to drive to school and work without Jas and I arranging our schedules to fit his. I would not take Cal out of the private Catholic school even though it was so far away. Cal's new car would sure help. I added the Camaro to my insurance with my house and other vehicles. Somehow the 'peace offering deal' seemed too smooth, but I know Daniel wanted everything to appear wonderful. I was careful. Appearance was what he was all about, not truth and honesty and reality. How did he always slide by in life that way?

Maybe my life was getting back on track and I had to be patient. I kept a close eye on everything. I was still receiving mail and calls requiring payment. I forwarded the mail to Daniel and let him know of the calls, though he claimed they had him mixed up with someone else and he was going to straighten it out. No big deal. One of those companies had my name on the bill for a place in a northern state, where I had never lived. They had all the details from my identity and it was over seven years old. I did not know Daniel seven years ago and called the company for help. I explained I only wanted my name removed and had no idea how it got there. They asked me if I was married to Daniel and I replied legally but we were never together and briefed them. Their decision was final and I was responsible for payment in full. Under law, they explained they had a right to put a lien on my current home for payment since I refused to pay. Why was I not surprised that something like that would happen? Another one of my fears was now reality. After many frustrating calls, I spoke with a woman who was sincere and she gave me more information than what I had in writing. Originally the charge was six hundred forty-one dollars for the residence. Late fees and charges were since added and continued to increase the balance due. The woman could find no past history or info on Daniel and Jane (me). We worked for months on the problem. Daniel's birth date and social security number they had on file was different but all my info was correct. She could not understand what was going on and who the other person was. She asked if I was sure of his social and birth date. Then I put more pieces of the puzzle together and called her back. I did have some reports that matched her info on him and it was one he used for other things, but all of them were him. Then if that person was not real or the info was not valid, I would be the real person responsible. She tried to help and spoke with supervisors and would get back to me. It was the tangled web Daniel was so good at weaving. A real professional con artist. Researching this bill and my notes I found that Daniel had a business which repaired credit reports. He and another person were listed as owners. More pieces of the puzzle for me to put in place. Was everyone related to Daniel involved and use fake names and personal information?

Sorting through the investigation report in my spare time, I found two women listed as living in the apartment above Daniel. One was his daughter's age and the other was his age. What a surprise that the young one had the same last name as his. It should not have shocked me but I admit I was stunned. Then I found an investment company on the main level listed too. It matched the name on some of his investments. There was no such thing as a coincidence with these people. I had no idea where to tie it up or where to look next. It continued to fall into my lap every time I searched for one thing. It never ended and I could not keep up because the more I looked, the more popped up. If I found one thing, ten more would automatically follow. He must have been scamming before his kids were born because his son has his exact same name. Anything to throw off the trails.

During the calm, I drove up to his apartment out of nowhere, and called him. I let him know I was bringing up ATM receipts and his mail and he could meet me. I wanted him to see the bank statement and receipts for all his withdrawals. I went into his building and checked the residents listing. I could not believe right in front of me, in black and white, were the names I had in the reports. I knocked on the door but there was no answer. I quickly went to his floor just in time. Daniel came by and I pointed out to him someone had the same last name as his right there in the apartment above. I had to be careful how much information I let him know I had. I knew not to upset him and asked if she was a relative. He claimed he had never even seen that name before on the listing and had no idea who she was. He claimed it another coincidence so I uttered the other company name I found and he had never heard of it. Oh, I told him they were supposed to be a great investment company. Daniel had never heard of the company and did not know what they did. I explained they dealt with 401k's and investments and he told me he did not know what any of that was. I told him I thought somewhere I had seen his name on something from them. He claimed he knew no one in the whole building and never had. He told me I was imagining it because I could never remember anything anyway. One of his reinforcements since I was not mentally capable of much, as he continued to tell me. Why would I ask about that girl with the same last name? I just wondered when I saw it. I had to let it drop so he would not be suspicious but I wanted to ask more detailed questions. No, I could not go any further. It would be evident that I had something on him and he would be wild. It was going to take longer than I wanted, but what other choice did I have?

Change?

There was no change. It rolled into the next day and the next week and the next month, unchanged. I was broke and tired and wanted to get rid of all that was hanging over my head. I did not feel I was making progress because it was slow. I wanted to do it right and work with the facts. When I tried to explain any part of it to someone for help, they were lost because of the extensive details. I would explain one little segment and they would shake their head in bewilderment and each question they asked me, I answered and that continued to lead to another crisis and illegal matter. There was no end. Everyone found it so difficult to believe. They would tell me how it was like the movies on TV, but not real life.

Daniel and I met for dinner to talk. I explained that nothing had changed and we should close the joint account since he was living so far away and had a bank account up there to use. It would be easier for him to use an ATM and deposit his money. I had no more money to continually drive twenty miles and deposit so he could withdraw it. It was not fair to me. He needed to use his own money. He refused because he had no money to open an account. Exactly my point. Since he could not afford to deposit his paychecks, he needed to use my money which kept me broke. That way I would never be able to dig my way out from under him and keep what I had owned. I would never be able to fight him in court and pay a lawyer. I wanted to pay for my own bills and payments and take care of what I owned and he could pay for his. He knew what he was doing and was very good at it. Practice makes perfect. I was sure I was not the first and I would not be the last. He claimed he was only trying to help me and I should be grateful he was there for me. The opposite was actually true. I would say nothing and bite my tongue. He continued to tell me that if I really loved him, I would see the psychiatrist that he wanted me to. I was worried about nothing and there was something wrong with me. So selfish. All the girls he knew would die to be with him. I do not know if he truly believed that or just used it on me. He talked about a couple of places we had been and I told him I had never been there with him or anyone. Then he laughed and claimed it was me with him and told me what we did but I did not remember as usual. His point about the shrink and how he always tried to help me. He knew he had been caught by me and he was trying to cover up what he had done with someone else. That way he could make me feel 'crazy' and doubt myself. I told him I knew where I was and who with in the last few months. He kept pushing and telling me I needed help and I was delusional. Why would I not accept all the help he offered because the marriage would be perfect if only I would do what he asked? I refused and told him he needed the help without details. I wanted to continue in more detail, but let it drop. His life was great and he had all his friends and always had something to do and somewhere to go. All I did was stay home and work. It was a complete turnaround from my whole life before him.

Then came the story about the sex clubs again. I could go with him and have fun. Everyone up there did it, well, everyone that was anyone with money. I was a country girl and did not know what went on in the real world. I was backwards and slow and behind the times. It was simple to set up meetings on the internet. Sometimes they were young kids and teenagers, but it was their own fault because if they did not want to do it they would not be online. No one could blame him for what these adolescents were doing. The articles I gave him months ago where the FBI set up adults and then arrested them for doing exactly that, had no effect on him. He showed no concern and laughed because no one would do anything to him. It was just sex. So what? I shook my head and felt ill. Daniel said it was everywhere he went. Even when I told him he was sick and I would have no part of it or feel sorry for him if they caught him, it was me with the problems. Daniel explained how normal he was and how I was not. He brought up the show on TV again; the one he had called me to turn on. They were all upper class people like doctors and lawyers. Daniel wanted to be wealthy like that, but on the back of someone else. He asked me to go to one of his meetings. If I went I would understand that he had to do one of them or all of them. That was how it went. Was he justifying what he did? Were there that many people out there that had that 'monster that had to move around' like he told me? It was bizarre to me. I had no desire to know or sit around with these people and listen to their sick stories. Did they all think it was amusing? I did not know how much he was making up. Daniel called it a 'monster that moved around' because that was him to a T. It was a perfect description of Daniel. He met men, women, kids, and groups for sex. They would meet at each others apartments after setting it up in special chat rooms. Married couples advertised for 'partners in sex'. Every type anyone could think of. It was funny to him as he explained it all to me. This time I listened to his story. He showed me online how to go to the websites and communicate with these people. He began to actually follow through with it and wanted to set up a 'meeting' with some of them he knew. He said that as his wife I should take part in those sex games with him. I told him I had to leave and wanted nothing to do with that. When I got home I wrote it all down. It was too much for me to absorb. I assumed I could in no way be involved because we were totally split up and I reported the story to law enforcement. They were not interested in any of it. Maybe they did not believe any of it because to me it was so far fetched. Or maybe they were familiar with it in a negative or positive way. I was not sure except that they wanted nothing to do with any of the internet child porn and sex clubs.

Daniel continued to try to convince me to take out

a second lien on my house or file bankruptcy because I had no choice. He informed me what my balances were on my credit cards and if I was a good person and wife I would help him and his kids out temporarily. Another solution he had was for me to give everything to him so he could get his name on my house. He was unable to teach me anything and it was only for my own good. If he left me he could take everything from me anyway, so I should listen to his solutions.

Everyday was the same as I continued to spend time with my kids and attend their events, work, keep the ranch going, and work on my 'investigation'. There was not much time to sleep and even when I tried I was wide awake with thoughts of how to keep Daniel out of our lives. He could keep all his twisted lies. I just wanted out and away. Many legal officials told me to walk or run away and let him take whatever he wanted because I had no way out no matter which way I turned. Like there were no laws or what? Was there a justice and legal system anywhere? No one cared. Too much time and work to convict any of them was the basis of most responses. There were no laws set up to handle a case like that. I felt I was losing ground as it became more extreme and complex.

I understood I was the only one who could help myself. I learned as much as I could, as fast as I could. I decided to persuade my bank to remove my name from the joint account. At least I would be relieved of his ATM withdrawals almost daily. Daniel used more money than he made and I had to stop it. I would not continue to cover his debts. I made an appointment with the Bank President. I had worked with him for twenty-five years and he was the one to give me my home loan at eighteen years old when I built my house. He was shocked by the few problems I had updated him about. He decided I should write up a letter to remove my name from the account and no longer be responsible. After I had that finished I called Daniel to let him know what I had done and was no longer responsible. The bank had a letter for me for proof of name removal. I left money in the account and was sure all checks that were out had cleared. Daniel continued to use the debit card and overdraw the account and call me to put money in the account. I refused and told him that letter covered me legally. He thought I should still cover his overdrafts and told me I had to legally take care of it. I knew he would realize it was done and I no longer had to keep paying for him. It would not go over well once he realized I was keeping everything separated and I no longer had to cover his withdrawals. That would not go against me and he could not use my money, keeping me broke. Now my paychecks were for my payments on my house, autos, insurance, bills, and my own kids. It had been less than a year, but seemed like an eternity. I had accomplished one very important step. His brother had even told me once I was a survivor. Now I know what that meant. I guess I was finding that out because I know I would not stop until I was able to keep my home. Everything else I had might be lost but my kids and I would have our home. I was not sure what he would settle for so he would leave us alone and go away.

Daniel called a few days later to let me know he would not give me a divorce and that I had no way out. He claimed he tried to help me and I would not keep the appointments he made for me. I believe he set me up with many of his 'friends' in the suburbs telling them I was crazy and had mental problems and he tried to help me and did everything he could for me. He also claimed he bought me everything I had and built me a beautiful horse ranch and bought me horses and on and on. I made it a point to speak with a few of his 'constituents' and they all knew what he was doing and did not want to be involved in any way because they were basically afraid of him and what he could do. Apparently they were all familiar with how he operated and got whatever he wanted. I was not the only one who he threatened and used; the list was extensive. They wanted to keep their families safe and asked that I not use their names after each conversation. The more people I spoke with that knew Daniel, the scarier it was.

The threats were real and Daniel was serious. Anyone that did not go along with him would pay. I finally talked him into copies from my Camaro purchase that I had signed when he met me with the paperwork. I told him my insurance company needed the information and he surely was not going to pay for any of that. When I received my carbon copies of what I signed, surprise, Daniel's name was added. Now he owned half of that auto with a signature. I should not have been surprised because if there was a way for him to collect and own anything, he knew the loophole and had the criminal mind. He had grown up with the knowledge and deceit of a criminal. I had to convince myself it was all real and criminals were not only on TV. I called the dealership and told them he had added his name to the car I made the down payment on and signed for. We discussed the deal, but all the paperwork was processed so it was final and if I wanted his name removed it would be a legal matter. They apologized for what he had done. I thought it was a final deal as I signed the contract, but should have known Daniel had an illegal way around everything. No one dared to confront him or pursue any legal action. That family was smarter than the law and it seemed they made the laws.

After trying to rectify my car purchase contract error, I called Daniel and he laughed and told me it was done and not to worry about it. It was not a big deal. Well, no, not for him because with his signature and no money he became half owner and had another tie to me. I knew he would never put one penny towards that car or my insurance, yet he would claim half. I had made another error by not understanding how a criminal operated. That would cost me.

Daniel was on my new Chevy ZR2 4x4 and new Camaro, too. One step backwards. Was it not enough that he made the commissions and whatever on the side from the sales to me? Daniel never had enough scams. He knew I was upset about it but could not afford to hire a lawyer and fight over it. I could not even get a divorce from the con artist because I had to come up with more cash than I had just to begin the case. It would have been cheaper to give him back the autos and lose my deposits and payments. My kids and I worked so we needed the transportation. I did not want to go back on my promise but I thought about it. Daniel stuck with his claims that I did not really love him and never planned on staying married. That should not have bothered me but it did. When he told me I was a three time loser, it bothered me, and coming from him it should have meant nothing. I was a bad person and needed help and refused to share with his family. When someone continually tells you something, it wears on you. It sticks on your mind and you begin to doubt yourself even though you know the facts.

Out

I wanted out, knowing the losses I would take. Daniel had his life up there and I could not have my life back until he gave me a divorce. He claimed everything as his and told me he would never give me a divorce so I may as well go along with him. I asked a few times on the phone and he would have nothing to do with it. It only proceeded to get worse by the day. Daniel's threats became more extreme because he was not getting what he wanted. I guess he knew by now I would not add his name to anything more, especially my house and other property. I refused to take out a second mortgage on my house or file bankruptcy for him. I would not borrow money from my parents or sell my antiques or kids' things. Those things were not his to claim. I refused to give him my social security benefits statements and accounts my kids or I had. My life insurance policies and all other assets I owned were going to remain mine. My will would not be changed as he begged and claimed it was only fair to him because he married me. Yet before I wanted the divorce he constantly threatened to leave me and take everything I owned if I would not give him my credit cards and paychecks to use. I would never give him thousands of dollars for his latest business scam. Nothing Daniel did was legal or ethical. It would have been easier if he would have given up and put all that nasty effort somewhere else. Did Daniel ever really expect me to do all that? The marriage had nothing to do with me and everything to do with every asset I had. If he put as much 'work and energy' into a real job, he would have had some money instead of swindling everyone out of everything they had. It would be less work for him, but he did not know how to give an honest days work. He had not done that his whole miserable life.

Since he had to take care of his own ATM withdrawals and use his own paychecks to pay his bills, Daniel's aggressive behavior was endless. But I would not budge no matter what he threatened me with. He would not give up.

I was onto what he did and how he lived. I made many calls and checked out everything I had in print. One call was to the building manager in his apartment building.

All of our conversations were by phone and I thank God that he had stayed away. His phone calls upset me and worried me, but at least I did not have to handle him physically at my house or around my kids. He would tell me I was crazy and everyone agreed with him. Now that we were married it was all his. He checked and could legally have me declared insane and take control of it all. My kids would see nothing and I would be locked up. The scary part of that was he told me they did that with his mother and he knew all the angles better than any legal authority. It was like the family joke. How did they get away with that? How cruel and pathetic. My proof that these are people that would go to any extreme to get what they want.

Daniel still begged for another chance. I would have more money than I knew what to do with if I gave him three thousand dollars to join his family in their new business. It was not just with me that he tried to make 'deals', it was everyone he came in contact with. I wanted nothing to do with him or his family. I told him I had no money and he believed I did and could easily take out another mortgage on my house because his friend had done the appraisal and I had way too much equity. Why would I refuse to help them? I tried to smooth it over without too much drama. I knew he had access to all information about my finances and everything I owned. That in itself was scary. He made it clear that he knew. I knew he had never planned to go through with anything we discussed before the marriage. It was part of his deal. That marriage certificate was Daniel's contract for ownership. He made it all sound so real and everything I liked and wanted, so did he. He never planned on a real relationship or marriage. I was a real person, not a fake. I never set people up for appearances or tell stories that have one thread of truth to them. But it sounds great and interesting. I loved privacy and paid what I owed. Bad people like Daniel have to live in cities and move around because they would otherwise be discovered as to what they do and who they really were. That type of person would not get away with what they did living in a small rural community. What Daniel did not realize and expect was how many people I knew for so many years living in the same house. As an avalanche rolled down the mountain it became faster and larger and more extreme. It wipes out everything in its path and grows while doing so. I did not want to know the end result when it stopped and was over. But that was my goal. Stop it and end it forever. Maybe I could remove that nasty piece of my life and it would go away. He had to realize that something was going to happen soon. It had to give. I struggled to keep what I had and worked as much as possible. In the long run Daniel was coming out ahead financially by staying married to me because I was paying for everything while he claimed half. But I could not stop paying because he would claim all instead of half and reminded me when ever we spoke. I was getting nowhere trying to split up and cut the ties even though I was being cordial. I was on a high wire doing a balancing act and the stakes were extremely high if I lost my balance. Every day of my life had become a high wire act and I had never done it before.

I was not sure if Daniel would become desperate in his final stage of taking as much as possible from me. He obviously went to extreme lengths to have that opportunity so how far would he go to walk away with all I owned? I had seen his dark, evil side. The majority of his life that he kept well hidden before marriage. There was no doubt that I had only touched the surface of what he was involved with and how "bad" it really was. I tracked down only what involved myself and my kids in the few months of marriage and had no desire to find what ever more was out there. It was already too late for some of my possessions and I was willing to give some up to get out. There was no marriage, only a business deal for Daniel. The deal was he signed a piece of paper in June and then he owned everything I had and I would continue to fund his life. That was simple to him. It did not matter to him that the piece of paper was a marriage certificate. That was only a formality.

I wondered how these people were not in prison. Since the files had become so extensive and contained so many illegal activities, I decided they should be stored elsewhere and copied for me to work with so if anything happened a few people had the facts. I felt I was playing a part in a suspense movie. I was the eye of the hurricane and it was moving all around me and I could not stop it.

Finally, I decided to attempt the word 'divorce' in my next conversation on the phone with Daniel. At the right moment I could slip it in and hope he would go for it. The next conversation with him did not go well as I led up to the legal split. Daniel did not care if we were split up and not living together or even if we ever saw each other. As long as there remained a legal marriage certificate on file, anything went for him. He told me he would never give me a divorce and if I ever tried to file for one I would be sorry. He continued to threaten to have me removed from my house and locked up. He knew how to get that done. I let him know I believed he was into illegal activities and I wanted out with no involvement. That was amusing to him. Other threats he made were avoidable, but now he let me know that if

my house burnt down, half the insurance money was his
and if he could have me put away it would all be his. I
would lose everything either way in the end. He already
had it all figured out. Yes, I knew he could get away
with it. The problem was that I believed he would do it
and get away with it. He had no idea I knew about his
past yet. How had he gotten away with all of that in the
past for all those years with no arrests? A professional
criminal. So his story that he was taught by the best,
raised by the best, was the best, and no one could touch
him, a truth or another story? According to what I had
investigated it was all true. He was proud of that fact
even though his father spent time in prison. I told him
that was not something to be proud of. The puzzle
slowly came together. There were too many pieces and I
only wanted a small corner finished. Daniel continued
to tell me I never wanted to stay married and was bad,
selfish and would not share with him and that was our
problem. I would not make it without him on my own.
That was so off the wall untrue that I thought of it as a
reinforcement instead of a negative. It helped to give
motivation to not listen to him and pursue the divorce. I
believed Daniel and his family were very dangerous.

Sometimes it crossed my mind that Daniel might
be right. I continued to dig myself out. The more I
tried to remove myself, the more intense he became. He
reminded me that his friends would do anything he asked
them to do. Before I knew what was going on, I thought
it had to be my fault like he said. He justified everything
he said and did and it always ended up somewhat logical.
I had tried so many times to fix what cannot be fixed. I
always had to tread lightly no matter what it was about.

The harder I tried, the worse the situation became. Every time it ended up the same. No way to fix it and no way out. The first few months I only saw the surface and listened too intently to what Daniel said. The more I listened to him, the worse I felt. Daniel always had a story. Then it always ends up the same old story and he continued to use it over and over. He always told me he wanted the same thing in life as me. In all actuality, he wanted 'my life' and was willing to do whatever it took to acquire it. Not help physically or financially to get it, but to take it for free because he could and thought it was owed to him. Daniel spent his life learning how to take from everyone and anyone he came in contact with. It took me so many months to figure out the deep, dark person he was. I thank God I had my parents and friends for support. That was always a problem with Daniel if I had anything to do with them. He could not stand the fact that my kids and I were close and tried to sabotage our relationships. I kept close to home whenever possible.

The collusion story came up again when Daniel called one day to tell me he had spoken with a lawyer friend of his and they would prosecute and decided my bank we had used had committed a crime. The bank and I were in collusion because the additional property purchased did not include adding Daniel's name to my house and all other property I had owned. Again, there was that collusion word. He told me I would go to jail for sure and if I tried to file for a divorce I would find out what he could do. He kept yelling I would be put in jail and it would all be his. This time I told him he was crazy. I hung up the phone and thought about it. Then I called a lawyer I knew. I explained Daniel claimed the bank and I drew up the loan on that property secretly without telling him he would not be added to my existing home loan. But we were all there at the table at the bank and went through all paperwork and loan agreement and had a lawyer present and asked specific questions. I specifically asked that the new additional loan on that property be completely separate. We all acknowledged that fact in detail. That was one detail I wanted to be absolutely clear on. Besides the process with me purchasing that additional property was already in the works before Daniel was around. To him it was an addition to the marriage deal. Daniel claimed my house was partly his. I also called the bank President to be sure Daniel had not somehow added his name to my house since my last call. He reassured me nothing was changed. What a relief to find he had not yet manipulated that detail, not that he had not tried or was in the process. If my property taxes on my other property and house were manipulated adding his name illegally at the courthouse, I was sure anything else could be manipulated in the same way by a professional criminal. Still, I continued to pay for it all because I did not know the consequences if I stopped. I paid and Daniel claimed it. I was not even sure if he would illegally end up with it all anyway. He used fear to control and manipulate.

I wondered if any one had ever checked his credit report. If they had he would never obtain any type of loan. Daniel had only debt and no assets. Maybe it was a fake credit report he had done. That was one of his businesses I had found, altering credit reports to obtain loans. All of my assets and collateral prior to marriage were used because he had none. Daniel insisted if I tried to do anything and not add his name to my house and other property, he would charge me and my bank with collaborating against him. We were in collusion. New words.

Daniel made sure he had something on everyone and then used that to get what he needed. He told me about those involved in the sex clubs with him because they were the ones that would help him so they were not 'publicly found out'. Their secret lives remained safe with him as long as he had that protection. I began to believe his threats because if it were true, those lawyers, insurance agents, law enforcement officials, doctors, and the others, would obviously cover for him in their little sick network. From what I had seen, it was true. I had no doubt about that. It was more pieces of the puzzle I put in place.

I had a few very good friends that helped me keep going. I did not have much stability in my life then and they supported and helped me through it all. I did not have the answers and would not upset and worry them any more than necessary. Jas and Cal were still kids but I would not lie to them. Cal was so impressionable and it confused him more than Jas. There would never be an explanation or solution. I would always say 'if only I had known'. All that was left was to get out as quickly as possible.

The more I made, the more I had, the more Daniel wanted. Daniel had to have spent a lot of time and money to find out all the information on me. He did not miss anything because he believed he was entitled to it all. It did not matter that I owned those possessions and property my whole life because he felt entitled to everything tangible and of monetary value from my past, present, and future.

Keeping track of my bills and overdue payments, I realized just how much I had lost. Unknowing to me Daniel had added his name to my new vehicles and all the insurance for the house, property, and autos. If I had anything of value, Daniel claimed while I continued to pay for it. Maybe he was right about being able to convince women to do whatever he wanted, like he had always bragged about. He absolutely had no conscience. I told everyone that Daniel was the kind of person that could murder someone and be able to justify it in court. Law enforcement would probably even help him drag the body where ever he needed it to be. Daniel would walk away laughing. That was how I saw what he did to me and my family. He was so flawless in how he operated, I had nowhere to turn. I would continue to get caught in the web he had spent his whole life weaving.

I wanted my quiet, comfortable, fun life back. During a conversation on the phone with Daniel, I asked him to leave me alone and prepare the divorce papers or I would. He explained there would be no divorce and he would never leave me alone because he did not have to. I was to continue to pay for everything and it was his whenever he felt like coming down to my house. I told him he should not come to my house. He screamed into the phone that this was his house and he would do whatever he wanted. It was all his and I would see. He would have it burnt down and collect the insurance if I did not give him half of everything. He could take it all if he chose and no one would do anything about it, he promised. I knew something would happen because I did not make the deal he wanted, but I felt he had no right to everything I owned. He already managed to go through all my savings plus more in a few months and that was it. He warned me it would be the biggest case the county had ever seen and he would drag it out and cost me thousands of dollars and he would walk away with everything. My kids and I would be homeless and have no vehicles to work. He told me I would not go public in court and talk about his sex clubs and scams because I was a private person and I would be too embarrassed. I refrained from telling him I had all the other information from investigations. All of the information that he had never breathed a word about to me. He tried to scare me and it worked. I told him he was so obsessed about me adding his name to everything I owned and taking out another lien on my house to help him and his kids, but it would never happen. I would not give up. It was a game to him and he had nothing to lose because it was all mine.

Daniel had portrayed me as a bad person, crazy, and needed help, to his co-workers. It was all part of his plan. He claimed he spent all his money on the ranch and horses he bought for me. I wondered how many people believed him until I realized I was one of them. I spoke with a few people when I had questions. They knew what was really going on the whole time and apologized. They did not want Daniel to know they had any conversation with me. I promised them I would never do that because they believed he was dangerous and manipulative. He was sure to set up the story for following events. That way he felt he was covered when he proceeded with his plan. It was a big scam and he thought he would get rich quick. It would have been better than all the other scams I found he was involved in. All it took was a signature and a lot of lies, which he was excellent at. Then it was his. No work, no investment. And it was almost instant.

The death threats were constant and then he started with Jas and Cal. My kids or I would have an auto accident and no one would ever know. He would and could have me committed and locked up. My house would burn down. He thought I was terrible for not adding his name to everything I owned, yet Daniel owned nothing and had nothing to put my name on. It was a one way deal. I was to give everything to him. It did not make any sense. I had a tough time understanding the whole idea. Daniel had to know I would not stop pursuing the split and wanted out. He thought it was common and even ok to threaten to kill me or have me committed if I filed for a divorce. Daniel had the knowledge and resources to do things that I never knew existed or were possible. There was so much to comprehend that it hurt my head and made me sick. I would lie awake at night wondering what I could do and what would happen next. I believed he would send someone down to my house and burn it. Yet, that would not be as terrible as Jas or Cal having an accident. I would never forgive myself for the situation already. It could be worse. Maybe I should let him have it all and that way I know my kids and I could walk away. That was my thought process as I slid through each day not knowing what or when something was going to happen. It hung over my head and it was so hard to sleep, even with the watchdog outside standing guard. But every noise seemed to keep me awake, even the dog.

Daniel knew how much we loved our animals too, so he could easily kill or poison them. He would think that was amusing. He made sure that I knew he was able to 'have things done' if I would not go along with his deals or spoke with anyone about it. I tried to avoid his calls since I had nothing more to say to him. I was unsure of what step to take next.

I thought about all the times I would sit quietly in public so he would not embarrass me. I knew not to disagree or say anything to upset him because that meant an escalation into huge, nasty, abusive confrontations. The embarrassment came more from the fact that I allowed myself to be involved in any way, especially the marriage, with him and not that he was mean and abusive in public. Daniel's abusiveness was not present until the marriage and began to escalate immediately after. That was what made it so hard for me to believe. I pondered the thought that maybe it was me and that was why I worked so hard at pleasing him in the beginning. Daniel continued to tell me it was all my fault. It never mattered what or how much I did for him, it was never enough. I never realized how terrible the relationship was and how devious he was until after I completely understood all the reports I had studied and pieced together. That process took so long; I was having a hard time letting the coincidences sink in. It was the same whether in person or on the phone. Since that began after a few weeks of marriage and continued to increase with intensity, I wonder what it would have been like had we lived together? I cringed at the thought. That part was over.

The times I answered the phone I was prepared for the verbal abuse, controlling and manipulative stories, and threats. Daniel called me at work and continued his 'hammering' to teach me a lesson for my own good. It was difficult to work after those calls. I was under a lot of stress. Sometimes I would hang up when he said he would come down and cause problems for me if I did not listen to him and do as he said. I spoke as little as possible, but no matter it ended with the same threats from him. I did not want him to come to my house or be anywhere near us. Daniel and I had been at the point of no return for a while and there would never be reconciliation, yet apparently he thought it would happen with his stories and threats. He continued to tell me how I was so stable, it was all he ever wanted, and perfect. I never loved him and shared with him or his adult kids; there was something wrong with me. Of course he continued to tell me it was all my fault the marriage was not working. Perfect for what? Stable? All he ever wanted? I did not give and give and give and it was my problem and fault the marriage had not worked? It was always one-sided about what he wanted from me. I had nothing but debt, stress, misery, and financial hardship from the day I signed the marriage certificate. It was over. I would not let him mess with my mind any more. He needed to move on to his next victim. I continued to work on my way out.

As expected, Daniel showed up at my house one day. I had not seen him come down the lane and walk up to the patio doors. He knocked and I did not let him in and asked what he needed. He could have broken the glass in the doors if he chose. I remained calm while he explained he would not sign any divorce papers so I would have to live with it or else. Then he explained the or else and I told him I still wanted out and could not continue with the 'marriage deal' he offered. He told me he would never leave me alone and pushed his way inside my house. He became very loud and began throwing my antiques and banging his fist on the table. Then Daniel told me to leave. He told me to leave my house immediately. He was staying and I was to leave with nothing. He screamed for me to get out because it was his now. Over and over he continued I would never be able to make him leave and he would show me. I was crazy and everyone agreed with him, even my friends. He had talked with my friends and they agreed with him. Daniel was calling to have me removed and locked up; he had it all set up. I froze and just stood there wondering what was next. In my mind I quickly doubted myself, as he had a way of making me do that, and wondering if he had found a way to get it done. If there was a way, he would find it. I remembered his story of how they locked his mother in an institution because she would not go along with them. I questioned myself, like many times recently. Could he, would he? After all, I knew what they were capable of and I had it in black and white.

I had not been prepared for that confrontation. I hoped the divorce would be over before that happened, but now it was too late for hoping. It had happened and I had no idea what to do even though I stayed awake most nights praying for closure. Not knowing how to safely get that done. There was no safe way and that was why I could not figure it out. Not with someone like Daniel. Had I not been the one it happened to and found the hard evidence I did, I would never have believed any of it. He could convince anyone of anything. That I know from experience during the last few months. It was so hard to believe all that had happened in less than one year. It seemed like a lifetime or two.

The Threat

I refused to leave my house which enraged Daniel into one of his abusive tempers. I tried not to listen and stood back from him while I tried to keep him from coming further into my house. He pushed inward. I told him I would call the Sheriff's Department if he did not leave. I went for my phone across the room on the counter and he followed me into the room. Still screaming and calling me names, he grabbed the phone from my hand and threw it. He told me I was dead if I did not leave and no one would question him. He could have it all that way and I would be gone. That is what I called crazy, but I was in fight or flight mode. I retrieved the phone and dialed and he hit it out of my hand again and I ran outside hoping he would follow. That did not work. While I was on the phone Daniel continued to threaten me. He told me he had contacted the DCFS because I was a bad parent. He would call the IRS and have me thrown in jail for doing my taxes without him and that was illegal. He would call the Health Department and turn me in and I have no idea what that was for and neither did he. He was using all these threats to control and manipulate me out of fear. Yet again he threatened that Jas, Cal, and I would have an accident and no one would ever know. Daniel was using anything that he could think of to terrify me, believing I would do whatever he wanted to avoid his threats. He really believed I would stay with him and not go through with the divorce out of fear. After I dialed and someone answered the phone and I began asking for help, Daniel raced to the car he was driving and squealed away. I had called a relative, not the Sheriff's Department. A deputy would take a half an hour to get there and I wanted someone closer. I was embarrassed that I married him and allowed myself to be in that situation. I thought I could handle him through the divorce. I watched him drive down the lane and away. I was not sure if he would return, maybe with a gun, which he told me he had. He had a terrible temper and expected everything to go his way. I had someone stay there for a while until I thought it was safe and made sure my gun was loaded and ready. I was done living in fear of what Daniel would do next. Many things flashed through my mind. There would be no doubt that Daniel had gotten the picture of what I would and would not do. There was no chance of a quick or smooth divorce. He did not want the truth out and he had no idea how much I would be willing to reveal. He was still unaware of my investigation and findings. What was he capable of and how far would he go to keep his lifestyle and illegal activities concealed?

Did he think I was afraid of him enough to give what he wanted and walk away? Could he find someone to keep me quiet? That would be more like him, let someone else take the fall if caught and cover any connection to himself. So many questions kept running through my head. If I continued my investigation, what more would I find and who else was connected. I believed he made deals with those involved in government and law enforcement. It was his blackmail tactics that would keep him in the clear no matter what he did. That was why he had continued to get away with his acts. Had he left me alone and not pushed with his threats, I would have stopped investigating and believed it would be over.

I knew I would be the one to file for the divorce because Daniel would never do it. He would end up losing his free ride if we were divorced. After all, I continued to pay and build the equity of what he was going to claim. He would only gain and had no chance of losing anything. That was if he had anything. I was not sure what was real or true anymore. I only knew what I had found in black and white through months of investigating.

Many weeks went by and I gathered as much information as I could on my time off. I tried to keep our lives as normal as possible under the circumstances. Cal had football games and I made them all. He loved the game, but worked whenever he could. Jas had a boyfriend and worked. They helped me whenever I needed it. We used to have brunch every weekend, but now it was only once in a while. Breakfast was the cheapest to eat out and seemed to fit all of our schedules. We talked about what was going on and that I had no idea what my future plans with the cabins and horse riding business or the restaurant purchase. The problem with pursuing any type of business or purchase was that Daniel would claim half just by being married to me. Of course he would jump on that. I was going to be divorced soon anyway, but it was all on hold for the time being. My kids and I wanted to move on and try to collect our lives and return to the pleasant way of life we had before Daniel. I had taken a drastic fall without knowing and I needed to get back up and out of the black, bottomless pit. My kids were supportive and patiently waiting to help in our business we had planned. I insisted everything would be okay soon but the whole situation was so stressful and wearing. I had a difficult time seeing an end to any of it.

Daniel and I spoke a few times on the phone which resulted in the same old story. I was so worn out and tired and had no energy left to fight him. I spent all my time off researching reports and putting the puzzle together. As I piled the files higher, I consulted with lawyers, searching for someone I could afford to pay upfront and then keep what I had. Fees were anywhere from twenty-five hundred to twenty thousand upfront and fees accordingly by the hour after that. What a cost to keep my life I had only last year. What a mistake I had made. Just one signature and my life was no longer mine. It became someone else's life. Someone else's everything. I did not even know how it happened. I waited for him to file for the divorce as I asked him to do many times. It would have been cheaper for me, but he was going to go the distance and wanted anything he could think of. I know he had access to my personal information and finances through the dealerships. He knew the value of what I owned better than I did. I began to realize exactly what my kids and I had. Only when what you have begins to disappear, do you realize what you had. Not that I took it for granted, but I had always had a good life with my kids. It would be an uphill battle, but I had no choice. All that was left was to choose a lawyer and pay to proceed with the divorce. Once he was served, I knew it would be dangerous for Jas, Cal, and I, but I had no other option.

It was not long before Daniel called and wanted to meet me to talk and I thought he was giving me a divorce. We were two adults so we would sit down and take care of the details, not expecting to agree on everything. If that was what it took to get the divorce, I was all for it to be over. He told me there would be no divorce and I had no way out because he knew what he was doing. Nobody messes with him because he was the best at what he did. Then he hung up on me as I told him I only wanted to be left alone.

A couple of days passed and Daniel showed up at my house again. It could not be good. He began to raise his voice. When he refused to quiet down and have a conversation, I suggested that we go elsewhere. He told me he had been driving all over looking for me. Had he been at my house earlier? He had no key to get in, luckily. I had never even locked my door before I met him. Why had he not called me instead of 'driving all over looking for me"? Something did not sound right. I would not continue that discussion with him while Cal was home. I did not have high expectations and told him we could go to a restaurant to talk just north of my house. A public setting would be best. I was not leaving the county, but I did not want him close to my house. I did not trust him and decided it was probably a set up. He wanted me in unfamiliar territory and to go with him further away. I agreed only to talk in public where I knew people. He was being very nice and agreeable. I told him I would meet him outside. Okay, that was set up. Cal was home because we had just returned from a political event. Jas was at work. I asked Cal to stay and I would return shortly with his dinner, but he wanted to go to a friend's house. That worked out well. Daniel convinced me to get into the car he was driving. I was scared, but at least I got him out of my house. I wanted to drive separately. We began to talk about how he had acted previously and told me it would not happen again. I did not believe him, but I listened to the same stories that he wanted to stay married, and on and on. I made him that way and it was all my fault that things were as they were. He kept on and on about trying to make me a better person and help him out. It was the same story I had heard for a year now. The stories were always the same. The end result was always the same. Now that he realized I wanted out, I thought he had decided go through with the divorce. Maybe it was his last attempt to win his game. He never lost and I suppose he knew he was not on the winning end with this marriage. I wondered why he had been so agreeable and nice. I told him I still wanted a divorce and he tried to persuade me otherwise. I stood my ground and was very cordial and used simple explanations. At that point there was no need to say anything else. No need to go into details. No need to go over the same old issues. It was always the same but each time we discussed 'us', it became more dramatic and severe in threats from him.

We ordered our food and I told him he would have to pay the bill. He agreed and the conversation became increasingly negative and going nowhere. I really did not want to hear his same old stories again because it did not matter. I asked if he had found a lawyer to file for divorce. He had not. He must have thought he could manipulate or scare me enough to change my mind and stay married. He grew louder and when I asked that he keep it down, he told me he did not have to and continued. He would not stop. At some point it must have sank in that I was not agreeing with him because he explained if I ever thought about getting a divorce, I was dead. He smiled and snapped his fingers in the air and told me he would make one call and I would be dead. He repeated it again, snapping his fingers. To him it was that simple. It was his solution. He wanted to know if I understood. He never blinked, wavered, or hesitated. He was calm, cool, and collected and knew exactly what his plan was. I sat there looking at him because he was not whispering. I said nothing. I was shocked and I froze. At first I thought I misunderstood and then when he repeated it, I knew it was the last time I would attempt to talk to him and only wanted to see him in a protected courtroom. He went on that no one would or could ever touch him no matter what he did. He knew all the angles and he was the best. I could do nothing about it. I was going to die and he would bury me. No one ever crosses him and gets away with it. I had no way out and that time it was not a threat, it was a promise. I told him I was tired of his threats and wanted him to leave me alone. The waitress, who I had known most of my life, brought the food and asked if there was anything else we needed and if everything was okay. She looked straight at me and waited for an answer. I just sat there staring, then got up, not sure what to do next. I was sick! I was not sure if he had a gun or if he had someone waiting outside. Daniel was very unstable and verbally and physically abusive. The waitress asked again if everything was okay, looking at me because I had not touched the food. I finally unfroze and told him to stop threatening me and do it. Get it over with. I was calm about it because that was what I was used to with him. I should have screamed or something but for some reason I was quiet, trying not to draw attention to myself. Daniel said he would, with one call. He would take care of everything with his call right now. He told me I did not know who I was messing with. In my mind, a flash of what extremes he had already gone through to add his name to me and everything I owned. The only way he would ever have anything was from me, he had nothing. Through my investigations, I began to realize what a bad person he was. How evil someone could be. I rushed to the bar area where many of my friends sat. I could not think clearly. If he could sit at that table and tell me that with people all around, what next? Where would I be safe and how would I get there. I wanted to go home. It was still my home and my safe, private place. I looked around to see who I should ask for a ride and thought. Some of them saw the look on my face and asked if I was okay. If he saw me leave with a male, he would want to kill him, claiming that he was my boyfriend. If it was a female, she would be afraid. It was not fair for me to involve anyone in such a serious situation. I got myself into this mess and I would get myself out. It seemed like a long time but was realistically a matter of seconds. I knew how Daniel worked and I decided not to involve anyone else. I flew out the front door while on my cell. I made five calls and could not reach anyone. I left a couple of messages. I walked to the side and back of the building so if Daniel came out he would think I had left. I wanted him to leave. No such luck. I finally reached someone and they were on their way to pick me up. I told them what Daniel had said and that I needed a ride home quickly. Daniel came around the side of the building and heard me and tried to get me into the car he was driving. Who knows whose car it was. I refused and he grabbed my arm and told me he was taking me to my house. I still refused and told him my ride would be there in a few minutes so he needed to leave me alone. He insisted I do what he told me and I kept moving away from him and told him I called someone very close and he should stay away from me. I redialed and called to see how close they were so Daniel could hear. I was petrified of what Daniel would do next. People were leaving the restaurant and walking to their cars and Daniel took off without another word. So I remained close by the door. The only safe spot I knew. A few people asked if I was okay or needed anything because he left in the car and I was still there, shaking. I wondered if he would go to my house or drive straight back to his apartment and get out of the county. I was still sick. I hoped my kids were not at the house and tried to call them. I prayed and thanked God that they were not back yet. I was a wreck and did not want anyone else to see me like that, especially Jas and Cal. I had no idea how to explain any of what had happened so how would I explain that incident? That was extreme to me but common for Daniel because he did not get his way. I would not do as he told me and it was again my fault he has to go to that extreme. He had to make me understand. Those were his 'lessons'. I had 'learned' enough. I was ashamed that I had not been smart enough to not have been tangled up with such an evil being. Being, yes, that was what Daniel was. Not a person, some kind of being.

My ride and I were pulling into the lane as I glanced around to be sure Daniel was no where in sight. It seemed to be clear as I rushed in to check that no one had broken into my house. After some thought and discussion I decided to call the Sheriff's Department to file for an emergency order of protection. He had to be stopped and it was up to me even if I was afraid of what his reaction would be. Did I let it continue too long and go too far? Was it my fault as Daniel always told me? Was there something more I should have done? So many questions were going through my mind and I wanted to know why he had done that. Why? How did I end up in that position and in that situation? What else could I have done to end it sooner before I needed law enforcement's help? Why had I not seen what would happen? If I would have done this or that, only if...I would not be in that situation. I blamed myself one hundred ten percent. Why did I believe or trust him? What ever made me think the marriage could be saved? Why did other people see through him but I did not? I had no answers to my questions. Did anyone else? I should have been smart enough to catch on earlier and put the puzzle together. So many people did not want to get involved so they remained quiet about what they knew. Why?

I stayed at a family member's house to try to calm down and wait for the Deputy to arrive. I had a tough time sorting through what had happened because it seemed so unreal, as though any minute I would wake up and realize it was only a vicious, sick nightmare. Upon realizing I was nowhere near the end of the nightmare and it was real, I had to gather any strength I had left and pursue the inevitable. The end! It was time to end the nightmare and be strong enough to follow through with the divorce myself. No one could help me with that. I was afraid of what would happen once I started the procedure. I knew it would be an avalanche to say the least. Would my kids and I be safe? We lived on a back road, out in the middle of the forest, ravines, creeks, and only a few homes nearby. No one would ever be able to come quick enough if we needed help. But that was where I grew up and what I loved about my ranch. All that was left was to keep praying. I had to pray for strength and safety for us. Why would Daniel not just disappear? He had his own life up there and this life was definitely not his. That was the easy way out, but not his way. All that Daniel ever promised me was 'no way out'. That was not what I meant when I told him there would never be a divorce. That was prior to marriage. It never meant that he could do as he pleased and use me and my assets at will with no limitations.

That was Daniel, one personality to the next without a blink. I never knew which one it would be. When I told him he needed help, he would admit he had issues, but believed that was how it was supposed to be. He had more than issues. It was very deep and dark inside. That was what made him so evil. He had no conscience!

I tried to sort through all the words that were said because it was the end of the line for the 'marriage'. The Deputy arrived with his papers and I sat and cried and told him what had occurred. That was probably the moment it all began to hit me and seem real. Up to that point in the last months it was a blur and I was not let the facts seem real. But as I repeated the evening and what had lead up to it, it all hit me and became real and sunk in. Was I really involved with the story I had to reveal, all the facts that came out? How could anyone else believe it when I could not bring myself to believe what was going on and what had taken place? He wrote up the report as I explained and he told me my options. He was very sympathetic and understanding while we went through the events that evening. I tried not to miss anything though there was so much to tell. I promised I would go to the court house and file for an emergency order of protection the next day. They would patrol my road and watch my house and kids and do what they could. I refused that he be arrested if they found him because I explained his brother would have him released on bail immediately and that would only further his anger and threats. He was used to everyone following his orders or else. Well I had gone against everything he wanted and it would not be a pretty sight. Maybe he would snap all the way. I worried about Jas and Cal. The Deputy explained that they would try to find him if he had not left straight for the suburbs. I thought he would head north and his brother would keep him hid. His brother always covered for him and I guess that was why they always lived together. No matter which state or city or car dealership. Everyone agreed I should also file for the divorce at the same time because Daniel would be furious when he was served anyway, so the best process would be to get all of the paperwork done as soon as possible and proceed. I agreed. I know I should have filed for the divorce as soon as things started to turn ugly, which was just after we were married. I mean within forty-eight hours of the signature on the marriage certificate. It was the end of the marriage now because I would never turn back no matter what was said or done and it was in black and white for all the world to see. That was what and who Daniel really was. Now everyone knew and I had nothing to hide or cover for. There was no need. When anyone would ask about the marriage, I could tell them what had been going on the whole time. Well, that was during the last year of my life. I was out! Finally it was over, the end. All that was left was the paperwork. In a way it was a very heavy load off my shoulders and I could breathe. I could try to get my life back and move on with my children.

In the beginning I prayed it was just Daniel's new adjustment from 'being married'. I wish I had put the pieces together so much earlier before it had gone to such an extreme. Now I would have to be prepared for the wrath. Daniel had to know what would come of that evening.

Givers And Takers

Daniel was an evil being and there was no way around it. His goal in life was working for the devil. He felt it was his right to take all he could from everyone he could. It was his game of life. He worked harder and put more effort into using people than if he had a job and worked like most people. He never knew what an honest living was and had never worked an honest day in his life.

Maybe that was among the many reasons he told me he had to watch what he said on the phone and was paranoid of being recorded. Someone else must have been watching him. Other times Daniel would complain he had to watch everything he did now. I did not determine why he had to watch everything he had done and said now, as if something had recently happened. Or was it because we were married? If he was doing nothing wrong, why would he have to 'watch everything now'? Why was he unable to explain that when I asked him? The only answer he gave me was that he had to watch it and be careful now. That was all he would say. Something else had happened with someone else. All I knew was that it was all too much for me!

After being involved with such an evil, unstable, abusive person, I understood bad relationships and why women are afraid to get out of them. There is so much more to understand and without going through it no one could possibly comprehend. It becomes easier to remain in that relationship than to try to leave. It takes an enormous amount of strength to fight it and get out and away. Some of these "men" are impossible to get away from and they never have to leave the women alone. No one can stop them. Women become emotionally and financially abused. The result is low self-esteem and the inability to see the forest for the trees. They get lost and do not know how to get out because it is too difficult and dangerous. In many ways it becomes easier to remain in a bad relationship. Family and friends are a must but not everyone has that option. Some have nowhere to go. How could anyone understand without personal involvement with that experience? That was another world. A very evil, wicked one.

At first I had believed him and thought he would be that nice person I knew before the marriage because he wanted the same things I wanted and he was ready to settle down. I believed he wanted me, not everything I had. Daniel wanted it all......literally. He was so careful not to let the real Daniel emerge when I was present until the marriage certificate was signed. It was difficult to understand and comprehend that it was all so perfect, sounded so perfect before the marriage for a reason. I had not been able to handle the threats and abusiveness and had run out of everything psychologically, physically, and financially. It was the first time in my life I had been what I called 'broke'. Always the same ending and I never figured out what he wanted or needed. I gave and gave until nothing was left. By the time I realized what he had planned, it was done. Basically, I was his bank for free money, like a money tree. Money and assets that became Daniel's to claim once I signed the marriage certificate. Since I refused to volunteer my assets to finance his life, he tried to 'hammer and teach me a lesson for my own good' to coerce me into giving up and doing whatever he wanted. When that failed he attempted to force me into bankruptcy so he would 'inherit' my assets, as he tried to 'help me'. He needed a fall person and address to cover for his illegal activities, always keeping his name in the background. With nothing working as he had planned, he reverted to more extreme tactics that were common to him. Daniel set up his plot to have me committed, locked up, or have a fatal accident. Even worse was the threat of my kids. No one threatens my kids. Their safety was first in the whole situation, so we kept close contact with each other. It did not matter to him which plan he had to proceed with. As long as he got the job done. He was perfect at reversing the fault and blame on the other person without blinking. Almost perfect. Now I could see how his threats and actions escalated as I refused to surrender what I had left. Daniel became more extreme in his ways as I became more concerned. One fact I was sure of, Daniel was the perfect specimen of every human flaw to the extreme. He would be a psychiatrist's dream case study. When someone blames or claims the entire fault to be yours and you know what you did and did not do, it is exactly what that person did. It took me months to realize that fact. When Daniel turned around a story one hundred ten percent and blamed me and explained how it was my fault, it made no sense. That was unfamiliar territory that I had no experience with in my life and that was fine with me. He was an emotional and financial holocaust. I could not understand where he came up with some of those stories and accusations, until later when I realized it was he who was doing just that. That was why it made no sense to me because I was not the one doing it. Daniel was. Why had it taken so long for me to figure that out?

It made sense that no one had gone against him because of threats and blackmail techniques. Maybe I was the only one he never blackmailed. After our legal split, I attempted to obtain all I could in writing. One gentleman I admired had sent me a copy that I needed. The only promise I had to make to him was that Daniel never know where it came from. He told me he and his wife thought a lot of me, but he had to protect his family. He told me they wanted to call me to let me know about Daniel so many times but ultimately decided to stay out of it to be safe. He let me know how sorry they were about what Daniel had done to me. They were all aware of how bad he was, but they had families to protect. I found I was correct even though I did not want to believe I was involved with someone so evil. Daniel found something on everyone to make them do what he wanted. He always claimed he could have any woman and she would do anything he needed and asked for. That was what I found as I investigated further. All the stories were the same about Daniel. That was the way he lived his life.

Unable to proceed with any type of business, I continued to work for my friends and part time for the Federal Government. It gave me another support outlet. I was safe and met many new people. I did not feel safe at certain places. I knew Daniel was very unstable, devious, and vengeful. No one dared to go against him or tell anyone what he did. I continued to receive overdue statements, past due letters and demands to pay from collection agencies, businesses named with my name and address, and home mortgage applications that were not mine. It was all more than I could trace and investigate. There was so much that it became more than a full time job. I had to draw the line somewhere so I could tie up any loose end involving me directly. The problem became evident that there was no end. No end to anything Daniel was ever involved in. The leads continued forever and went back as far as I could trace. The leads included so many people and businesses that there was no end to find. I had to leave many of them open and try to pick up the trail on the next lead. Suddenly all these leads I traced had my name or address involved. Everything from a government agency or a used car business or a past due invoice or collection agency. They involved many states. It was not believable, even though I read it in black and white. There was literally no end to any of it. I traced so much of it back for many years before I knew who Daniel was. No wonder I could not get a divorce. There would no longer be a fall person and address for him to use. He spent many days transferring all of his, and his family's, illegal scams and deals to my identity.

No one had ever heard of this so I had no where to turn. I wanted no one's sympathy, I wanted justice. The law would surely not tolerate what I had spent the last many months producing and documenting of illegal scams. Right? That was what I had thought. No one would tolerate all that illegal activity when all the investigation was documented in black and white and handed on a silver platter. Someone, anyone could jump on it. The laws we have protect us from criminals and their illegal scams. There should have been no problems for the legal system to do the job at that point. I was not sure that there was any reason for me to spend anymore time and money to further investigate the scams.

Point Of No Return

Now I was at the point of no return and no one denied that. Everyone was afraid for my safety and my kids. I listened to everyone's advice and kept it all in mind. I had been in unfamiliar territory and needed advice. Only I could decide how to proceed and what I felt would work best in the situation I was left with. No matter where we went, my kids and I had our cells and kept in close contact. Jas and Cal understood enough to know that I wanted nothing to do with him and that I wanted him no where around us. He was bad and all that surrounded him was bad news. There was nothing good around him and he left a path of destruction. I assured my kids that we would be okay and our lives would soon return to normal. We would have our lives back. We would be able to move on and put it all behind us and we could forget what had happened when I married Daniel. I believed we were on the road to recovery and Daniel would be a terrible memory that I could forget. Even though it was actually a few months, it felt like it was more than a lifetime of terrible circumstances that most people would never be involved in through their whole life.

All of the necessary paperwork was completed for the order of protection and the divorce. The worst was over I thought. It was the nightmare from which I would awaken and return to my life. The good life that I had with my kids. Every morning I woke up, if I slept at all, was an extended nightmare. My kids and I could not get out and have our lives back. Daniel would not let that happen. I think he thought he could scare me into dropping the divorce. I know he was capable of very bad things. It had been just over a year and we were really never together even when we were first married because he always had an excuse which ran into more excuses until he ran out.

I researched the state's law which states that at the time of marriage if either party committed fraud, the other party has the right to seek an annulment. The problem was I could find no lawyer with enough knowledge to proceed with that annulment. They were unfamiliar with it and knew of no one who had proceeded with an annulment due to fraud. That became no surprise to me since I found no one that had a clue what fraud was. Not one law enforcement official knew what to do about it or even how to proceed. The more information I gave them, the more stunned they were. They were not just stories I told but it was all documented. The facts could not be denied; I showed it all in black and white. To back up my findings I had other documentation from other sources to back me up just to prove what I had found was all too real. No one could deny anything I said or produced in legal documentation. They were all stunned to put it lightly. No one could believe any of it. But they had to when I produced the facts. It took me a long time and lots of research but I had what I would need. I searched back to many years before I was in the picture so I could prove who and what Daniel was. There could be no doubt, not a trace. I had no intention of turning back or letting anything drop at that point. Why would I? Facts that were all documented so that no one could ever question what had happened. In a way I had to do it to prove to myself that it was real and I was being used for my assets and as a cover. Maybe in the back of my mind I still thought something would pop up and point to someone pretending to be Daniel and doing all this bad stuff, like he tried to persuade me to believe. I could not understand how it was possible for a family to knowingly be involved in so much illegal activity and walk around bragging about it and flaunting and boasting to everyone that they can do whatever they want and no one will touch them and that they are so good at it. Daniel explained that they knew how to and what to do because their father had gone to prison for some of it and they "learned in court how to get away with doing things" while they watched the trial. So they not only learned how to get away with it, but they learned how to expand on all illegal activities and advance to the extreme. It was like some kind of joke to Daniel. Did he make a deal with someone to be able to continue his life of crime so that everyone would look the other way and forget? Something was very wrong and made no sense.

No wonder he threatened that he would never have to give me a divorce. Because he could. Because he needed my identification for illegal scams. My research continued and it was only the tip of the iceberg. Daniel had his credit report fixing scam business, insurance fraud, auto and mortgage loan fraud, title fraud, and so many other businesses. People even paid him to teach them how to run used car scams and set up shop with his 'mortgage companies'. Car dealerships hosted his 'seminars' as they all collected the money. The list of 'companies and businesses' is endless. The worst part is how many jumped at the chance to run fraudulent businesses for him. Some of his business constituents were in office and allowed the illegal activities to continue to grow. They were in on the cut. Some people have no care as to how they get their money as long as they get it.

When I filed for the divorce, I requested that Daniel and his family discontinue using my identity and address for their illegal scams and businesses. That never happened. Was everyone that afraid of him and his family, or were they that ignorant of the facts? The facts that were produced in black and white. The facts no one could believe when reading and requested even more back up which I provided. I continued to provide more each time someone asked for it and the piles grew and grew. There still was no end. As I continued to research and investigate over the next few months so I had plenty to produce in court, I found how extreme the fraud had become. Each week it seemed to become more extensive and widespread as it flowed into many other states. That becomes a Federal crime over state lines and through mail but still no one stopped or questioned Daniel. Why?

Law enforcement officials were lost and looked at me as though I was reciting a fictitious TV show. That does not happen here.

Most records were apparently kept at the used car business Daniel's father owned. It seemed that was the place they had 'secret meetings'. That proof would never be attainable because they were too smart to get caught. Maybe they had someone on the inside to warn them. They would never be attainable. Even with what I had already produced they should have been in prison. It was very evident that these people involved covered for each other and would get the money from the scams no matter what it took.

I continued to try to have the marriage annulled, but every lawyer I spoke with assured me I could not do that. Why was it so difficult for me to get my life back so I could move on? Many of them explained to me I should be happy my kids and I were alive and just move on. Yes, hard to believe that I was told that many times by many men in the legal departments. Some others told me to get on with my life and leave him alone and just forget him. Well, I have been trying! What did they think it all was? Did they think it was a game? There was nothing simple or funny about the situation. I wanted no one's sympathy. I wanted someone to give me a divorce. I wanted to keep what had always been mine and stop Daniel from using my identity and address for fraudulent businesses. What could be so difficult about something so illegal? Why should I even have to hear someone tell me something so absurd! I was furious. No one even wanted to stop them. Was it too much work? Did any of them together have enough brains to put a stop to the criminal I could not separate from? What was it? Why did no one have an answer? Are there laws in our State? Any laws in our Federal System? Anyone who even cared to stop a criminal when all the work was done and handed to them? What was wrong with these people? What were they there for? As long as it had not happened to them, because nothing like that would ever happen to them. Unfortunately for me, Daniel and his family knew all the laws and had their inside protection. What did that leave me with? At the rate I was going now, Daniel would never have to give me a divorce and could continue to use my identity for scams. While I was married to him, as the laws states, one spouse cannot testify against the other. He had it made. Why would he ever give me a divorce? On with the crime spree and to the extreme as he saw no one would stop or even slow him down! These criminals knew the laws better than any law enforcement official I knew or had contacted. The more I investigated, the more I found and the more visible the escalation. There was no stopping them and no one smart enough to stop them. It became extreme beyond my imagination and I had already thought I had seen it all. Well, I had seen enough to last me the rest of my life.

I had all types of fraud attached to my name and address now. It continued to escalate and I had no recourse and no way to stop these criminals from using my identity. My kids and I tried to keep our lives stable and move on. It was not easy and there was a lot of stress. I worked for my friends and was able to spend quality time with Jas and Cal. I was thankful for that. It was a test that I was to go through for some reason. Only God knew why.

I wondered what and how much would come back to me. No one cared. Only me. I got myself into the mess and I knew only I could get myself out. But I was doing everything under the sun to get out and it was not helping at all. I wanted terribly to totally remove myself from Daniel, his family, and everything he stood for. Daniel's favorite saying that 'I was raised by the best, taught by the best, I am the best and no one can ever beat me at it' meant exactly that. That was how they lived. They were proud of the fact that they continued to commit fraud against people and businesses and get away with it. Since the used car business Daniel's father owned was 'sold' there would be a new set of records even though it was a family member who now owned it. No one cared to look into them anyway when they were informed of what they would find by my investigation. The used car salesman cover. The perfect fit. He ran every scam on the side he could slip in and buyers had no idea what they were signing. The insurance companies set up a deal with him for each signature and he received a check in a special post office box. Selling titles and no cars to lending institutions. Credit report access for identity fraud. The list goes on and on, like the famous record keeping with cash payments weekly by me to the 'business' and checks for the others. It makes sense now that I am in the position of documenting all the money transactions to prepare for court. I had so many files it was almost impossible to break down into categories for those unknowledgeable in the courtroom to understand.

I had to keep it somewhat basic and simplify that which I found only pertaining to me and the divorce.

Many of the papers and instructions from Daniel to me about his 'new business plan' were kept in my piles of files. I knew they could not be legitimate, since nothing he ever did was. It would probably have to be used for future reference when another business or past due payments started popping up in my name and address. Everyone it seems knows how his games work and they keep their distance when it comes to his 'business dealings'. No one would ever say anything to him, only when he was no where around and then did so secretively. They explained to me that they feared what he would do if he found out they had said anything about his illegal activities. Why was everyone so afraid of him? Why did they let him continue his evil deeds?

In a way I felt better after I spoke with people that knew him.

It was not me and I knew it deep down, but still had a tough time understanding why Daniel was so cruel to us. We had never done anything but help him. I helped out financially with his adult kids and never once did any of them thank me. It was expected and demanded. That was how they were raised also. One generation to the next. I think of all the times he threatened me and told me I was nuts and needed help and it was my fault the marriage was not working. At first I trusted him and somewhat started to believe what he kept repeating to me over and over and over. That was a tactic he used to get what he wanted, but it never completely worked on me. There were so many people that it did work on and he did get whatever he wanted. A great con artist works that way. Same old stories for Daniel, just another person to use. Same thing, different day. How did he keep it all straight? Well, I had caught him a few times mixing me with someone else in his stories.

I did not want to learn anymore but there it was. Thrown at me like a concrete block to the head. Another headache because my head was so full of bad stuff all of a sudden in my life. I still tried to keep most of it from my kids because it was not going to do any good for them to worry and I tried to make it all go away as quick as I could. Jas and Cal used the computer and internet for school. I was trying to go through to see if I could copy anymore of what Daniel had been on the few times he used it at my house. Surprise! Large print on my screen 'you are being watched'. That was the beginning of what was to follow. It became impossible to use the internet or get my e-mail. It continually crashed and had viruses. I spoke with my internet provider and they had never seen what I had. Weeks went by as I tried to use it and continued to try to fix the blocks and viruses. There were threatening messages and it became more intense. Many computer techs tried to help but were unable to keep it out. They tracked down the problems for part of it and explained someone at another location was inside my computer at the same time. Basically, the techs told me there was nothing more I could do, especially about my email. Even though I told them no one had my information to get into it, they said someone hacked into everything. My kids did not even have my passwords to do it. We were learning another lesson about how far Daniel would go and what he was capable of. Or what he had someone else do for him to keep himself in the clear. There were many others involved and they figured the stakes were high enough to pursue all that I had. I believe what I was trying to retrieve from Daniel was incriminating and they tried to keep a no records policy. So I never completed my task of copying what he had in my computer. Sounds like a far fetched story, but just another tip of the iceberg. Now it was me that had to be careful of everything I did. I could not make a move that he did not know about. No matter how I tried to fix my computer, it always showed up the same messages. My complaints to the internet company did nothing. I could go to the F.B.I. because that was the only way to stop them. But in the year 2000, the fraud was just beginning and no one knew how to catch a hacker and prosecute. Another wide open crime spree opportunity. The Mohy's were always two steps or better ahead of the law in everything they did.

I knew Daniel was always on the internet. He is a sick person and I knew the evil would continue if he did not get what he wanted. There was always a reminder of what he was capable of and he wanted to be sure I knew that he was in total control of my life. Unfortunately, he was. I could do nothing but sink and run out of money and willpower. I was stubborn and had always been. Maybe that kept me going because I wanted to keep my life my kids and I had. Why did I have to give him my life? No one had an answer.

We were unable to use the computer for anything and I could see that coming. Everything Daniel touched was toxic. He was toxic himself. A black aura surrounded him. Next were the problems with messages no matter what we tried to do on the internet. The messages were all negative about being watched and being caught and someone knowing everything and threatening. Sometimes the message was the same and sometimes they were different. The internet company went through many departments to try to help but no one could stop it because they said it was a professional hacker and they were always a step ahead. I tried everything they asked. We were unable to use websites or e-mails. It was frustrating. Finally I called and told the internet company that I had to cancel my service and they apologized that they could not resolve the problem or stop the person from doing that. They had no problem with the cancellation. Jas and Cal would use their friend's computer when absolutely necessary. We slid by for a while and then when so much of their school work depended on the internet, I tried a different company. We made name changes and passwords again and it seemed it would work. I never used my e-mail because I was afraid to see what was on it. Now, we were the ones that had to be careful. Not because we were doing anything wrong, but because Daniel would not leave us alone. Then it started again and I tried my e-mail after calling the new internet company and explained to them what had happened. They went through each department and called me back and told me they had no idea what to tell me because they had not heard of it before. What they had found was that when we tried to access the net someone would kick us out and we were not allowed back in. The company told me each time I called about it that it was one of us at a different location but using the same passwords at the same time. I explained that was impossible because the three of us were there as we were speaking about it.

They claimed it had to be one of us and we argued that was not the case and I wanted to know how that could happen. They finally realized each time I called that I was telling the truth. No one at that company had seen that done before either. The only way for that to happen was for two of us with the same names and passwords on two different locations at the same time trying to access the same thing. That was the only explanation anyone had. As we sat at the computer on the phone no one had a solution. We continued to be kicked out. I went back into my e-mail with the help of the company rep on the phone and found more problems. Did Daniel have someone watch my internet twenty-four/seven and hack in whenever we tried to get online? How could someone do what was being done? NO ONE KNEW! Again, how can no one know? Daniel must set around and/or hire people to do just that to threaten and put the fear into those who disagree with him. I followed the new directions from that company like I had the last one.

It was far beyond frustrating now because I could do without a computer and the internet, but the kids had so much homework which required it to do reports and research to obtain good grades. Why should they have to endure Daniel's wrath? That was exactly what it was. They did not suffer, but it caused more stress.

Daniel had somehow added my name to an e-mail list of some kind for sex ads involving child porn. I asked the company to look at my e-mail and to be sure to let every department know what was happening to see if they could resolve the situation. I wanted to continue my internet but had to have some help. Calls were made back and forth and everyone at that company tried and gave advice and direction but to no avail. During that brief period of time I had subscribed again to the internet my e-mail became flooded with all child porn sites. All day and night it continued for weeks. I was unable to use my mail. As I was instructed I copied some of the sites and e-mails randomly through the pages and pages because they wanted copies. Law enforcement and my lawyer would not believe someone could and would do anything like that, so I had to print out copies for them too. They were also unfamiliar with it. No one knew what to do and this was my second company and second time around. Daniel would never let us have our lives back. We were once again in a terrible situation at the hands of evil. No matter what we did or where we turned he was there to stop us in a sickening way. There was no stopping him as he became disgustingly sick with his child porn sites. I could no longer search through all his sex sites to retrieve one of my own e-mails to each hundred of his sick listings. I called the company and told them to look at my e-mail and they apologized and commented on how terrible that must be to have someone able to do that to us and get away with it. It was harassment, a violation of privacy, and the new type of stalker. I never wanted to see the sex seekers and prospects popping up in front of my face each time I went to my e-mail. They all tried again to stop it and I finally asked that they shut it off for good because I could no longer stomach even turning on my computer and my kids were not going to have to tolerate such a sick and demented person's handiwork. After months of frustration and reminders of the sick person I married, I was worn thin.

There was a virus that no one was able to remove

whether I was on the net or not and my whole computer had to be dumped and restored from the beginning and yet still never worked even to type school reports. I gave it away. A three thousand dollar set up, but I wanted it out of our house. It was like it was an evil on its own that no one had control. I had some of the copies the internet companies asked that I keep and print out.

When I returned for an appointment with my lawyer I had a new box in hand. He was actually shocked that I was able to produce what I explained had happened. It was not a divorce story like he was used to seeing and hearing about. He was speechless as he read through that file and shook his head. Now they were starting to see what I was trying to deal with and remove myself from. It was not a marriage, but a piece of Daniel's newest scam. Like his old friends said; Daniel was always working on his next big scam trying to make a million. They were right.

I needed sleep but worried about the threats from Daniel. How did he have the money to do all he was doing? He knew I was tapped out because he continued to drain me. He knew where every penny I made went. I went forward and had no plans on stopping.

Documentation was my new word. I kept two sets in two different places. With each new piece of evidence, every new person and business a new file name was created and placed in boxes in alphabetical order. Then I started on my second box. When I was asked for some new evidence to back up a file or letter, I went to work and investigated until I produced what was needed. No one believed how much there was until I produced the proof. Then one led to another and another and another.

A few people suggested I contact every County, State, and Federal Department that pertained to the fraud I had found. At first I wanted to use what I had to get through the divorce and run. Then it became apparent to protect myself and my kids in the future, I should at least make the contact with dates and names and responses recorded. It took a while to find a contact name for each department and send the information accordingly. More files and more boxes. Lots more time. More stress and less sleep. Of course, I know these agencies would not let all the illegal activities I have investigated and documented to continue. At the least I thought they would prosecute because they had the resources beyond my comprehension to find as much as they dared. The best part was that it would be out of my hands and Daniel would have to leave me and my kids alone.

It took some time but I collected phone numbers and addresses for every county, state, and federal department I could think of. I tried to narrow down the files into categories like insurance fraud documents, title fraud, mail fraud across state lines, identity theft, fake businesses and addresses, and so many more. I also made copies of each and kept elsewhere, in case my house really did burn down or I had an accident as Daniel had promised me. I had copies of what I owed and owned. I called the banks to get the exact balances. It was all up to me to put it together anyway because the cheapest lawyer I found that was able to understand half of it wanted twenty thousand dollars to just look at it and sort through it. After that they would charge by the hour and then there would be the court costs and I knew Daniel was going for the whole package and it would be a long, drawn out process.

They all agreed I could not afford to take him to court because it was so extensive that it was overwhelmingly unbelievable. There were so many people involved. No one wants to believe or admit a person was capable of all of that. As Cal said, "And get away with it".

At the same time all my friends were helping me collect contact numbers and names. My credit report was a prized possession since it contained many leads. After all, I had known what was mine and what was not and it was very clear to see what had happened since 'the marriage to Daniel'. Each time I ordered a copy from a different company I had something new to follow up with. I took the time to literally pick it apart and learn every code and letter and what to do with it. There it was, my life before and my life after. Clearly it read a different person now. It was a comfort and relief to have it all in black and white. My backup of the backup of the backup. Anyone could follow the trail if they could read. There was a new combination for my names and addresses and businesses. Further into the report I found all the inquiries from mortgage companies Daniel had attempted. The 'transportation business' I had at my home address. I needed all the backup because without it no one would understand where it was coming from. Such as the local newspaper ads invoices to my name and address for used car sales and loans. Yes, it was in my name though I had nothing to do with it and no knowledge of it. How was he able to pull that off? I built my house right out of high school and raised Jas and Cal there in the middle of nowhere on a back dirt road. My ranch was listed as non-residential! Different names and birth dates and addresses and businesses. How could that be? Who could get away with that? Daniel and his fraudulent life had been attached to me. That explained why I continued to receive mortgage applications for my home. I tried to have all the fraud removed and was unable to even after speaking to the supervisors. They tried to tell me that my information on my report was correct and true. It was upsetting and made me investigate deeper. I explained I should know what was correct and what was not since it was my life. I did not need someone to tell me that my name and birth date and addresses and businesses were correct in their files and I was wrong. Some of them blamed me for trying to lie about what was on file. One that really irritated me was the fact that Daniel was able to get away with using all my information falsely for his gain and even show that he owned my ranch and lived there. I would have to continue to document and call and send by mail every month or so until I cleared that part of the mess up so it could show the facts.

Months seemed to be days that swept by and it was like a heavy fog over my life that I could not get out of. Severe storms replaced the fog and were not even having any effect on me now. I wondered if I had to live that way from now on or if it would go away. I thought it was a temporary situation, but at least we still were a close family and were able to talk about what was going on because I wanted their lives to remain as stable. We always had our ranch and animals and each other.

At the County level, I filed fraud reports as I was advised. That was to suffice the State Departments I had began to work with. That was just a required formality because they had no knowledge or protocol in the matter and told me it would need to be taken up with higher authorities. They said it was a divorce matter and the county would not be involved. They had no jurisdiction in such matters at that level and it was way more than any local Department could handle. Not one person within the County level had ever heard of such scams. Some told me I should hire a lawyer and sue. It sounded simple. But I already tried that scenario. No one knew how to do that. I needed no one's sympathy. I wanted justice! Plain and simple. I was not asking for something from someone, I wanted out and Daniel removed from my life. That was all! Nothing from Daniel, not that he ever had anything. He had nothing but what he was taking from me! I wanted to keep what I had my whole life. What was so difficult to comprehend about that? Why were they so afraid to be involved? Why would I spend more money to sue Daniel because all he had was mine? He had absolutely nothing, nothing but a criminal background. I did not want that. No one had answers, only the run around. Each contact sent me to another department, but I followed through every person, department, company, phone number and address, in writing and by phone. Many would not put in writing what they told me. I was not surprised at that point. I had heard it all.

Each State Department I had contact with brushed me off too. I got the run around and lack of knowledge. I did not want to know what I found, but I had to know it. It was my life all tangled into a criminal's life of crime without my approval or knowledge. I wanted it stopped and I wanted it stopped yesterday. Why could or would no one stop it? I spent everyday of my life working on that in some way. Not a day went by that I could have put it out of my mind. The longer I waited, the more I tracked, the more it grew into my life like a cancer the rapidly spread. It spread into every aspect of my life no matter what I did to stop it. It was toxic and out of control, yet Daniel continued knowing as he always told me that no one could stop him because he was that good. Was I the only one to cross him and not allow him to poison our lives? Why had no one else stopped him? My mind never had a break and I slept less and less as the fraud became more flagrant and extreme. It was like I was the test and the more he got away with, the more it increased. The more tangled the web became, the more no one had the knowledge to do something about it. State Departments helped very little and even told me there was nothing I could do. They apologized. So what! I still kept many notes and every detail recorded. It was so hard to believe even after documenting the facts that no one knows what to do with it. How did I figure it out all by myself? I am not a federal agent. It seemed to me it did not matter what the laws were if you made it difficult to untangle the web, no one wants to take the time. But you can not drive your car without your seat belt on unless you want to be ticketed and pay the fine. It is the law. How simple. Drive a few miles over the speed limit and you broke the law and will be ticketed and pay for that illegal action. Never mind that the house you pulled in front of is a known drug house and those that live there have never been ticketed for their illegal activities. Is selling and making drugs illegal or harmful? What is the law? Who follows those laws? The honest, hard working, law abiding citizen. Those that try to do what is right and not harm others or their property. They follow The Law. God's laws. Those are the real laws. Even our constitution is no longer upheld. No one cares until it effects them. Now we have laws to explain laws to explain those laws. Why? Is there right and wrong anymore? Just how much can one afford to not have to follow the laws? Now I was learning what it was all really about.

Most County Departments and offices explained that my situation would be a civil matter. Why would all of that be civil? Because no one knew what else to do. They told me to just hire a lawyer. I used to shake my head and take my notes. It was much too big to try to have anything done at the local level anyway, but it was documented in their records and mine. Time to move on.

Next I went to the State level. What a learning experience I was in for. I tried to do too much at once because they all scratched their head and thought I had to have made it up. Everyone I met with or spoke to on the phone had no idea what to do or where to find help. No one was familiar with the laws, but felt sorry for me. I was not looking for sympathy and that only infuriated me further. I was there for help in prosecution and to remove myself from him. I no longer wanted myself or my kids associated with Daniel in any way. I wanted him to be stopped from using my identity for all his fraudulent crime sprees, I explained again I was stuck with all my files and documents and no one to do anything about it. I had spent so much time collecting what the lawyers told me I would need in court for a divorce and still had to find an end somewhere. There was no end and as I continued my investigation to document and keep myself clear. It continued like he was flaunting how much he could illegally get away with. I was not sure how much more time and energy I could put into the disaster. Disaster was a very mild word for what was going on. I do not believe there was a word for it.

I prayed. I needed an enormous amount of strength to keep going. I was so worn out, but I kept telling myself it would all be over soon. With all my documentation I felt I would be granted my divorce and a stop to all Daniel's crimes against me. Then he would go away and find a new victim. I did not want to be his victim anymore.

The State consisted of so many departments and none of them knew what the other did. Most of the time I heard it was a civil matter and would be settled in a divorce court. Their departments would have nothing to do with it. "Maybe you should take your kids and go to a shelter". That was absurd! I should go to a shelter and leave the criminal to his antics. I should leave my home and animals for him while he frolics around the system. Please! What was wrong with these people? I heard "sorry and hope it goes well for you" so many times. Again, the sympathy. Do these people think I called them and have gone through all I have for sympathy? I finally began to tell them I had not called for sympathy; I called to have something done. My lawyers explained it was criminal and would be a criminal court, not divorce. A divorce court would have no knowledge of these crimes. That made sense but I did not really care which court handled it as long as they handled it. I could even comprehend the fact that as long as Daniel was legally married to me he could continue and expand his criminal life and buy more time to cover himself. By covering himself it meant he would use other people and different names, social security numbers, dates of births, addresses, businesses, keeping his 'real person identity' off the records. I honestly do not know Daniel's real name, date of birth, social security number, address, phone number, and so on, since many, many documented identities are supposed to be him. All have variations of what I would guess were the real Daniel. I did not know who I married. That was nauseating. I did not know and will never know and did not want to know anymore. It made me sick whenever I had to 'work on it'. But it had to be done because either no one else knew how to do it and had no conception, or they would charge by the hour and I would have to mortgage my ranch. Those fees would be astronomical because I knew how many hours I had already put into it and I would be further ahead financially to 'give it all away' and start over with my life. I had thought about that many times during the investigation. As it was, I had to 'teach' each lawyer what each document meant and how to read them.

When I called the State Title Department to inquire about my new Camaro and ZR2, I was in for another surprise. I thought they had to be about over. Weeks were flying by. They explained to me there were two lien holders on the car and the truck had one. Both were titled in my name and Daniel's. My vehicles were necessary because my kids and I worked and the kids were in school. I had the new vehicles before Daniel in only my name. As far as I knew, Daniel never owned a vehicle. Daniel was so manipulative from the first day of marriage and kept everything in my life in such a turmoil twenty-four seven that I did not know which end was up. I never had a day of rest since that day last June. Daniel was like a huge, rusty nail stuck in my side. No one could remove it no matter which path I took. Prayer was all I had. It seemed that the 'car salesman' added the dealership as a lien holder. So that made the first lien holder the car company and the second lien holder the car dealership. How about that! Still a learning experience. The woman I spoke with was very knowledgeable about title work and sent me a copy of what she had after I explained my dilemma. I told her no need to apologize. She told me I would have to go through the dealership where Daniel worked to get my title signed off and release interest because there was no other way around it. That was the law. No need to worry about the balance. I knew it would never go that far.

The proof would be in the signatures because I would never have allowed a car dealership to hold interest along with the car company, two liens on one car! No way. Someone forged my signature on legal documents, contracts. Someone also signed my signature using Daniel's last name as mine. Wrong again, it was not me. I jumped through all the loopholes again and went through all the departments to no avail. All they told me was that I would have to prove it was not my signature. Look at the copies and tell me it looks anything like my signature! No, I was told, it does not matter. I would have to prove it in a court of law. How much more proof did anyone need? If I had anymore PROOF, I would need to rent another building. How much black and white did I need? Every time I turned around and took a breath, someone wanted PROOF! Yet, no one was willing to use the proof I gave them on a silver platter.

Another solution I kept running into was for me to hire a handwriting expert and use that in court, though that was a very expensive process and not one hundred percent accurate. Nor did anyone have to enter it into evidence. So why bother with that kind of expense because I knew it was more money and time for me out the window. I had it with our wonderful legal system. Our legal system is there to protect the criminal. The victim is required to have and pay for two hundred percent PROOF and then someone may consider looking at it for a fee. We must protect the outright, flagrant criminal, not the victim. One would only know had they been in that situation firsthand to fully comprehend the absurdity. To know and document the facts of many crimes and no one willing to bother with it. The State Departments acknowledged it would be too time consuming to prosecute so many illegal activities. The State budget enforced too many cuts and they had very little manpower for that type of situation. There was no one available to work on that extensive amount of illegal activities. It would take too much time and cost too much money. How was that for an honest answer from the State? So let me understand what I was told. The State does not have the manpower or money to pursue criminals if they commit a lot of crimes or if it takes too much work. Yes, I understood it in full. Of course, they apologized many times! Big deal. I had about as much of our justice system as could be crammed down my throat. To sum it up, the State had no money, knowledge, or time to bother with the real big time criminals. Sorry my ---! Those crimes were okay to commit. I could not get through my mind that someone was able to commit as many crimes as they wanted and continue becoming more extreme and no one cares. Who was signing my name and why? How many legal documents and contracts were out there with my signature? I had no way of knowing and if the State could not afford to do anything about it, what was I doing? They had easily available, free resources and I had nothing available or free! It was all quite expensive and time consuming and stressful. What were my options? Let it all continue and give up my life and everything to a known criminal? That was what the State gave me as an option. None of them could understand why I continued the investigation which trailed back to my identity. One Secretary of State Official told me "just leave him alone and move on with my life". That ruffled my fur. The State Insurance Department's top man, Bo, told me after many conversations, "honey, do not even worry about it, move on and leave him alone and be glad you are alive". I wanted to come through the phone and let him know what I thought to his face. I told him I was happy to be alive and I was trying to move on with my life but was unable to because I was getting no help from the State. Again all I got was "Oh, do not worry about it, we will take care of it". He would make some phone calls and take care of it. Who was he calling? How could that be a solution? That was all he had to say as I gave him the insurance fraud information. My fur was more than ruffled then. It was a great thing that he was far away and only on the phone. I tried to remain calm and professional because I needed any help I could get. I continued to record all that each department was going to do as they told me there were really no laws to protect me. Another brick in the wall. I kept running into that wall. Law enforcement helped me to run into it. How nice they assist me with that. I spoke with Bo many times and gave him updates each time I found more insurance fraud but all he could do was tell me he would call and have it taken care of. He kept telling me not to worry about it and just get on with my life. To say the least I thought very little of that Department. Did any State Government Office have a real function? Did they do anything? Not as far as I could see. Nothing had changed in my situation because the fraud with two very large, well trusted insurance companies continued after I called, faxed, and wrote directly to each different department within each company to no avail. Fraud departments and management were well aware that their agents and clients continued insurance fraud and did absolutely nothing. All the documentation was useless. They did not want to be bothered. Their apologies were not accepted and I told them so. I only wanted them to stop the crimes using my identity. No one stopped it. Why? I wanted it over. Who would help? I asked them what would happen if I did that? No response. Was I supposed to commit crimes like the Mohy's did? I knew how and it would have been very easy. No response.

It seemed that all I had from the State was 'no response'. No one cared to know anything. Everyone I contacted seemed to let me know that if a person was smart enough in crime, they could do whatever they wanted and it was okay. The more crimes committed, the more it was okay. That was a true and correct. I found no one to deny that. They actually agreed with me. It was a new, evil side of life I never thought I would have to be involved with or learn about. The devil's advocate wins the souls here on this earth so easily. I have seen firsthand and I believe that with all my heart and soul. We would all change our ways if we knew. Some of us do know. I have dealt with him directly face to face. There are many of them.

I continued to contact and document all those on my list. It took weeks and responses were like snails. There were more demands for payments that Daniel had sent my address from his life insurance company, credit card companies, ads for his scam business, bills for out of state residences, and so on. They all continued to claim that I was liable to pay. Legally they expected me to keep paying his and everyone else's bills connected to him? His wives, girlfriends, kids, relatives and a mix there of. I refused and told them so even though some became argumentative, I did not back down. How ridiculous. I did not know these men, women, kids, businesses, and did not want to. Oh, legally responsible? Well, there was no 'legal' anything I could find. Only what one can get away with.

I called the State Insurance Department to ask what had been done and Bo told me he called the insurance companies and it was taken care of and would not happen again. That was so simple and I was sure it was taken care of....not. It was just more b. s. He could not understand what the big deal was. There would be no progress through that department and definitely no legal action. Insurance fraud is okay. He told me I had no monetary loss so there was no real problem. I explained I had been tapped dry, what was he talking about? My insurance company raised my insurance because I was high risk. That was all they could tell me about all the accidents they showed. Bo told me the amount of the difference in my insurance costs for that crime was not enough to bother with. It was too small of an amount if I would check that and compare. What was he talking about? That was crazy and I made him repeat it. I told him he was very wrong and I wanted that in writing. He explained there was no need and laughed. Bo would never give me anything in writing when I asked for that because he could take care of it with a call. 'No need', he told me each time. So I repeated myself many times to get his exact words and told him it was because I wanted to be sure to write down exactly what he told me, the way he told me. He was very helpful with that every time I spoke with him. He would never send me anything in black and white, all by phone. I wonder why? I cringed. Bo found it was amusing.

The Secretary of State Police were of no help. They asked that I write up the complaint I spoke to them about on the phone and they would process it and look into it. There was no response and it had been weeks. After a couple of filings I contacted the Captain. They also were short on time and money. There was too much for them to follow through and investigate. The Captain explained there was nothing they could do, but I could file a civil suit. He could not see anything that was really illegal. There was the 'sorry' again. I told him sorry did not help, everyone was sorry. He was cold and could care less giving no direction or hope. I told him I could not believe what I was hearing because we had laws and that was what they did: catch criminals, right? He must not have liked my question. I asked for something in writing because that was not the end of my investigation. I would continue to document and wanted his Department's response for my files in writing. He told me he would see if there was anything to send. How nice of him.

The Internal Revenue Service was also on my list. What a pleasant surprise to find the gentleman on the other end of my phone to be polite and accommodating. It was a piece of blue sky in the storm. Each time I spoke with him and gave him information I was pleased that one out of all the departments I had contacted so far was actually nice and took me serious. He was careful to get each piece of information I had correct. I believed him when he said they would definitely do something and that it was illegal. Someone that knew we had laws. I explained my biggest fear was that all of these illegal businesses Daniel had set up using my identity would come back to haunt me or my kids. He was probably using Jas and Cal's identity also. He thought I should be very careful. Most of the crimes just popped up out of nowhere as I researched and investigated my own identity. Imagine what it was like to find out all that illegal activity associated with myself. That all began with a long past due out of state utility bill with my name and information on it by the collection agency. That was a snowflake that turned into an avalanche. An avalanche of terrible destruction that wiped out everything in it's path. Or another name for it would be Daniel. I wanted to do whatever I needed to insure that would not continue. He promised with the information I gave, we would be okay. Well, okay for the IRS part of it. He thought it was very brave to do what I had done and agreed that was the only way to receive protection. I told him I would add that information to my files and he gave me all the information he could. I told him about the threats of death and accidents and that he wanted to burn my house down to collect insurance so if something happened to me or my kids look for him. Daniel planned on having me locked up. He was amazed at how much I had found and that I would pursue it. I wanted everything, and I mean everything, documented and recorded everywhere with everyone. That was how serious the situation was because I explained Daniel was capable of anything and knew how to get away with it all. Laws did not apply to him because he believed he was the best and knew how to stay two steps ahead of any law. I wished all the departments I had to contact were so efficient, knowledgeable, pleasant, and took their positions in the State and Federal Government so serious. If they did we would have a lot less criminals committing such heinous crimes. He appreciated my comments.

Whatever Daniel wanted, he stole. Even if he wanted someone's identity, he stole it because he could. Daniel continued to weave and expand his web of crime as I tried to survive. It was survival because I always had to be careful that he was not around me or my kids and I never knew what would happen next. Anything could happen now. I had seen that to be true. At any time Daniel could burn down the house or we could have the car accident, just as he promised me over and over. I know he would get away with it. No doubt in my mind that he would not blink twice. He always talked his way out of everything. I had uncovered such terrible things about him that he would not want public or in court. I would use all that I had. I was left no choice.

Social Security was another wonderful department. They were very professional and polite and took all that

I explained very seriously. A very nice lady worked with my case. We went back and forth for a few months and all they could come up with was for me to change my identity. They would give me a new social security number and I could come in and sign for a new identity. I could be a new me. They thought that would be safest. She would meet with me and begin the procedure. I told her that was so confusing and I would think about it. There was nothing more than to file a complaint to show what had happened and continued to occur. I had to think about the mess and what that would mean. They thought I should change all of my identity and move away. I was not sure I wanted to be a new person because all I wanted was my life back. What about Jas and Cal's identity? Same thing. It was like the witness protection plan and I felt ill just thinking about it and told them that. I would contact them later after I thought it through. They were very helpful and protective. Another smart group of people. My issues were all a domino effect. It was the severity of the situation and the danger that made these women concerned for our safety now and in the future. That was what made me realize I was lucky to be alive and keep my kids safe. How far did I have to go to do that? There was no one out there I had found that would do anything to stop Daniel and his partners in crime. I believe they were afraid to do anything because of pressure from someone on the inside, Daniel, and his entourage. They had quite the set up and connections to be able to obtain the information they used and to keep from being arrested. My options were on the table. Why did I have to run and hide and become someone else? I did nothing wrong. I wanted to understand why our government would rather go to all that trouble and, to me, extreme measures to resolve the 'problem' instead of locking up the known criminals. Lock them up and throw away the keys. They are a waste of good oxygen, as my friend told me many times. The decision not to change my identity and move away took some time and a lot of sorting through scenarios. I did not want to be someone else because my kids and I had a good life here. It was such a drastic ordeal. I had no idea what the future would hold and what kind of life we would end up with. That was a chance I was not willing to take for Jas and Cal. If it were not for my kids I would have probably thought otherwise. Why would we give up our lives for a known criminal? That was the bottom line. Somehow, somewhere the criminal justice system would surely step in and lock the criminals up. We have laws that protect those that uphold them, right? These people would not be allowed to continue their expanding crime spree and laws not apply. The good guys and the bad guys are no longer. Those days are gone. No more black and white, only gray. And money. Money gets the white collar criminal a protective shield.

The Attorney General's Office could file a report, but there was no such department to handle such a thing as identity theft and fraud. Oh, that was too bad, but we do not handle anything like that and the apology.....sorry. Again I told the lady sorry fixed nothing and did not help and that I needed no one's sympathy. No one had any knowledge there to do anything with it and I told that office they had better be prepared because there was big money involved and it was going to be an explosion of crime as I watched what Daniel had accomplished in such a short time. They did not have much to say, like I was making up a crazy story. They had no information for me as we spoke a few times on the phone, hoping to find a solution somewhere. I continued to contact their office and update them with complaint forms anyway. That office could have done something.

I filed a complaint with the Inspector General's Office. There was no such protocol for my situation and no one had any knowledge or guidance. I sent a few forms to them anyway and told them I wanted them on file. They agreed and gave me other contacts I should try. I followed up with every contact anyone could possibly think of. The notes and files were still growing.

The Governor's Office had no knowledge of these crimes but gave me leads and other contacts. One young gentleman I spoke with on many occasions filed complaint letters for me but in the end that was all they could do. Oh, they told me that was too bad that happened.

The Senator's Office and State Representative's Office were unaware of such crimes. Were there laws about identity theft? What were any of these people aware of? The list was longer by the week and sometimes I had to wait for responses for a month or more. Why would I stop now, I thought, most of the case was done. It was a matter of making contacts, though I admit I believed it would only take a few calls and a couple pages of my documents for someone to jump on it and run. No such luck. I spoke with a Senator and a State Representative that I knew many times. They had made calls and given me other contacts which I followed through. They were shocked that I had married a con artist, but then so was I. Reports were again filed and for the life of me, I cannot figure out where all these reports ended up. If they were anywhere near the same place, a red flag and siren should have gone off. Someone should have been tracking someone down. No, nothing. No one had answers or solutions that had any effect on the crime spree that continued. Why? I know they made calls because they called as I sat in their office. I knew some of them followed through when I returned for a status update. Hard to believe after months of complaints filed by phone, fax, and mail to every and any department within the State, nothing was done. So I moved on to the Federal level. It did not matter at that point to me who I filed my complaints with.

The F. B. I. and the F. T. C. were a little leery of my reports because I was still legally married to Daniel. Though I explained as I went through the whole story, Daniel would not give me a divorce. I tried. Did he think I would walk away and give him everything I owned after all I had been through? No one really understood the whole situation or were they trying not to? Wait, what did 'legally married' mean? There were no laws if one chose not to uphold them. I did not want to be legally married, so why did I have to live it and give up everything because I had signed a marriage certificate? What did that mean to anyone? Nothing to me but a signature to commit crimes. Then it was allowed by law? Something was not right and I saw the whole thing in a different light. I was not going to cross over and be a criminal like Daniel, but someone was going to do something no matter what I had to do! I made up my mind to continue the contacts and repeat them over and over until something was done.

The F. B. I. was very vague but the gentleman was

thorough and took down all my information and asked questions and explained what he would do. It would take some time and he would contact me to inform me of what he found. They also were short on staff, but he would see what he could do. That was fine with me because so far no one had really done anything but file a complaint. What did a piece of paper mean? I was sure they all had millions of reports. Then I moved on to the next contact on my list.

The F. T. C. was an important lead because of all the out of state traffic with fraud and titles to vehicles. The vehicles seemed to be lost in thin air but tiles were held by banks for money, not knowing about the scams. Some banks chose not to deal with Daniel's group of criminals because they had experiences with their title fraud. I had spoken with a few. They were tight lipped about their problems because they had to absorb the money they lost on their deals. It was common practice for the lending institutions to sweep it under the rug as a bad business deal because they could not afford the publicity of fraud and crimes committed in their companies. They would lose too much business so they wrote it off and moved on. But it was all still swept under the rug. Very few people were aware of those transactions, especially the public. Banks and lending institutions had an image to project. The public had to view them as secure, stable, smooth, calm, professional, and most of all 'legal'. Who would deal with anything other than that? Without that image, they would not exist. Titles, vehicles, and businesses across five states that I had tracked. There were more but I did not care to follow up with more just to add to my huge pile of files. I looked at what I already documented and thought if no one could do anything with what I had so far, there was no need to continue. Five states or twenty, which was closer to the total, what did that matter. One or one hundred was still illegal. I was not looking for more, but more crimes continued to show up with every transaction. What a web Daniel had woven. A criminal mind can do so much damage to other peoples' lives. A criminal has no conscience and a sociopath has no conscience.

Federal laws apply because of all the scams between states. The F.T.C collected all of my information and filed reports and complaints. They were accommodating and knowledgeable, but as far as taking any action, it was like the others I filed complaints with, that was the extent of their purpose. More files and documents. I returned all the appropriate complaint forms and that was all I could do. The rest was up to them, like all the others. The gentleman seemed to have a genuine interest in the complaint. By that time nothing would get my hopes up. It seemed to be a standard formality and procedure with those I had contacted. Where did all the paperwork go? Why they could not unify these reports into one system for all departments, was beyond my comprehension. Our government needs to simplify and downsize because no one ever really gets anything done from what I had seen and been involved with. We could all take down information and file reports. It is what is done with that information and those reports that count. So far nothing had counted. Why?

I fully understand that my story was taken lightly because I was trying to get a divorce from this criminal. If any single department or contact I filed a complaint with had seriously looked into the matter, they would have been appalled. Did they think it was a case of a scorned woman going through a divorce that wanted to cause the ex problems? Did any of them even look at the information or follow up on any of it? My case had nothing to do with a fighting, upset spouse. Nothing remotely close to a divorce case situation. It was a legal, criminal dilemma. I was trying to move on and remove myself from the trail of crimes. All departments continued to tell me it would be a civil matter and the lawyers told me it was state and federal. So no one wanted to touch it because no one knew how. In the meantime Daniel continued to perfect every criminal act, covering his tracks, and staying two steps ahead of the law, laughing all the way. I was not laughing or finding any humor as each week passed. All those involved told me to be careful with Daniel. I already knew that.

The order of protection was in place, but that would never stop Daniel from what he wanted. He contacted my friends and asked questions about me and harassed them. They were upset and worried about their kids because they knew what he was capable of. I worried about them too. They tried to avoid the calls and then when it continued, they hung up and told them not to call again. I reported that to my lawyer and he explained there was nothing to be done to stop it. Of course not. Daniel knows the laws. I knew he continued to check out the ranch he thought would soon be his. It did not intimidate me anymore as long as my kids were safe. I did not catch him on my property, but there were ravines, timber, creek, pastures, and almost thirty-nine acres so I doubt I would.

Nothing stopped or slowed Daniel down. Another company I had been in contact with many times was a private vendor contracted with our state to gather auto and personal information for insurance companies. The company worked with me and we gathered information from each other in an attempt to correct my report that was used for my insurance company. Another scam unknowingly unveiled. There was a plethora, a Pandora's box of illegal activities and leads. It became obvious once I began to study and break down all the information. That took me over a month to learn how to read it and begin making calls. It could be done with patience, or out of necessity. I had to. I had another web to untangle that Daniel spun around my identity. The money to be made from what I found was astronomical. Unbelievable. No wonder Daniel's insurance agent was so accommodating. It paid very well for the criminals and cost me dearly everyday. But no one else seemed to care even when I would explain to them how someday they would because it would be them next. They would be in the same position as I and then it would be a catastrophe. But not until then. They did not want to know about it until that time. It would come soon.

That contracted company was all about fraud and illegal scams. I found one woman in the company that seemed innocent of the facts. She worked with me for a while on my file and tried to clear the illegal, incorrect information. Others I spoke with claimed that was correct or it would not be on my records. It had to be me. Some tried to tell me I was falsely trying to change my own information to hide the accidents. I sent documentation and within months some incorrect details were removed.

My documentation and complaints would resolve that problem. The fraud should never have showed up again. Well, I saw no decrease in my insurance premiums. My insurance agent was shocked about that little tidbit when I informed her of that small detail of fraud that I was dealing with and trying to clear. My identity was all over and involved in so much I could not keep up. Would that be something if the feds knocked on my door for an arrest? That was exactly why I had no choice but to continue to try to clear myself. It continued to cost me in money, time, and stress. The criminal commits the crime and the victim pays for it in so many ways forever. I ordered another report for my insurance and picked it apart and there it was....more fraud. That continued to happen even after my complaint reports filed with county, state, and federal agencies. My reports continued to show vehicles I had never had, addresses where I never lived, accidents I never had, injuries to other parties, Daniel's family on my insurance with all their accident claims, and more. They thought I was giving them false information about myself. They claimed I was falsifying info. Hard to believe. It was a free for all and no one told the truth because that was not required. I paid the consequences. It was big money for Daniel and a big joke how he was getting away with it and making so much money. He finally perfected the crime to make millions.

The scams were growing by leaps and bounds and I made it clear to everyone I contacted over and over that they were never to come knocking on my door. They had all they needed and they sat on it. It was on them.

I called the insurance company that was involved with the fraud and reported their agent's illegal activities.

317

I gave them all my documentation from my research. They would look into it. Later, I contacted them to find that agent still working in his office as though nothing had happened. The large well known insurance company held all the fraudulent claims that were filed through the fraud department at various corporate locations (so one would not sweep it under the rug). That was the end of that. Nothing was done and the responses from my contacts ceased. Letters came to me stating it was me and my identity and my accidents and vehicles and addresses. That was their final decision. They would do nothing else on the case. Closed. Another letter, another file.

Every contact would continue to receive complaints from me until it was fixed. That was a promise to them with each correspondence. I was not giving up no matter how long it took. Many people begged me to contact a television station about a story of stolen identity. They did not even know how to begin such a story. It was too unbelievable. I told them I had been living that over a year and still have a hard time with it. It was becoming a part of my life.

I threatened a lawsuit to the insurance company and the agent. I still did not have a resolution. Daniel's son lived in another state and had since he was a child. He still used my name and address fraudulently. Daniel's daughter, also out of state since a child, and using my name and address fraudulently. Her driver's license and car were titled and registered in her name at my address. The Secretary of State showed she resided at my address. They had been in my home briefly one time. I know where I lived and who lived there, my kids and I. Daniel's father and mother also used my address for insurance purposes fraudulently. Since his father spent time in prison for fraud and scams I was furious and made sure everyone in those departments knew it. Still no help so I remained on my own to fight the crimes.

It was time to order another credit report. It came and there were more scams. I was no longer surprised, but actually expected it. My ranch showed non-residential, businesses, transportation services, loan companies, insurance broker, publications, dealer business, internet businesses, credit repair business, car donations for 'charities'. Charities are big business and tons of profit to the used car business. It seemed to work so well and be so profitable to continue to use my identity.

The internet businesses Daniel had were illegal scams growing every day. There would be no way to correct so much fraud and crime if it were to come back to me later for taxes or payments.

Then I found records showing that Daniel had sold his half of that condo he owned with another woman in a northern suburb. The date of the transaction showed exactly the month after Daniel married me. So it was processed at some point at that time yet he claimed that as an asset on the bank loan application and told them all about it. He already had it sold. Where did that money go? The whole time he was broke and needed money and could not pay for anything once we were married. He should have collected about one hundred thousand dollars. But I believed he still owned it and could not sell. All that money went somewhere while he broke me and my kids and ran us into financial hardship.

Someone knew what was going on and gave me a copy of an annuity for Daniel and two other women. Maybe mother and daughter. The daughter had a husband and though it had one of Daniel's suburb addresses, the others had an address in the same building directly one floor above him. The name listed at that rental was the younger woman and male. They each had various last names. Then those names were connected to other addresses and states. After I made attempts to contact them by knocking on the door and by phone, they were suddenly gone. Moved. I was on to more. Once on the phone she claimed knowing no one with those names ever living there and after that she hung up on me. The younger girl was one I had questioned Daniel about when we were seeing each other and he claimed he knew nothing of her. The company renting that apartment told me she left abruptly with no forwarding address or information. The older woman left also at the same time. They disappeared and no one ever knew who they were or where they went. When Daniel was involved there was no such thing as a coincidence.

There were six women very strangely and closely connected to Daniel and many believe he was married to some of them and one was his other daughter. It was all kept so quiet. But that fit the life of crime. Who will their next prey be? Very calculating.

Stories always come out after the fact, but I never believed stories and had to find out for myself. Daniel never had a real life because it was always someone else's. He was never satisfied and always had to pretend and never told the truth. He had never paid the price or the consequences as a user and taker. He was always in the red and in financial ruin. That was always someone else's fault. It was evident that Daniel was taught to use other people's money and did, like he bragged. Like a leach, Daniel would suck the life out of everyone. According to Daniel it was never his fault and everyone used him and owed him. That was his story, how great a person he was, everyone should feel sorry for him and try to help. These types of people open their mouths and the stories roll out without skipping a beat. I wondered how I had missed that and not seen through his stories. He wanted everything I wanted and said everything I said. He lied. It sounded good. Sounded too good to be true. It was. Someone always lived with Daniel-always. Was it to take care of him? Was he incapable? Daniel was one person when I married him and another the next day and even worse each day after. The reason for his moves in apartments, work, banks, the whole change at least every two years is because too many people started to catch on, then Daniel's gone on to the next place before anyone realizes the full extent of his crimes. He tried to get everyone around him in as deep as he was to give him his way out, backup, cover, keeping them on his hook to use when needed. Was Daniel really broke? Where was all that money? Was it gambling, partying, drugs? Was he stashing it away in another identity? Or identities? There are some people that move around with him when he moves and I could not tell if they were real or fake or he just uses their identity. Some are kids, relatives, and made up. When I started to contact them, they were gone. Just like the two women and one man in his apartment building.

Daniel looked and played the part of the used car salesman. Or a professional con-artist. If he wore a t-shirt and jeans and did not shave, and was not a smooth talker he would have been in prison a long time ago. He talked his way out and got away with it. Just like he spoke of his father, that was what made him so dangerous. Daniel told me he learned from the trial of his father. Those that did not really know him thought he was a nice guy. But then so did I!

Is It Over Yet?

A question that had no answer. We tried to move on but Daniel would not allow that to happen. Since the ranch was all tied up and we were not able to make the income we had planned for our business. We were stuck. We were still close and talked about what had happened and why our lives had taken a downward spiral. They understood our finances were not at all as they had been. I tried to keep it low stress when we talked. They had comments, ideas, and questions. The most important thing was that we were a family and we were stable. Daniel had no place in our lives. We were devastated and confused and there were no answers to most of it. Our lives would continue as best we could. We had each other to depend on. Why would someone do what Daniel had done to us? I decided to speak to a counselor to keep our sanity, or maybe just mine, because I wanted to do the best for my kids without too much emotional damage. I had no explanation for what Daniel had put us through and continued to do. It was not okay and my kids knew that. I felt guilty for making the mistake of being involved in any way with Daniel.

Cal was in football and that kept him occupied. He worked after school and kept busy. His grades dropped and the school called me to see if they could help. They understood when I explained I had married a con artist without going into detail and told them it was a very bad situation. Daniel was dangerous and Cal was concerned for me. We were making the best of it and I was trying to get a divorce. They said they would try to help him and keep him on track because he was so solemn and tired in class. I talked with Cal and asked if he thought a counselor could help him to understand why? We decided to think about that. We could wait. Cal and I had pep talks. It was important to him that I say as little as possible about Daniel's disaster to our lives and I agreed.

I told my kids we would be okay and we would return to our lives soon. Soon never came, so maybe later. Many months had gone by since I tried to get a divorce. I felt depressed that I allowed someone like Daniel into our lives to destroy it. They had given up a lot and helped me.

Jas seemed to get through it and let it slide more easily. Maybe it was because she was older and female. We had our talks and were supportive of each other. She had a boyfriend and that was going well. I was happy to see her keeping busy and enjoying her life. We were uneasy about the danger with Daniel and we all decided to keep close contact with each other when apart until it was over. Hopefully it would not have a negative effect on her later. Jas and I watched a movie one night and half way through it she said, "that sure reminds me of Daniel". We talked about how that story was like my life. The way the man set everything up was an identical scenario. I felt like it was someone else and not me living the current life.

We were ready for it to be over. We believed Daniel's stories and fell for the promises about the way it would be and what we would do. A perfect life. Lies, but it sounded great. How could I go wrong, I thought?

Jas and Cal seemed to be adjusting and we were getting by, though it was a different life. In a way we tried to pretend none of it had happened. A person should not live off of another and use them at any cost to pursue a goal. A criminal goal. I was raised to work for what you want and if you want more, you work more. If you cannot afford it you, you do not get it or need it. Was I the only one raised that way and the only one raising my kids that way? That was life. There is no honor in using everyone. Would my kids survive in the world that I was learning about. It was so acceptable. No one wanted to believe the story I had to tell because it was easier that way. Just pretend it did not exist and do not get involved. I wanted to. Who could you trust? Why trust anyone after what I saw and heard during the last year? I wanted to shield my kids from as much as I could.

I had beat myself up over and over trying to understand what had happened and why. I wanted to pretend he tried to change for the good and wanted to settle down. Really it was his other life and not stress of the new marriage.

Before we married he would never have laid a hand on me or called me names. The abuse was immediately after and continued to become more severe. Daniel always explained why he had to do the things he did, unethical and illegal, total justification. It was never his fault, but everyone else's. Then the story how he only needed a little help to get on his feet financially and catch up a couple of his bills before he could move down with me at my ranch. I fell for that, but was uncomfortable when his kids continued to require weekly bailouts from me. It turned into three cons running scams as fast as they could. That was the simplest, most honest explanation. I began to keep notes after the marriage because I had kept diaries since high school, so it was not out of the ordinary. Now that I look back it was a lifesaver in many ways.

It was about someone fighting for everything they had owned, trying to survive and keep their life. It was not a marriage, but a professional con artist's grand scam to set himself up to have the status and stability he would never have. His fantasy and other life was immediate when he married me. One signature and it was a life on the downhill for me and my kids. It was all uphill for Daniel in a win-win situation. His stories were lies as he posed as the victim and always turned everything around. The real monster cannot hide for long before it comes out. Daniel was a chameleon because he blended into wherever he was and whoever he was around, trying to be someone he was not. He was very dangerous, manipulative, obsessive-compulsive, controlling, a calculating predator, pedophile, multiple personality, pathological liar, and abusive. That was a few of Daniel's traits that come to mind. There were more.

Daniel thought he had completed his grand scam, but I threw a wrench into his plan. He thought he had perfected the perfect crime and rolled it all into one nice little package. His biggest goal and challenge was to see if he could pull it off as well as all the other scams he got away with over the years. I needed to follow the whole crime spree through to the end until I was freed from any connection whatsoever to Daniel. I was still not sure who I married; which name, social security number, date of birth, and address belonged to him. One of the many ID's and lives he had. Oh, and I wanted a divorce.

It was time to settle on a lawyer so I wanted the least expensive and most competent. Since I had compiled all the research, records, and many years total that I had investigated, it should have been a breeze. It was all there and if you knew legal and illegal and some laws it was done. We would set up the court date and the rest would fall into place. I tried to simplify my files so they could all comprehend. My boxes were ready. Simple. Honestly I wanted to take my case to court on my own without a lawyer but the courts would never allow that. Everyone has to get in on the money. It was part of the game. The divorce was a minute piece of the problem. It was the fraud, scams, and identity theft I was worried about and wanted over. My head wanted a break and I wanted my life back with my kids. I was tired of trying to prove who I was and what I was doing. Women would never go as far as I had with my investigation and I was sure it surprised Daniel. My costs were outrageous. I thought it was over, but it was just beginning.

The fraud using my identity continued without fail as though Daniel knew no one would touch him no matter who I contacted. I had heard oh, that was too bad, sorry, do not worry about it, and it was no big deal, way too many times. In the end it was all up to me. It was all mine to pay for. The burden of proof was all mine!